LORD EDGINGTON

BOOK II

A KILLER
IN THE
WINGS

A 1920s MYSTERY

BENEDICT BROWN

COPYRIGHT

For my father, Kevin,
I hope you would have liked this book an awful lot.

Daly's Theatre

HUGO JAMES

presents...

"A Killer in the Wings"

A DRAMATIC MYSTERY WRITTEN BY

MARIUS QUIN

Adapted from his novel of the same name

Inspector Rupert L'Estrange..	GABRIEL NELSON
Edward Buxton...	OLIVER HARTLEY
Clive McCormack..	BRIAN GRIMAGE
(Young) Edward Buxton...	PETER CANNING
Marjorie Whitstable..	LILLIAN BRADSHAW
Miriam Buxton...	TALLULAH ALANSON
Carolina Buxton / Emilia Buxton....................................	HARRIET TAFT

Other roles played by
MARMADUKE ADELAIDE and DENNIS DANZANTE.

Produced under the immediate direction of

COLIN G. WEST

Presentation Programme

READER'S NOTE

Welcome to another "Lord Edgington Investigates…" mystery. This book is really two mysteries rolled into one. You have the main narrative featuring my detective and his loyal grandson, Christopher, but there is also the play that is being put on in Daly's Theatre that we slowly get a sense of as the story develops.

With the dual identities that the actors all have, the character list at the very back of this book may come in handy. You will also find a glossary of antiquated, unusual and dialect words, a list of some interesting historical facts and an explanation of my reasons for writing.

As with all the books in the series so far, this is a spoiler-free story and does not give away the names of the killers in the previous mysteries.

PROLOGUE

"I don't believe you ever loved me." The woman's tortured voice rang out around us, and every last person watching just froze. Her make-up had run so that a thick black line descended from either eye.

Soaked by the storm that was raging through the window behind him, her husband put both hands out to reason with her. "Darling, let's talk about this. There's no need to be upset."

"Upset?" She emitted a shrill laugh, but there was no joy in it. Her every move was coloured by her anger. "I'm more than upset, Edward. I'm a ball of burning fury; I am wrath personified."

He took one step closer as though he wished to embrace her but changed his mind at the last. "You're seeing this all wrong, my love. Emilia is just a friend. I swear, there's nothing between us."

Shaking as she held the gun out in front of her, the wronged woman continued as though he hadn't spoken. "To think that I loved you, Edward – I truly loved you. I gave you everything, but it was never enough."

He pushed one hand through his sodden hair to wipe the rain from his brow. "You're not thinking straight, my love. Your mind is all confused. Try to concentrate on the life we've built together. Think of our family and the future that still lies ahead of us."

She attempted to gasp then, but the sound became strangled in her throat and emerged as little more than a moan. "You don't even have the courage to look me in the eye and tell the truth." Her sobs were amplified by the silence that enveloped them and, as no reply came back to her, she spoke again. "Just admit it! Admit that you betrayed me."

Edward's eyes were fixed on the savage black pistol – his pistol, which he kept in such good order in a drawer in his desk. He watched as the barrel jerked about with every twitch of his wife's muscles.

"Very well, Carolina. You're right. I never meant for it to happen, but can you really blame me? Emilia was there when I needed a dose of human kindness." He looked up at the ceiling of the stately sitting room and breathed in deeply before summoning another word. "You were kind to me yourself, once."

"How dare you..." Her expression had hardened. "You're a despicable coward."

"Darling, you don't have to—"

Carolina was distracted by the argument and couldn't have imagined that her husband would jump towards her at that moment. I looked on in silence, unable to move, unable to think as I watched the terrible scene. Edward grasped the gun, and everyone there awaited the fatal sound, the ear-splitting bang and the smell of burnt powder, but it never came.

"Sit down and stop talking," he shouted once the danger was averted.

Shivering and distraught, Carolina remained on her feet.

"Did you hear me? I said, sit down."

It was clear that she could no longer grasp the events that were unfolding around her. The whites of her eyes seemed to consume her pupils, and she looked about the room as though she didn't recognise the home they had lived in for years.

When she didn't move, he pointed the gun at her, and his voice rose higher. "Carolina, you had better sit down on the sofa or I don't know what I'll—"

BANG!

Everyone watching jumped a few inches in the air as the shot rang out. Even Edward was terrified, and he was the one who had pulled the trigger. Perhaps Carolina was the only exception. She looked oddly peaceful as she slumped to the floor, and a red stain bloomed on her perfectly white blouse.

"No!" Edward screamed, and he ran to her limp body. "No, Carolina. Not like this. This isn't how it was supposed to happen."

He knelt down in front of her as a sorrowful piece of music began to play. The line of people nearest to the action looked at one another, their haunted faces etched with fear and perhaps the slightest hint of excitement.

Realising the trouble he now faced, Edward peered around the Victorian lounge. He looked at the ticking clock in the corner and the huge suit of armour standing on a plinth against one wall. He looked through the window at the lashing rain just as a flash of lightning illuminated the world outside. Presumably accepting that his wife

10

really was dead, he trailed across the room, mumbling to himself as he went.

"It was never supposed to happen like this. It's all gone wrong." He came to a stop in a pool of light beside the old armour. "You weren't supposed to die here, Carolina. I'd planned to kill you somewhere far away. Somewhere the police would never find you."

That was the moment at which the kettle drums in the orchestra struck up and the axe that the hollow soldier was holding swung down on top of his skull. At first, no one in the audience knew what to make of it. They all assumed it was part of the show, but then previously dead Carolina sat up in the middle of the stage and shouted to her co-star.

"Peter, what's happened?" She scrambled across the floor to look at him, leaving a trail of fake blood in her wake. "Peter? Talk to me."

She screamed then, and something in the frightful sound she made revealed that this was not part of the play. It echoed about the audience and the people in the dress circle were the first to realise what had happened. They had the best view, after all. Almost as though they were trying to communicate with the woman on the stage, several people produced horrified cries of their own, while others offered half-formed questions which the actress would soon answer.

"His skull's been cleft in two," she shouted to the side of the stage. "The poor man's dead!"

CHAPTER ONE

My hands were shaking as I seized the pair of tweezers, carefully gripped hold of the cotton and attempted to thread it through a hole the size of a speck of dust. Admittedly, it took me ten or so attempts to achieve my task, and I had to get a bigger magnifying glass to see what I was doing. Oh, and I cut my finger on the hook at some point and ended up bleeding all over myself and having to stop to put a sticking plaster on the wound.

I only needed a few more attempts, though, and then I managed it! I felt a small thrill at a job well done.

Sadly, this was only the first step. By the end of the morning, I would have several plasters on my fingers, and the fox fur and feathers I had used would be rather bloody. However, I eventually succeeded in producing two lures (and a few failed experiments).

"What I don't understand, Grandfather, is why we're tying flies if you know how terrible I am at fishing."

For his part, the great Lord Edgington was still working on his first, but it was a thing of beauty. It looked just like a colourful moth and was made with any number of tiny fragments of feathers from exotic birds that I couldn't identify.

Instead of answering the question that I'd spoken aloud, he answered the one in my head. "I've used a sheath of married strands from a peacock's wing and a golden pheasant's tail, narrow strips of barred wood duck and green-winged teal, hints of lesser florican and bustard and the main curving feather at the top is from a junglefowl."

"It's exquisite. Really it is." Looking from the other side of the table in the petit salon of Cranley Hall, I had to pause for a moment to appreciate the intricacy of his work. "Now, would you mind answering the question I actually asked?"

He had one eye closed and was tying a thread ever so slowly around the end of the hook. "I couldn't hear what you were saying, as your thoughts were so noisy."

"I asked why we're tying flies when there is no chance on earth that I will become a competent angler."

"I would have thought that was obvious." By his standards, this was a fairly revealing response.

Instead of saying the first thing that came into my head, I thought carefully about what this obvious reason might be. "Are you teaching me to do this seemingly unrelated yet painstaking activity because it will in some way improve my abilities as a detective?" This seemed like the kind of thing he would do, and I expanded on my initial suggestion. "By learning to focus on this task, will I be able to concentrate better on the minutiae of our cases?"

He had taken a strand of feather between the tips of his tweezers and was pushing the end of it into a small bunch that he had already secured. "No. Not at all."

"Then are you helping me to hone my motor reflexes so that, should I ever need to aim a gun at someone, my hand will remain steady?"

"No." He didn't look up at me as he spoke.

I clicked my fingers, certain that I had finally divined the solution. "Then it must be related to hand-to-eye co-ordination."

He peered around his looking glass to cast his sardonic gaze my way. "No, Christopher, that is not why we are engaged in this superlative activity. We are tying flies for the simple reason that we haven't had a case worthy of our talents for some months, and this is one of my favourite hobbies." He returned his attention to the fake moth. "Perhaps you have forgotten that I am retired and had planned to spend this period of my life engaged in leisurely pursuits. I've barely had time to play a round of golf or paint a sunflower because I've been so busy overseeing your education."

He'd been unsettled for some weeks. He was often like this when deprived of the attention of our adoring public. I suppose he was like a prima ballerina or a film star in that respect.

I stood up from the table to stretch my legs. "You've just contradicted yourself, old man. First, you complained that we haven't had a juicy murder to investigate for some time, and then you moaned that you haven't had the opportunity to indulge in your pastimes. You should make up your mind which bothers you most."

"Moan?" was all he took from this comment. "The former bloodhound of Scotland Yard does not moan."

I smiled at his cantankerous response, and he must have known he was in the wrong as he threw down his tweezers, and they went skidding off the table. It was quite the most delicate tantrum I'd ever witnessed.

"Very well, Christopher. You have found me out; I am in a funk." He leaned back in his chair, and I thought he might lash out once more and knock the really very tiny fishing fly from its vice. He presumably realised just how dramatic this wouldn't have looked and changed his mind. "What upsets me most is that I can't relax. I thought that I would spend the remainder of my life engaged in intellectual and sporting diversions. It turns out that all I want to do is seek out evildoers with you at my side. It's most perplexing."

"I'll try to take that as a compliment."

It was at this moment that our factotum Todd arrived with a pile of letters. Actually, the word *pile* doesn't do it justice. I'd seen smaller stacks of books on the floor of Grandfather's ever-messy library.

"Please tell me there's something of interest in amongst all the missing dogs and swindled toast racks," he begged his second favourite employee – no one could compete with the woman who prepared his meals.

"Good morning, M'lord. I have not yet opened your correspondence, but we will soon discover who has written to you and what the senders require."

Grandfather simultaneously managed to nod whilst shaking his head. It was a little confusing, but Todd always understood his master better than I could.

The smart young man took a letter opener and, with the precision of a surgeon – or a fly tier for that matter – sliced open the first envelope. "This one is from a little boy in Sheffield who—"

"No," the Marquess of Edgington declared before we'd even heard what the poor northern tyke wanted. "Children rarely have anything scandalous to report. They only ever write to me requesting help with missing toys or because they think the men their mothers are courting have 'suspicious beards'."

"Ahh, I'm afraid you're right, M'lord. Timmy from Sheffield is writing to report a man with untrustworthy facial hair."

Ever since the trial relating to our last case had been covered by the national newspapers, Grandfather had been inundated with post from admirers and detractors alike. It was as though half the population of Britain had suddenly remembered he was alive, and they all wanted something from him.

Upon opening the next letter, Todd's face turned a little grave. This triggered a hurried question from his employer.

"What? What is it?" I think he was hoping for an interesting crime, but his employee would only disappoint him.

"Sorry, M'lord. It's another letter from a child." He cleared his throat before giving a fuller account. "And I'm afraid she really isn't a fan... I didn't realise that young ladies possessed such colourful vocabularies."

Grandfather issued a resigned sigh. "What would an artist be without his critics? What would God be without the devil?" I had to wonder with whom he most identified in this metaphor.

"Here's a more interesting one, sir." Todd held the missive aloft. "It's from a man in Leicestershire. He claims that his three sons are all trying to kill him."

The old detective sat up in excitement. "What's his handwriting like?"

Todd grimaced for a moment before answering. "To be quite honest, it's a little untidy." He turned the message around so that we could both see. It did not meet my grandfather's high standards.

"Blast!" He collapsed back into his chair once more.

"Why?" I felt compelled to ask. "What does his handwriting tell *you*?"

Glancing out of the window towards the grand lawn, he no longer seemed interested. "It tells me that he's looking for attention."

"But we had a very similar case that started with an old man who believed his children were trying to kill him, and the messiness of his handwriting turned out to be a key element to solving his murder."

He still wouldn't look at me. "No, Christopher, that was entirely different. For one thing, the old man in question was a self-made millionaire and, for another..." He didn't actually give another reason but whistled a bright tune instead. I really couldn't fathom what this was meant to imply.

Seeing no other way to placate my mentor's bad mood than to find a case worthy of our particular talents, I went to help Todd. Seizing a handful of letters from the silver tray, I ripped the first one open. It was from a farmer who'd lost his sheep. I'm not joking. He didn't even claim that they were stolen, just lost.

The next was from a little boy who had presumably written to the wrong person as he was asking for advice on the best type of conker to use in a school tournament. The next was from a girl who thought it suspicious that Lord Edgington happened across so many bodies and yet people rarely considered his guilt, so I tossed it into the bin. The one after that was a bill from the local garage for repairs on my grandfather's many luxurious cars. You wouldn't believe how much he spent each month on engine oil.

"Ah, this is more interesting," I said as I read through the next letter. "A woman in Litchfield says that a rare diamond, which has been in her family for years, has mysteriously gone missing."

Todd, I and our golden retriever Delilah, who was sitting in the sunshine by the French windows, looked hopefully at my grandfather.

"Tell me more."

"It's been in her family for years—"

"You've already read that part."

"Don't be so impatient." I might have snapped at him then, but he deserved it. "Been in her family for many years, taken to Britain from India by her great-grandfather, worth over a hundred thousand pounds and not seen for a month."

"Christopher," he began and raised his right hand to his left temple as though I'd given him a headache, "can you tell me whether the government has introduced some kind of tax on subjects and auxiliary verbs?"

I had no idea what he meant. "Not to my knowledge. Why?"

His voice grew in volume and tetchiness. "There must be some reason that you refuse to speak in full sentences." He got up from his chair and wandered mopily about the room. "Now, I will grant you that, on the surface, the letter in your hand sounds as though it would be of interest. Diamonds of that value and antiquity do not vanish into thin air. However, I have one question for you."

"Yes?"

"How does she conclude her letter?"

"She writes, 'Yours most truly, April Abigail Moorefield'."

He stopped moving, and his eyebrows scaled the south face of his forehead. "Is that all? There's nothing else?"

"Ummm, she also drew a small heart and…" I had to count them. "…twenty-one kisses."

He clapped his hands together, happy to solve this minor mystery. "I knew it. The woman is a time waster and a fraud."

Todd retrieved the letter and put it in the wastepaper basket in the corner of the room. He explained my grandfather's feat of deduction as he passed. "Lord Edgington has a lot of lady admirers and sometimes their attempts to get him to visit their homes can go a little too far."

"I should say!" Grandfather put his hand across his chest as though he were a great statesman about to make a speech. "The women of this country seem set on marrying me or marrying me off to their elderly aunts. It is quite daunting."

This summary of half the citizens of Great Britain was followed by a sudden bang on the window. Delilah jumped up to bark at a figure who had pressed his face up against the glass. The sun was streaming in behind him and, at first, it was hard to make out much more than a silhouette. Todd rushed forward to open the door and a lanky young gentleman with a messy mop of curly red hair fell to the floor where Delilah had previously lain.

"My goodness," I exclaimed, walking a few steps closer to make sense of the scene. "Are you dead?"

CHAPTER TWO

Don't worry. Not every fragment of this tale is going to end with the revelation of someone's death and, as it turned out, this one was greatly precipitous.

"Of course I'm not dead, Chrissy." Marmaduke Adelaide, my former school friend turned… well, friend I suppose, jumped to his feet in one impressive movement, much as a monkey would. "I'm an actor now; I have to make a dramatic entrance."

He brushed himself off and went to inspect my shocked grandfather's face. It was rare to see the dear man fall speechless, but that is what had happened.

"Doesn't he talk anymore?" Marmaduke whispered to me. "I distinctly remember him walking about and that sort of thing. I suppose such inactivity creeps up on old folks and, before you know it, they grind to a halt."

His comment brought Lord Edgington back to himself. "I'm not that old, you impertinent pup. I was simply amazed that you had managed to get onto the grounds without either the guard at the gate or one of the footmen stopping you."

Marmaduke smiled his usual mischievous smile. "Oh, they tried, but I worked my magic."

It was at this point that our ancient head footman Halfpenny burst panting and breathless through the door. "I'm sorry, M'lord," he began as politely as he could.

I was worried that these would be his last words, so I rushed over to him with a chair. He was far too good a servant to sit down in his master's presence and managed to stay on his feet.

"A thousand apologies, sir. The young fellow got around me at the front of the house. I tried to stop him. Really, I did. But he was too fast for me."

Marmaduke had taken a seat in an armchair beside the open doors onto the terrace. I don't know how he'd obtained it, but he already had a glass of port in his hand and took a sip of it as he observed the curious scene. "Not bad stuff, this."

Grandfather stood where he was and tried to make sense of the chaotic character who had blown into his typically ordered world. "I did not realise that we would be honoured with your presence this morning, Mr Adelaide."

"You're very welcome," my friend replied with a cheeky smile.

Delilah walked in a circle around Marmaduke's chair and seemed most entertained by our guest. Her owner, meanwhile, did not. "It is customary to receive an invitation before appearing at a gentleman's house, you know. You might at least have waited to be shown through to us."

"Waited?" Marmaduke pronounced the word as though it had some vulgar second meaning. "Life's far too short for that. Look at you. You must be nearly a hundred, but I bet it was only a week ago you felt as if you were twenty-one."

"I still feel as if I'm twenty-one," Grandfather replied through gritted teeth, and I was worried that he'd throw my giant, ginger friend back the way he'd come.

"Now, now, everyone," I said to restore some decorum. "Why don't we calm down and have a cup of tea? There's nothing like Earl Grey to soothe the nerves."

No one looked convinced by my entreaty, except perhaps Delilah. That clever hound knew that tea was usually served with cake or biscuits, and there was a high chance that some morsels would fall her way.

"Wait just a moment." Lord Edgington was still on his feet and towered over Marmaduke impressively and imperially (not to mention imperiously). "What were you thinking, coming here in such a manner? Considering my background in the police, you must have known what I would think upon seeing you collapse before us on the carpet."

"I did indeed." Marmaduke had finished his drink and set the empty glass down on the walnut cabinet behind him. Being a truly excellent employee, Todd swept over to seize the offending object before it could leave a mark.

Grandfather's eyes narrowed. "I know that you are far cleverer than you would like everyone to believe, so perhaps it is time to explain what you are doing here."

Even though we had been close friends for over two years, I

20

still found Marmaduke an incredibly strange sort of person. When we were at school together, he had first been my tormenter and then my protector. The son of a former criminal, he was one of the toughest boys at Oakton Academy, but, beneath it all, Marmaduke had harboured a love of theatre and music. Instead of following our friends to university, he had spent the previous year training to be an actor, and we were due to see his first role in the West End that week.

He looked uncertain as we awaited his explanation. It was as though he didn't quite know what he was doing there and was searching for the words to explain it.

"First things first…" He glanced down at the floor and, despite his bravado, I could tell that something was terribly wrong. "First things first, I apologise for disturbing you, Lord Edgington."

This seemed to reassure my grandfather a little and, with the required concession obtained, he motioned to Halfpenny that tea was, after all, an acceptable idea.

Neither of us interrupted, and Marmaduke understood that it was his job to talk. "The thing is, I've been having a rather worrisome time of late, and so I decided to motor down here to see you both." I'd rarely seen him so restrained. He was like a candle whose wick had got too close to the wax and was at risk of going out altogether.

Grandfather finally decided to help him along. "I believe that you are rehearsing a new play in London at the moment."

"That's correct." This cheered him up a touch, or he put on a brave face at least. "It's right down your alley, your lordship. 'A Killer in the Wings' is a mystery by a wonderful writer named Marius Quin. He's been there throughout the production, and he's an inspirational figure. He really is."

His interviewer's white eyebrows squashed together to do an impression of a moustache. "Yes, I'm sure he is, but perhaps you should concentrate on whatever has upset you so."

I thought he'd phrased this rather strangely considering the cheery scene that my friend had performed for our benefit, but then Grandfather was a master at ignoring the superficial and focusing on what lay beneath the surface.

"Of course." Marmaduke still spoke in that muted tone. "You see, I originally had a tiny role in the play. I was selling newspapers on a street corner in one scene and working as a waiter in another. I only had three lines, but then I got a sort of promotion."

I was the only one still standing by this point, and I went to give him a celebratory punch on the arm. "Congratulations, old friend. That's wonderful news. It's your first play, and you're already making progress. But why are you so worried?"

Grandfather shook his head ever so subtly, and I decided that I should stop talking. No matter how much I might have improved as a detective's assistant, there was a certain naïveté to me that I struggled to lose.

"Well… I'm worried because I only got the bigger role after the first actor was killed on stage."

"I believe I read something about this in *The Times*," Grandfather began, then realised this point was moot and encouraged my friend to keep talking. "But I'd still like to hear what happened in your own words."

Marmaduke had apparently forgiven me for my previous foolish comment and looked in my direction as though he needed my support. "We had an early performance for friends and family. There was even a local school invited to make up the numbers. We're not opening until the weekend, but this was a good opportunity to practise everything with a real audience and Colin – that's our director, Colin West – Colin thought that it would help us to see the progress we'd already made and the areas upon which we could improve."

A hint of a smile graced his lips, and I knew he was going to make a light-hearted comment in an attempt to hide his troubled state. "I thought I did a perfectly good job as a newspaper seller but felt I still had some way to go to convince anyone that I was a waiter." His jovial tone was soon forgotten. He became serious again and looked at my grandfather with a glimmer of despair in his eyes. "That's not true. We were only a few minutes into the performance when the accident happened."

Grandfather pounced on his words. "Are you certain it was an accident? I know that's what they said in the press, but I rather wondered if you had some other knowledge of the thing."

Marmaduke was evidently suffering the telling of his tale and would need a moment to compose his thoughts. "That's what everyone in the theatre said. You see, the first scene of the play features a couple who have struck more than just a rocky patch in their marriage, and the woman is about to shoot her husband."

I was really very tempted at this point to tell him not to reveal anything more about the plot of the play. I can't stand it when people chat away about a story as though you already know what happens. Instead of interrupting him, I tried not to listen to what he was saying and sang an old song in my head.

> **You are my honey, honeysuckle,**
> **I am the bee,**
> **I'd like to sip the honey sweet**
> **From those red lips, you see.**
> **"And then the husband seizes the gun from his wife**
> **and…" He was still talking!**
> **I love you dearly, dearly,**
> **And I want you to love me,**
> **You are my honey, honeysuckle,**
> **I am the bee.**

"Then the axe from the suit of armour came swinging down right on top of the actor's head," Marmaduke continued, but I think I'd avoided hearing the details of any important parts of the play by this point, so I decided to listen again. "His name was Peter Canning, and he was a very nice man. It really is terrible what happened to him."

"I imagine you took his part when he could no longer perform?" It was a little insensitive of my grandfather to state this in such blunt terms, and I could see the effect it had on my friend.

"I didn't take his part. I was his understudy. And it's not as if he was the main character. He was only in that scene at the beginning, and then he played a smaller part later on. You see, in the play, his character is actually the younger version of the—"

I stuck my fingers in my ears and started to sing less quietly than before.

> **"You are my honey, honeysuckle,**
> **I am the bee…"**

Grandfather looked at me as though I'd lost my marbles.

"Christopher, what exactly are you doing?"

"Oh, ummm…" I was about to explain when I realised that it would only make them think worse of me. "Marmaduke, you were saying that it was just an accident, but if that's true, why are you so nervous?"

He stumbled over the answer. "I… The thing is, I don't believe it was an accident. We'd run through the scene just before the audience came into the theatre. We'd had the same gunshot and the same drum roll, and the axe hadn't fallen. It doesn't make sense that it did the second time."

Grandfather tried his best to comfort him. "That's very interesting. But what has unnerved you so? As frightened as you must be by Mr Canning's death, there is nothing to say that you're in any danger."

"But I am." There was more than fear on Marmaduke's face. As he looked directly at his questioner, I saw pure panic in his eyes. "You see, there have been several accidents since then, and perhaps a few before." He had to swallow as it had all got too much for him. "I'm absolutely convinced that Peter was murdered."

CHAPTER THREE

Evidently feeling that time was of the essence – and no doubt secretly over the moon that we finally had a case to investigate – Grandfather made a quick plan just as Halfpenny arrived with a trolley.

"There's no time for that, man," he said as though it had been our footman's idea to serve refreshments. "I am heading to London forthwith." He couldn't resolve any problem without a spell of pacing, of course, and he wore a path into the carpet before issuing more orders.

I hadn't had breakfast, so I sidled over to the trolley and helped myself to some vanilla cream sandwiches and a thimble or two of tea while Grandfather was busy.

"Todd, you'll have to drive Mr Adelaide's car. Marmaduke, you'll come in the Daimler with Chrissy and me."

"May I drive?" Marmaduke never stayed sad for long and was his incorrigible self once more.

"No, you may not. But I have a great number of questions for you, and we can talk on the way."

I must admit, I was rather excited by this burst of activity. It was all well and good living on a luxurious estate in the countryside, with staff on hand to cater to my every whim at the ring of a bell, but you can't beat life in the city. London is very much the centre of the universe, and there really is nothing better than a trip to the theatre. I was half tempted to telephone my regular companion, but I knew that Mummy was away for a few days helping my cousin Cora with preparations for her wedding.

Grandfather had finally noticed me (and the crumbs down my chequered woollen sports jacket). The old terror knew exactly what I was thinking and rebuked me accordingly. "We're not off on a jolly to the city, Chrissy." I rather liked his accidental consonance. "I can see from your friend's panicked state that something devilish is afoot. We are going to London to work and nothing more."

"We'll have to eat at some point," I reminded him.

"Obviously, we'll have to eat. One is not a plant."

He had not understood my meaning, and so I tried to explain. "What I should have said is that, as we'll be in London, and food will be consumed, I imagine that you will insist on dining at the Ritz or perhaps the Cadogan."

He shook his head and marched to the doors that gave onto the terrace. "Now you're stating the obvious, my boy. One is not a plant, but one is also not a savage. Where would you expect us to eat?"

"Well... what's wrong with a nice, humble sandwich?"

He looked as though he was about to tell me exactly what was wrong with a sandwich when he had second thoughts. "You have a point. Not all food has to be elaborate to be delicious. I promise to take you to an establishment that sells the most delicious sandwiches in the country at a very reasonable price. However, as we'll be spending time in the West End, the Savoy is the only obvious location for us to stay. After all, it was built on the back of a great theatrical success story."

With this curious enunciation made, he placed one hand on Marmaduke's shoulder and guided him from the room. Todd was usually an expert at hiding his feelings on any such scene he happened to witness but, once we were alone, he offered a few words of advice.

"If I may say, sir, I don't think this is the moment to challenge your grandfather. He's been searching for something to fill his time for weeks. Even if Mr Adelaide hadn't presented him with an intriguing case, I'm fairly certain he would have found a pretext to head into the city this morning."

We stepped out into the garden as I answered him. "I'm sure you're right, Todd. But if I refrained from challenging my grandfather, I would have few hobbies left to enjoy."

He did not show his amusement but bowed his head to avoid looking me in the eye. It's a hard job being a chauffeur and what have you. I often wonder whether staff at big houses undergo similar training to the King's Guard at Buckingham Palace. Why smiling should ever be frowned upon is beyond me, but they all do a very good job of keeping their faces perfectly straight.

Todd hurried off to get the car ready and, by the time I reached the driveway at the front of the building, the majestic blue Daimler was already pulling up.

"It's the car of kings, you know," Grandfather told Marmaduke. He'd already told everyone in the family, and he was running out of people to impress with this fact.

"I prefer sportier vehicles," Marmaduke replied as he got into the back seat.

I could see that grandfather was vexed by his response and would no doubt have liked to march him over to the barn to show off his collection of such cars. He had everything from Le-Mans-winning Bentleys to Targa-Florio-winning Alfa Romeos.

Much like a King's Guard, Grandfather managed to hold in his true feelings as he walked to the driver's side of the Daimler, and I got in next to him.

"You'll have to pack a few bags for us, Todd," he said instead. "We'll see you at the Savoy this afternoon."

"Very good, M'lord."

"And take excellent care of my car," Marmaduke shouted through the rear window. "She may not look like much, but she has the heart of a lion."

His tatty brown Vauxhall A-Type appeared to have rolled to a stop against a bush. I found it hard to imagine she had a functioning engine, let alone a heart.

Marmaduke stretched one arm out of the window to bang on the side of the car. "Off we go, driver. Straight to London, please."

Grandfather said nothing, but he would soon have his revenge. Once we reached Surrey's smooth, sparsely occupied country lanes, he pressed his foot down on the accelerator and went as fast as the sleek tourer would go. This was nothing new for my favourite speed merchant, but I noticed that he took each bend a little faster than normal so that poor Marmaduke was thrown from side to side on the backseat.

Once we left the hills and woodland of our home county behind, Grandfather slowed the car to be able to discuss the potential murder. "One question that immediately comes to mind is why was there a real axe on stage?"

Marmaduke had turned an unusual shade of yellow and spoke with his hand over his mouth. "I wondered that myself. The set at the beginning of the play resembles the interior of an old house. They evidently felt that the suit of armour helped create the impression that we were miles away from a West End theatre."

"Yes, thank you, Marmaduke. I do understand the concept of theatrical scenery, but it still seems risky to have a weapon on stage, what with all those actors prancing about the place." He fell to contemplation for a few moments before selecting another path of thought. "I assume that the police examined the armour for signs of foul play?"

Holding onto the seat in front of him, my friend leaned forward to reply. "They did indeed. From what I understand, there was a metal bolt that held the two crossed axes in place. They decided that the movement on the stage and the vibrations from the orchestra in the pit had loosened the nut. You can always trust the rozzers to get out of doing any real work. They refused to believe me when I told them there was something suspicious about it."

I'd barely spoken to my old companion since he'd collapsed through the French windows. It was about time I contributed more than sarcastic comments to the conversation. "And you said that you'd rehearsed the exact same scene a short while earlier and there was no problem with the axe?"

"That's right."

Grandfather seized the discussion once more. "And who had access to the stage during—"

"I was just about to ask that." We had been shut up together at home for too long, and I really snapped at him.

To give him credit, he was a gracious megalomaniac. "My apologies, Christopher." He somehow managed to pilot the car and give a courtly bow at the same time. "Please go ahead."

"Who had access to the stage between the two performances?" I smiled appreciatively at the old fellow as I asked this.

Marmaduke was unnerved by our bickering and answered in a hesitant tone. "Well, the cast. There are five main actors and a boy who dances. Oh, and there was a stagehand there, too, but now that I come to think of it, he left the stage when we did. He was talking to the writer and director at the back of the theatre, and they were still together when the play started."

"Six suspects!" Grandfather was more excited by the moment. "The perfect number."

I had to ask the obvious question. "Why is six the perfect number?"

"Eight is too many; it becomes difficult to remember everyone's name. Four is too few – I tend to solve such cases in a third of the time, and they offer little to test my wits."

"So what's wrong with five?"

He sighed as though I hadn't been paying attention. "Really, Christopher. You haven't been paying attention. You should know by now that I have no time for odd numbers. They're too messy. If I had it my way, we'd do away with them altogether."

I considered pointing out that he had three offspring and one dog, but a lord who has reached seventy-seven years of age is surely entitled to the odd bout of eccentricity now and then – or, in my esteemed forebear's case, approximately nineteen times a day.

"Of course, Grandfather. I'm sorry for asking."

"Wait just one moment." He was suddenly concerned by something and had to peer over his shoulder to look at our passenger. I truly wish he'd kept his eyes on the road. "How can you be certain that no one else accessed the stage during that time?"

Marmaduke was happy to have piqued the detective's curiosity, and he found his usual degree of confidence. "Well, for one thing, I was standing by the back door, so no one could have come in from outside. And anyone who attempted to mount the stage from the audience would have been spotted by the girls who work front of house."

"And there was only one stagehand?"

"I didn't say that. In fact, there are four in all: the one I mentioned, two who were having a cigarette out in the street, and the boy who dances – who got promoted to being an actor because the director took a liking to him."

"A mystery play with a dancing stagehand?" I muttered, feeling less excited about Marmaduke's debut than I previously had.

Grandfather apparently hadn't heard, as he clicked his fingers and looked overjoyed. "Six is the perfect number of suspects."

I tried to hold in my reaction to his reaction, but it burst out of me. "And what if one of them gets murdered? What will you do then?"

I believe he had the answer already prepared. "Are you saying that every dead person is innocent? There's no reason whatsoever why the second victim couldn't have been the first killer, and then we must look for two killers – but still from an original pool of six."

"Which is the perfect number," I said so that he didn't have to repeat himself (again).

"Precisely!" He stopped talking for the time it took to navigate a blind corner and then engaged our witness once more. "You said there have been more accidents since Peter Canning's death. Can you tell us about them?"

My friend looked at the autumn colours of the passing countryside as he replied. "At first it was minor things. There was some soapy water on the stairs onto the stage, and no one thought anything of it when I slipped over." An embarrassed grin lit up his face. "To tell the truth, it was quite funny. I went bumping down them on my bottom, much as if I'd done it on purpose."

"But there must have been something more frightening than a wet staircase." Grandfather had presumably forgotten how wonderful the number six is and was concentrating on the facts of the case. "From the way you spoke back in Cranley Hall, I thought you had a good reason to suspect foul play."

"I did," Marmaduke replied. "Or rather, I do. But some of it was subtle. Tallulah Alanson – she's one of the actresses – got locked in a room under the stage overnight. She said she could have died if she'd been trapped there any longer, but we all thought she was overreacting. It wasn't until yesterday that I became more certain." He steeled himself for this next piece of evidence, and I could see how hard it was for him to believe what he was saying. "You see… A whole piece of scenery fell on our star actor, Gabriel Nelson. He got out of the way just in time, but it could have killed him."

"Gabriel Nelson!" Grandfather had forgotten the gravity of the moment and grinned. "Oh, he's a fine actor. Truly fine. And he's quite the comic, too."

Marmaduke evidently had something more to tell us, so I helped him along. "What do your fellow actors think of everything that's happened? Do they believe that someone is behind all this?"

He looked through the seats at Lord Edgington for encouragement. If there is one person who's likely to instil confidence in a witness it's… well, anyone but me.

"They were sceptical at first, but as time has passed, most people in the theatre have come to believe the same thing."

"Then they agree with you?" Grandfather's voice seemed to drop an octave as he pronounced this important question. "They truly believe that your colleague Peter was murdered?"

"Oh, no. Not that. They think the place is haunted." He knocked his hair from his eyes with a careless swat of the hand. "They're convinced that a ghost stalks Daly's Theatre."

CHAPTER FOUR

We drove directly to the Savoy Hotel and pulled into its elegant, enclosed entrance off the Strand. There were a few taxis ahead of us, and I watched as several well-dressed gents and glamorous young ladies were ushered into the luxury hotel by the waiting porters. When it was our turn, the fellow on duty, in his long black livery with gold buttons and matching piping, looked less than pleased to see my grandfather get out of the car.

"Car parking is not a service we offer to chauffeurs."

I'd rarely seen the old lord look so affronted. "I am not a chauffeur. I'm the Marquess of Edgington."

By this point, the porter had turned a similar colour to the renowned aristocrat he had just insulted. As, just for once, my grandfather was not wearing his coat but was dressed in his neat grey waistcoat and shirtsleeves, it was quite understandable that he would be mistaken for a servant.

"Don't listen to a word this man says," Marmaduke sidled up to proclaim. "My chauffeur is forever playing such jokes, and I do not approve of it one bit."

He earned a clap around the back of the head for this impertinence, and I could tell that the porter would have liked to give him one, too. Grandfather ducked back into the car to retrieve his famous grey morning coat. With the article duly donned, there was no longer any doubt over his identity, and he seemed to relax now that he was cosily wrapped in his favourite item of clothing.

"Don't give it a second thought," he told the porter, and his moustaches gave a jaunty wave. "My man will be along in no time in another car."

He may have considered patting his beloved Daimler goodbye but settled for a loving gaze in its direction as we took off on foot towards Leicester Square. Much like Burlington Bertie in the famous song, Lord Edgington walked down the Strand with his gloves on his hands, past the recently reopened Vaudeville Theatre and the neoclassical Adelphi.

I was lucky to have been brought up by at least one parent who adored the vibrant centre of the city. Mother had taken my brother and me to countless plays, comedy musicals and spectacles since we were tall enough to see over the row of seats in front of us. Taking a trip to London's West End feels like going home for me, and yet, it is never truly familiar. The signs on every establishment can change from one week to the next. The names of the actors on the posters shuffle from one theatre to another and, far more frequently than would seem to make financial sense, the buildings themselves are knocked down and rebuilt.

The press calls it 'Theatreland', and it certainly deserves to be a nation in its own right. A nation peopled by the brightest, brashest and most talented of souls – where every emotion is felt as deeply as a knife through the back and every song requires a troop of glamorously attired dancers to accompany it.

We must have walked past ten different theatres in our short walk, and my eyes remained just as wide as on my first visit to that unique village that was enclosed within the greatest city in the world.

I defy any man to go to that glittering spot at the centre of Leicester Square and not be moved by the sights on show there. For all the stately homes and country piles I have visited with my grandfather, nowhere compares to it. I struggle to believe there are palaces in India as bright and beautiful as the Alhambra Theatre or any one of its neighbours. Even Grandfather looked a little awed by the spectacle, and Marmaduke hurried ahead of us like a guide to some foreign land, eager to show us the marvels of his home country.

Daly's Theatre sat in the far corner of the square. Though not quite as grand as some of the buildings around it, it still looked resplendent in the autumn sunshine. I'm not particularly knowledgeable compared to most in my family when it comes to architecture, but I can say with some confidence that it was built in Ham Hill stone in an Italian Renaissance style with neoclassical features. In the centre of the building were a number of fluted Doric columns which supported an impressive pediment that really attracted the eye, supported as it was by a more rustic base. Well… that's how it seemed to me, at least. You'd have to ask my mother if you wanted to be certain.

More pertinent to our case, however, was the sign attached to the front of the building. There in large letters were the words 'A Killer in the Wings'.

"It can hold twelve hundred people," Marmaduke said with great pride as we approached the entrance.

This may have impressed me even more than the façade. "Twelve hundred people a night are going to be watching you perform?"

"If tickets sell well." He almost sounded shy then. "The theatre could do with a hit play. I hear the owner has had a run of bad luck."

"How interesting." Grandfather purred at the possibility of a new motive to explore, but Marmaduke soon poured cold water on the idea.

"I'm sorry to disappoint you, Lord Edgington, but Mr James wasn't in the country last week when Peter was killed."

He considered the implications of this seriously before replying. "Well… good. I have come here in search of a mystery, not a simple case of sabotage in order to claim money back from whatever insurance policy the owner has in place."

Marmaduke opened the door for us, as there was no one on duty just then, and we swept into an entrance hall that looked much like a comfortable lounge. It had a welcoming fire burning in the hearth and was furnished with sofas and a pretty mosaic floor. This was quite disconcerting, as I'd expected to find myself in a grand theatre lobby, but there was more to discover inside.

"It's rather original, don't you think?" my friend asked, but he did not wait for a reply.

He rushed past us to another set of doors, and this was when Daly's Theatre really came into its own. The foyer itself was arranged over two levels and had an opening in the ceiling above us where we could see up to the floor above. There were palms everywhere I looked, and that's all that I had time to notice, as it was at this moment that a man came storming out of the auditorium.

"This is the final straw!" he shouted and, although the comment wasn't directed at us, he certainly was.

I had to step out of the way, as he was coming at such a rate of knots that he might well have knocked me over.

"Please, Mr West," a handsome man in his late twenties called after him. "We can't do the play without you. Please don't leave us now."

The first fellow had distinguished grey hair arranged in a wave on the top of his head. He came to a stop now and stared at his pursuer as though he'd said something offensive. "Let me give you some advice, Mr Quin. When a ship starts sinking, man the lifeboats. This production is cursed."

He turned and bustled off without a backward look.

CHAPTER FIVE

Before we go any further, allow me to make a brief account of my observations up to this point. From what I could tell, the man who had just left the building – and his job at Daly's Theatre – could only be the play's director, Colin West. The man now counting his sorrows in a luxurious foyer, meanwhile, was presumably… well… I hadn't got that far.

What I can say is that he had a mop of dark curls and a friendly air about him, even at this difficult moment. He looked as though he would flee the theatre himself but instead gave a deafening yell that shook the panes in the windows on the floor above. This was not enough to relieve him of his burden, and so he leaned back against the wall and slid to the floor.

He seemed vaguely aware of us as he offered a brief summation of his quandary. "That's it then. It's over. Why I ever thought this would be a good idea is beyond me."

As I didn't know what to say, and Grandfather didn't insert himself in the delicate situation, it fell to Marmaduke to intervene. My friend is afraid of very little, so he was the perfect candidate.

He knelt down before the man in the black three-piece suit. "Don't give up now, Mr Quin."

I'd definitely heard the name Quin that day, but I'd heard a lot of names and couldn't remember if he was an actor or a stagehand or…

"This is your play. You wrote it based on your own novel."

Writer! He was the writer. That's just what I was going to say.

My friend paused for a moment and looked unexpectedly optimistic. "Besides, do we really need a director at this stage? We open in two nights; everyone knows what we have to do."

Quin's floppy black fringe must have obscured his vision as he looked back at Marmaduke's sincere face. "I appreciate you saying all that, but we haven't even completed the dress rehearsal. Colin West knew this play better than any of us. He rewrote my script and decided where each of you should stand and when you should speak. I'm no director; you'd do a better job yourself. So I'm afraid this may be the end of the play." He added something under his breath which sounded distinctly like, "And of me, too."

"For pity's sake, man!" Grandfather clearly wasn't happy with this response. "You can't just give up. There are people relying on you. Now, get to your feet this moment and do whatever is required to save this production."

Marmaduke had always shown a degree of awe towards my grandfather. Never was this better demonstrated than by the speed at which he leaned forward to pull the playwright up to standing. I could only conclude that he was afraid of what might happen if Lord Edgington really lost his temper.

Mr Quin huffed out a long, harried breath before accepting the hand up. I don't know whether it was this close contact with another person, or the time he had to think about my grandfather's words, but in the second it took him to get to his feet, he began to smile.

"It doesn't look as though I have much choice."

"That's the spirit," his new commanding officer replied. "How difficult can directing be? You just tell people to stand exactly where they're supposed to stand and speak up a touch if you can't hear them. With enough time and patience, a parrot could be trained to do it."

It was at this moment that the young man took a good look at my grandfather for the first time. "My goodness, you're Lord Edgington." He sounded just as shocked as he looked. "I must have read about every case you've ever investigated when I was researching my next book."

Grandfather's bow was somehow both humble and smug at the same time. It was an impressive feat. "And you must be Marius Quin."

"You recognised me!" Marius grew even more amazed.

"No, I heard you referred to as Mr Quin and came to the conclusion that you were the writer involved with Marmaduke's play." The young man's smile vanished and so Grandfather hurried to explain. "But I have seen favourable reviews of your book in the newspaper. I was planning to read it, in fact." He held his cane in both hands and rocked back on his heels to reflect on this. "As a detective myself, I like to keep abreast of developments in modern mystery novels."

"That's right!" I waved my finger at him, as though he'd jogged my memory. "And then you can criticise me for reading such unrealistic drivel."

"That's very droll, Christopher, but not quite accurate. I read them in the hope that they will capture the essence of being a detective. I only criticise the ones that fail in that respect."

Marius gulped. "Perhaps you shouldn't read my book after all, then."

There was something reassuringly modest about this suave young character. He was clearly a talented writer to have not only produced a successful novel – which, I must admit, I hadn't read either – but to have it turned into a play in one of the most important theatres in the West End. And yet, he had a humble manner, as though he didn't quite believe he deserved his good fortune.

"Mr Quin?" A sprightly boy in a flat cap poked his head through the doors to speak to the newly appointed director. "Everyone's a bit nervous. Maybe you should come and talk to 'em." He had a thick cockney accent and was clearly born to tread the boards of an East End music hall.

"Very good, Denny," his boss replied and nodded his head a few times in order to summon the courage he needed. "I'll be there now."

Little Denny, who I could only imagine was the dancing stagehand that Marmaduke had mentioned, slipped back out of sight and we all moved to follow him.

"Wait just a moment, Lord Edgington," Marius said as we reached the doors. "Does your presence here mean that you believe one of us is responsible for Peter Canning's death?"

Grandfather put a reassuring hand on the man's shoulder and said something terrifying. "I suspect everyone and everything at all times."

Somehow, this perked our new acquaintance up once again. "In which case, I'd achieve nothing by worrying about it." He emitted a brief laugh as he held open the doors to the auditorium, and we went in ahead of him.

Now, I'm not going to explain how beautiful that theatre was. I've already talked of the wonder I felt on wandering through the streets of the city and just how impressed I was by our entrance to the grand old building. It would surely become repetitive if I were to describe how I felt when first laying my eyes on the rich colours that graced the walls around the boxes and at the side of the stage. Sumptuous ruby, Venetian red, silvers and golds abounded in several vignettes filled with mermaids, cherubs and Greek gods with tridents aloft. I won't even mention the pegasus flying high above the proscenium arch or the exquisite glass dome on the ceiling above the stalls, which seemed to hang down towards the audience like a drop of coloured water. No, I won't go into any such detail, but do allow me to say that, even by the standards of London's luxurious theatres, Daly's was a sight to behold.

"Marius, dear boy," a tall, plummy man on the stage pronounced as we approached, "I believe I speak on behalf of the whole cast when I say that we require some reassurance as to the future of this production." I recognised his face from several plays I'd been to see. Gabriel Nelson came second only to the great Henry Snow in the discussion of Britain's most admired actors.

"Hear, hear!" a conspicuously narrow man at his side spoke up in support.

"How unusual for you to put words in other people's mouths, Gabriel." A woman on the far side of the stage managed to both say this under her breath and be heard from the fifteenth row. It was surely a skill that only an experienced actor could possess.

"Very well, everyone." Marius put his hands up as though someone had pointed a gun at him. I could only assume this was an appeal for calm. "I'm happy to set your minds at ease." He had lost the nervous, negative edge to his voice and was ready for the challenge.

Grandfather presumably wished to observe the scene without interfering. He glided along one row to the central point of the stalls, right beneath the inverted glass dome that I didn't describe to you before. We sat down in two of the twelve hundred unoccupied seats and watched as Marius Quin took to the stage.

"As you will most likely infer from his sudden departure, Colin West is no longer the director of 'A Killer in the Wings'."

This triggered some hubbub on the stage as the three people up there who hadn't yet spoken joined in with the three who had. Denny, the dancing stagehand, spun on the spot and clapped his hands to signify his frustration.

"It is far from what I wanted, and Mr James, who has largely funded the production, will have to be informed." Marius's statement did nothing to calm the restless natives, but he moved quickly to address the problem. "However, your colleague Marmaduke Adelaide…" My bold friend inevitably took a bow at this moment. "…suggested that, as we are so close to our opening night, I might oversee the final rehearsals. I know the play well and have spent enough time here over the last few weeks to understand what is required."

"Well, hurrah!" that expressive actor Gabriel Nelson exclaimed. "I must say that Colin and I never got on particularly well, and I am exceedingly happy you will be taking the helm."

The woman who had already spoken against Nelson held her tongue this time, but her glare said enough. Hers was another of the faces I recognised. She was Lillian Bradshaw, Nelson's great adversary. The enmity between them was infamous, and it was incredible to see them in the same room together, let alone sharing a stage.

Looking at the group, I was certain that I'd seen most of them in one performance or another. The skinny fellow with a shock of white hair was Nelson's former music hall partner, Oliver Hartley. Just in front of him was a promising actress who had recently appeared opposite the effervescent Georgiana Cotton at the Lyceum. Sadly, I couldn't remember her name, but the cast list was a veritable who's who of Theatreland greats (plus my old school friend, a woman playing a corpse, and a dancing Cockney).

"I truly appreciate the trust you have placed in me, and I am here to support you, no matter what you might need." Marius directed his thanks to them one at a time, but a coldness that I couldn't entirely comprehend had returned to the room.

Marmaduke eventually spoke when no one else would. "I'm sorry, Mr Quin, but I think there's something that you haven't considered."

"Oh, yes?"

He looked at Gabriel Nelson in case the biggest star present should wish to respond, but Nelson waved one hand theatrically (how else?) and Marmaduke spoke again. "Yes, you see, it's good that you're taking over as director, but you haven't addressed the issue that caused Mr West to leave in the first place."

"Ah… I see." Quin's tone became more cautious again. "Well…"

"I still say it's a ghost!" A slimy-looking chap with black hair and a skinny moustache stepped out of the shadows. "It's the only explanation for everything that's gone wrong here."

This triggered a murmur of agreement from the more superstitious actors present.

"Thank you, Brian." Marius raised his hands to call for order. "But

I'm confident that the theatre is not haunted."

"I'm sorry to say it," Lillian Bradshaw, the older of the two actresses, intervened. "But I agree with young Adelaide. Peter is dead, and it's only down to luck that no one else has followed him along that shadowy path."

"Luck is just the word for it," skinny Oliver Hartley replied. "We've had a run of bad luck, but we can't give up on the play now. It would destroy our reputations for one thing, and the theatre would never survive if we did. I believe that, with Marius leading us, things are about to change."

Presenting a more considered response to the situation, the writer spoke again. "I'll ask the stage crew to keep an eye on all scenery and equipment. The orchestra isn't rehearsing with us again until tomorrow evening, so the vibrations won't shake anything loose. I really think that we'll be all right."

He smiled that winning smile of his, and they all seemed reassured. Unlike the departing director, he was not a showy person, though there was a quiet competence to everything he did. Perhaps I was naïve, but I, for one, was willing to believe him.

I can't say that Marmaduke shared my confidence. The stage was laid out as he'd described it for the first scene of the play, and he had stopped looking at his colleagues in order to stare at the suit of armour that had been responsible for his predecessor's death. I was happy to see that the axes had been removed.

If Marius was aware of any lingering apprehension, he did not show it, but called to his actors to take their places.

"Very good, everyone. We'll start again from the beginning of Act Two, Scene One."

He ran from the stage and, as he did so, a gang of stagehands appeared from the wings to roll certain furniture off the stage, rotate pieces of scenery and pull down curtains. In a few seconds, we were transported from a Victorian sitting room to the courtyard of an English coastal hotel in the summertime.

"That's remarkable," Grandfather muttered beside me.

"Have you realised something about the potential murder?" I had to ask him.

He shook his head. "No, no. I was merely commenting on the

ingenuity required to change the scene so speedily. Think of the time that went into designing something like that. Think of all the people who must have worked on it."

"Have you noticed anything significant about our suspects?" I tried again.

He rubbed the rough whiskers on one side of his face. "Yes. It's clear that the theatre has spent a lot of money to cast so many famous names."

This was all he was willing to tell me just then, and so I settled back into my seat to enjoy our first preview of 'A Killer in the Wings'.

"Mr Marius, sir?" the young lad came to the front of the stage to enquire once everything was prepared. "Would you like me to do my dance now? We skipped over it earlier."

Quin's expression vacillated between apprehension and relief for a few seconds before explaining the issue. "Sorry, Denny. I think that we're going to have to cut the dance. It was never my preference to have it. But don't worry, we'll find you a few more scenes through the rest of the play. In fact, you can take over the parts that Marmaduke was previously doing."

Plainly happy with this news, Denny jumped into the air and clicked his heels. I had a feeling that he would maintain the same level of enthusiasm no matter which role he occupied.

"Take your places, please." Now sitting in the front row of the theatre, Marius waited for a cue from the wings. "If everyone is ready, off we go."

CHAPTER SIX

The actors transformed into their characters as though a button had been pressed. In a moment, I lost sense of my surroundings and watched the scene as though it were not occurring on a stage but directly in front of me in real life. Of course, I considered putting my fingers in my ears, closing my eyes and humming a tune to avoid discovering what happened in the second half of the play. However, from the look on my grandfather's face just then, it was evident he considered the production itself to be a key part of our investigation, and so I trained my eyes on the actors.

Gabriel Nelson, the flamboyant, chubby-cheeked star performer, was standing over a body in the centre of the stage. To his right, the younger actress I'd previously noticed was crying into Oliver Hartley's shoulder.

"She's dead," Nelson said, and the young woman cried more loudly.

Marmaduke knelt down beside the corpse and, I can't say exactly why, but I got the definite sensation that he was playing a policeman. "It looks as though she was strangled, sir." He inspected the body for a moment and then looked up at Nelson. "There's a gold chain tied tightly around her neck. I would say she was strangled... to death."

There were a few gasps from the supporting cast and the most famous actor stepped forward to say something dramatic. "Even I, Inspector Rupert L'Estrange, have rarely seen such a wicked case as this one. For who did not love Emilia Buxton? Who did not admire her warmth and charm? It is a sad day for all of you and a sad day for Great Britain."

It took me a moment to place his voice, but it really reminded me of someone. "My goodness, Grandfather," I whispered as it struck me. "He's doing an impression of you." It is hard to laugh in an empty theatre without the actors on stage hearing you, but I tried my best.

"Don't be ridiculous, boy." He was a much better whisperer than I was. His voice seemed to manifest itself in my brain. "He sounds nothing like me. I'm not nearly so pompous as Inspector Rupert L'Estrange."

I silently snickered as he said the name in the exact same tone as the star of the production had. Grandfather nudged me in the ribs and so I tried to pay more attention to the scene.

"I, more than anyone, will miss her." Oliver Hartley was not the subtlest actor and delivered this line with far too much emotion. I'd only seen him in comedies before, and it appeared that drama was not his forte. "I loved Emilia like no other!"

At this moment, the svelte young woman in a pretty floral summer dress of white and blue heard the man's comment and stormed across the stage to throw an accusation at him. "That's right, Daddy!" She expressed this last word with such disdain that her bobbed hair seemed to shiver. Although I was seated several rows from the stage, I could almost feel the force of her voice. "You loved *her* more than anyone."

The fashionable creature walked into the wings, and it was Hartley's turn to overact once more. He held his hands up to the sky and clasped his fists in anguish. "Why? Why was Emilia taken from me?"

Marius had seen enough and rose from his seat at the front to interrupt. "I'm sorry, Oliver. This is all a bit too melodramatic. I know that you've just lost your wife to a madman, but we have to believe in your pain. This isn't Kabuki theatre. So could you try that line again with a more natural intonation?"

"Yes, of course, Marius." The poor man looked quite crestfallen but did as instructed. It certainly improved his performance. "Why? Why was Emilia taken from me?" He fell to his knees beside the body and caressed her hair ever so gently so that, for a moment, I actually believed she was dead and that I hadn't seen the woman lie down there (or breathe) just a few moments earlier.

"Why she was murdered is just one of the questions we must ask," Inspector Rupert L'Estrange – or rather, Gabriel Nelson – intoned. "When and by whom are perhaps even more pressing concerns."

"Is there anything to tell us what happened?" Marmaduke asked his superior, looking up at the nattily dressed officer with something resembling admiration. "Any evidence that a mere bobby like me might overlook?"

"Have you noticed the marks on her fingers?"

Marmaduke held the corpse's hand up to inspect it. "The nails are broken, sir. It looks as though she put up a fight."

"As anyone in her position would." Nelson moved a few steps

46

away to peer down at the dead woman from a different angle. "But look at the red marks on her palm. What does that suggest to you?"

P.C. Marmaduke clearly wasn't the brightest of officers and gave a comical shrug.

"Less humour please, Mr Adelaide," Marius called, but the scene continued as before.

"Think, man," Nelson continued. "Why would a woman like Emilia have red marks on her hand?"

I was eager to find out what this key piece of evidence might signify when a call went up from the wings.

"Watch out, Oliver!" Dancing Denny sped out from where he was hidden to push the skinny actor clear just as something plummeted from the ceiling above. There was an immense crash of metal and glass before silence seized the stage.

CHAPTER SEVEN

"That's it!" The actress Lillian Bradshaw had always reminded me of my imperious grandmother, and she was just as stern looking as she issued a proclamation. "We cannot continue with the sword of Damocles quite literally hanging over our heads. It's a miracle that no one else has been killed."

Grandfather shot forward to mount the stage at an incredible pace (for a seventy-seven-year-old man). If I'm being honest, I did think these last seven words, but I would never have dared say them in his presence.

"Lord Edgington, how did you...?" Nelson looked taken aback to see the man he was playing (in all but name) appear before him in the theatre. "I mean to say..." He apparently didn't know how to finish this sentence and my grandfather had no time to respond as he was surveying the damage.

By the time I climbed up onto the stage, several of the actors had crowded around the debris of the light that had crashed to the floor. I felt that it would surely have killed Oliver Hartley if fleet-footed Denny hadn't spotted the danger.

"You saved my life." The over-actor was lying on the floor a yard or two from where the light had landed.

"Wasn't nothing, gov," the little cockney replied with an abundance of modesty. "Anyone woulda done it."

He smiled as a couple of the other stagehands came forward to pat him on the back and ruffle his hair affectionately. His dancing was already much admired, and now he was a hero to boot.

The younger actress who played Oliver's daughter—

Actually, this is getting confusing. There were so many people up there, and they all had dual identities as their characters in the play. So, to make things easier, I took a programme from the prompt's desk, and discovered that the attractive young woman with ever so short hair who played Miriam Buxton was called Tallulah Alanson.

Where was I? Oh, yes. Tallulah Alanson pointed at Denny just then and, with her other hand raised to her mouth, said, "My goodness, you're bleeding."

The little lad looked at the back of his leg to inspect a gash in his trousers through which a line of bright red was visible. He did not appear fazed by the discovery and retained his sunny smile.

"I've 'ad worse. It's an 'azard of the job in this line o' work."

With his part in the drama played, he walked off the stage with his mates, whistling as he went. Grandfather was still looking at the broken light. I looked up to see where it had come from and noticed a metal walkway high above the stage, which the stage crew surely used to set up equipment. Anyone could have tampered with the lights up there.

As the others went to check on the man who could have died, Lord Edgington ducked to retrieve something. I couldn't see what it was, and before I could ask, Lillian Bradshaw spoke again.

"I mean it, you know." Her commanding voice caught everyone's attention, and we all turned to look at her. "No role is so important that we should sacrifice our lives for our art. Either this old theatre is falling apart, and we should get out of here as soon as we can, or someone has been setting traps for us. Judging by the presence of the most famous detective in England, I would have to imagine it's the latter."

Grandfather took a moment to enjoy this epithet, coming as it did from such a respected member of London's theatrical community. Oddly, Gabriel Nelson looked equally pleased, and it was evident that he had misunderstood her.

"Not you, you bloated fool." Miss Bradshaw was not one to mince her words. "I was talking about Lord Edgington. If you don't mind me asking, my lord, how did you come to be here just in time to see the latest episode of our company's misadventures?"

"I brought him," Marmaduke stepped forward to reveal. "I've ended up as a suspect in a number of his cases, and I knew he could help us."

The woman playing the dead body on the floor had sat up by this point and was listening to the conversation. She looked more frightened than anyone, though perhaps that was because she had watched the light fall from her supine position. It had landed right next to her.

"This isn't a murder investigation," the fake detective exclaimed. "We've had a run of poor luck. When I played Hamlet at The Old Vic—"

"Oh, please, Gabriel! No one watches Shakespeare anymore. I don't know why you think that's so impressive." There was no question about it; Lillian Bradshaw really didn't like her fellow actor.

"When I played Hamlet at the Old Vic," he continued regardless, "Rosencrantz fell off the stage on opening night and cracked his head open. The show continued because that is what an actor does." For a man who started out in a comedy act at the Hackney Fleapit, Gabriel Nelson was surprisingly pompous.

"Peter is already dead, and I do not wish to end up like him." Miss Bradshaw's eyes locked onto his and they glared at one another. "There have been too many supposed accidents to put them down to ill fortune."

It would fall to the makeshift director to keep everyone calm. "I know how you must feel, Lillian." Marius had to take a deep breath then, and I could only imagine that he was overwhelmed by the task before him. "But I'm begging you not to leave."

"I'm not going to die in this theatre, Mr Quin." She turned to walk away but didn't get far before he spoke again.

"It's not just the theatre that needs this play to be a success. If it fails, I will be ruined. I don't know how many of you are aware that I am one of the investors. Mr James assured me that this could be the biggest mystery play that the West End has seen, and I believed him. If we don't open this weekend, I won't be able to pay my bills for much longer." A hint of emotion had crept into his voice, and he had to pause for a moment. "Of course, that isn't your responsibility. I got myself into this situation, but if there was any way you'd consider staying, I'd do whatever it takes to keep you."

A few of the actors gathered around him at this point. Pretty young Tallulah Alanson had returned to the stage. The dead woman was up on her feet and Marmaduke was there, too. They clearly liked the writer and wished to support his plea.

Lillian Bradshaw's resolve had, if not weakened, then at least wavered. She touched her long grey fringe as though checking to see it was still there. "Oh… very well. I will stay, but with certain provisos." There was a brief cheer from the rest of the cast, though I wondered what Lillian might now request. "Before we go any further, the technicians and stagehands will have to check every piece of equipment in this theatre to ascertain that it is in secure working order."

"That makes perfect sense." Marius seemed a little heartened by this himself. "What else do you need?"

"Someone stationed night and day to ensure that no other traps or tricks are set. I have a feeling that the disasters we've witnessed were far from accidents, and I do not want even a chair to fall over from this moment forward. Ideally, I'd like Lord Edgington or his grandson to be responsible, but you can bring people in from outside the theatre if necessary."

"That's a brilliant idea." White-haired Oliver Hartley seemed less nervous than he had a short time earlier and had come to stand next to his colleague. "I'm sure Marius will do what it takes to avoid any more problems, isn't that right?" The former comedian turned to hear his director's response.

"I meant what I said. I'll do whatever I can." A serious tone had entered the writer's voice, and he sounded quite earnest. "Is there anything else you require?"

Lillian paused for a moment as she glanced around the assembled faces. "Yes, one last thing." We waited on tenterhooks to hear what final demand she would make. "I need a cigarette. Lord Edgington, would you care to accompany me to the roof garden?"

CHAPTER EIGHT

Lillian Bradshaw led us through the auditorium to the public staircases at the front of the building and then all the way to the roof, which had been laid out like an English garden. It was most curious to find such a scene in the centre of the city, but a lot of thought had evidently gone into it. There were neat flower beds with poppies, geraniums and… other flowers I didn't recognise. Between them, paths were marked out and, overlooking Leicester Square, there was a terrace where the audience could come to sip champagne during the interval and gentlemen could enjoy their cigars.

When we arrived at this spot, something occurred that I simply could not have predicted in a month of Mondays. The steely and self-confident actress sat down at a white metal table and burst into tears.

"I'm so sorry." Though almost in her sixties, she suddenly looked a lot younger. "I hadn't expected to react like this, but it is too much for me to bear. I thought that taking a role such as this one would be easy after all the gloomy melodramas I've appeared in over the last few years. I never imagined for a second that it would be the most challenging part I've had to play in a near forty-year career."

It was always hard to know whether my grandfather would show sympathy to a witness, or he would hide just how soft a heart he had. He was evidently in a generous mood, as he stood next to the actress and looked down at her with compassion.

"There is no need to apologise, madam. This is not an ideal situation for anyone here, and I completely understand your reaction."

"No," she said in a wail. "I don't believe you do. No one knows how frightened I am." Every sentence she uttered was punctuated by a sob or a sigh. "All my fellow actors see is my public face. They see the woman who played so many strong characters and they assume I'm just the same, but they're wrong… They're all wrong."

My grandfather has often told me that it is a detective's job to find the balance between force and tenderness – that which follows the letter of the law and that which is right. I could see that he was in two minds over the best way to approach the situation, but he sat down in the chair in front of her and spoke in a low voice.

"In which case, why don't you tell me how you really feel?"

I could see how surprised she was by his response. People were often amazed that the great Lord Edgington was a more nuanced, complex character than the newspapers made him out to be. In that respect, these two exemplars of their professions evidently had a lot in common.

He held out a clean linen handkerchief, and she took it before replying. "You know, when I woke up this morning, dreading coming to work for the first time since I began this job as a young woman, I couldn't have imagined that I would find myself up here with you and your grandson."

It had not escaped my notice that she knew who I was. It was rather an odd sensation when total strangers had read about my exploits on our cases, but I cannot say it was totally unpleasant.

"Life is full of such quirks," Grandfather replied in a philosophical tone. "But without them, I believe it would be horrendously dull."

He'd received a smile for his troubles and Lillian tried to compose herself as she dabbed her reddened eyes with the corner of the handkerchief. "You're probably right, though I think even the most boring existence would be better off without falling lights and swinging axes."

She looked up at the complex patterns in the sky above us and shook her head as she considered her predicament. "If I had any sense, I would leave this theatre and never come back. For some silly reason, though, I prize the livelihoods of my fellow actors over my own life." She sighed deeply and looked around the roof garden. "I don't understand what's happening. I was certain after Peter died that someone must have had a hand in it, but it's all so absurd."

"In what way?" I asked. At moments like this, my esteemed mentor often relied on me to cut through our witnesses' rambling.

She turned to look at me then and, as though my guileless face reminded her of why we'd gone to there in the first place, she reached into the purse she was holding. Having extracted a book of matches and a bronze case, she proceeded to light a cigarette. After she'd inhaled the first lungful of smoke, she let it out again and watched as the white cloud spiralled up into the atmosphere and disappeared. I was several feet away, and it still made me cough.

By the time she spoke again, I'd quite forgotten what I'd asked.

"Take the accident that you witnessed downstairs," she told me. "It was impossible for anyone to target one of us with any certainty. There was not even a drumroll from the orchestra this time that could have precipitated it."

My grandfather extracted something from this statement which I'd failed to understand. "Are you saying that you don't believe Peter Canning was the killer's intended target?"

"He may not have been. Perhaps it was meant for me... or Gabriel. One thing I can tell you is that Peter was in the wrong place."

"I beg your pardon?" Inevitably, I was the one who didn't understand what was meant by this.

"On the stage. He had been assigned a place to stand by our departed director, but he decided to move further to his right for some reason."

I turned to my grandfather as I thought this was a rather significant discovery, but he showed no emotion as he asked another question. "What was Peter Canning like? Is it so impossible that someone wanted to harm him?"

Something changed in her eyes then. It was hard to describe, but it was almost as if they were smiling. "Peter? Oh, no. It's very hard to imagine that anyone wanted to kill him. He was ever so easygoing. I'd known him since he won his first role, and I'd never met anyone who disliked him."

"He sounds a little boring," I said without meaning to, and though I instantly regretted my outburst, she sat up in her chair and clicked her fingers at me.

"That's it! That's exactly it. Peter was terribly boring but terribly nice, too. We were all very fond of him."

When she spoke so warmly, it was hard to imagine that she had made a name for herself playing hard, spiteful characters. In fact, her whole personality was quite different from the way I'd imagined her to be. Her ongoing feud with her co-star Gabriel Nelson was the stuff of legend and, if it hadn't been my job to say the wrong thing and mumble at unnecessary moments, I might well have asked her what had started it.

"I have to say, madam, that I have heard any number of reasons for why a victim couldn't possibly have been murdered." Grandfather's expression became a fraction more compassionate. "Families usually tell me that their deceased relative was too sweet to have offended anyone. The police regularly conclude that a victim was too poor to be of consequence, but you are the first witness to tell me that a man was too boring to be killed."

She showed no amusement but repeated her conviction. "I really mean it. Peter was a reliable actor who, to my knowledge, never put himself forward for big parts and so rarely stepped on other people's toes. He was not married, had no girlfriend, and was perfectly happy with his lot. To me, that is the definition of an unlikely victim."

"You may have a point."

My grandfather looked impressed by the woman before us, and I began to view her in a different light. Young fellows like me often fail to notice older folk, but it was evident that Lord Edgington was a great admirer of Lillian Bradshaw. I saw the actress through his eyes for a moment and noticed the beauty and charm she possessed. She had a heart-shaped face and sparkling grey eyes that were not so different from his own. Perhaps it was her theatrical training, but she had great poise too, and a voice that made you want to listen to whatever it was she wished to say. Not for the first time, I wondered whether the old lord wished to marry again.

They looked at one another in a lingering manner. It made me feel odd, and so I soon put a stop to it. "If Peter Canning wasn't the intended victim, who was?"

The pair of them turned to me and, ever the gracious gent, grandfather motioned for Lillian to respond.

"It could have been any one of us, assuming that there really is a killer."

"I'm only repeating what you suggested downstairs. You implied that there'd been too many accidents for this to be a coincidence. Something clearly went wrong this morning before we arrived, which is why your first director abandoned you."

Even though we'd been bickering for the best part of a week, Grandfather was quick to commend me on my good work. He clapped his gloved hands together so that I could just hear a faint *pat, pat, pat* as Lillian replied.

"That's right." She bit her lip for a moment, as though reluctant to explore this possibility. "There were hundreds of tiny metal balls spread between the stage and the dressing rooms. Luckily, Tallulah fell over them going upstairs rather than down. It could have caused a nasty accident."

"By which you mean to say that someone else could have died?" The detective beside me raised his eyebrows as he raised his voice. "You must tell us everything you know, Miss Bradshaw. Please understand that we have come here in order to investigate the strange goings-on, and I would greatly like to prevent another death."

"I'm not hiding anything from you, I just…" She paused to find the right words. "I just keep trying to convince myself that I'm wrong. I can't stand the idea that the poor man was murdered and that we may still be in danger. I've worked with almost everyone on that stage downstairs for years. The only two I hadn't met before were Marmaduke and the funny little dancing boy. I've always believed that we actors were best of friends. The thought of one of my colleagues harbouring some awful grudge is too painful to accept."

Even I could see that her thinking was muddled. She was both certain that there was a murderer treading the boards and unwilling to believe such a thing. Luckily, my grandfather was on hand to point out such inconsistencies.

"Come along now. It's an open secret that you and Gabriel Nelson can't stand one another. Even if I hadn't read the stories about you in the press, I would have guessed it from the way you spoke to him just now."

She was lost for words again, and a crease in her brow suggested that she was even more afraid than when we'd first arrived. "Gabriel is an exception."

"That sounds like another contradiction to me."

"Which makes perfect sense, as Gabriel is always a contradiction. I've known the man for the best part of four decades, and I still don't understand him."

Grandfather had a reply prepared. "And if Gabriel can be an exception, then there's always the chance that there could be another. Even in the police force, in which I served a similarly lengthy career, there are rivalries and grudges. Although it was our task to keep society safe and fight injustice, it wasn't easy to get along with a group of men with whom I had little in common. Could it not be that actors

57

are simply better at hiding their true feelings than most people?"

Instead of answering this question, she got to her feet and wandered over to the nearest flower bed. There was a magnolia tree in the middle of it which bore bright white flowers, and I finally realised that it was the wrong time of year for any such blossom. The poppies and whatnots were the same. It was almost October and yet Daly's Theatre roof garden was in full bloom.

Lillian took a petal between two fingers and something about the way it caught the light told me that it wasn't real. The whole garden was a fake, a fraud; a mirage of a verdant landscape created with wood, cotton and silk. I hadn't questioned it at first, as I had no reason to do so, but I now saw the place for what it really was.

"Actors are a lot of things, but we're rarely good at hiding our feelings. Not in real life, at least. Perhaps it's because we have to control our emotions in order to inhabit the characters we portray. In my experience, as soon as we step off the stage, it all comes pouring out of us."

I can't say I understood much of this, but my companion did so on my behalf. It was at times like this that I was grateful to be the lowly assistant to a genius. He tended to make sense of all the pieces of evidence that were beyond me.

Whatever she meant, the question he finally asked was, "So tell us what fractures you have noticed in your tightly knit group of thespians. Tell us what you've seen that could explain the fate that Peter suffered. Or do you suddenly believe that all the accidents you've witnessed were just that?"

CHAPTER NINE

I imagine that cleverer people than me might have guessed that Lillian Bradshaw would not answer his question. I imagine this because I came to that very conclusion. Instead, she made her excuses in a manner that suggested we'd forced her up there to talk to us.

"I'm really very busy, you know. It's almost opening night and there's no time for idle speculation." She dropped her cigarette to the floor and tapped the sparks out of it with the toe of her dainty silk shoe. "I'm sure you'll be able to catch the killer yourself – whether he be flesh or spirit."

There was a slight smile on her face as she turned to cross the garden and disappear back downstairs.

"How very strange," I commented once she was gone. The clouds had gathered and turned a few shades darker, and there was a feeling in the air that London's famous rain would soon arrive.

Grandfather continued to stare after her with that same admiring countenance that I'd noticed minutes earlier. I wonder if it was loyalty to my dead grandmother that made me interrupt him.

"I said, how very strange!"

"Strange?" he replied absentmindedly and then came back to the present moment. "Oh, you mean Miss Bradshaw. There's nothing particularly strange about her behaviour. She is a woman with secrets to keep, which she does not wish to disclose just because someone may or may not have been murdered."

"And which do you think is more likely?"

He finally looked at me. "We've driven all this way; do you really have to ask?"

I walked over to him as a crack of thunder sounded in the distance. "You infuriating old fox."

He did not deem this worthy of any more response than, "Please use full sentences, Christopher. I had hoped you were making progress with the issue, but it seems we are back to where we started."

"You can't get away with it that easily." I wouldn't let him change the subject. "Tell me what you really think. Was Peter Canning murdered or not?"

He rose, and we crossed the artificial garden to return to the auditorium. "I have already told you, Christopher. But now we will search for evidence either way."

This resolution pushed him onwards and, his cane swishing at his side with every other step, we descended the sweeping staircases, passed the palm lounge and made it back to the stalls where the actors had abandoned the stage to practise a scene in the aisle.

"Marius, we don't have the space to rehearse here." The actor who had previously broached the subject of the killer ghost was a greasy-looking cove with a tiny black moustache that kept falling off. I could only assume it was a prop for the play rather than – much as some bald men don toupees – his attempt to look more hirsute than he actually was.

"I'm happier down here than up on the stage, thank you," Tallulah Alanson informed him, and he looked a little guilty for voicing his opinion.

"Don't worry about your positioning," the new director reassured them. "In fact, this whole experience should help you to focus on the delivery of the words. I know it might be too late to change things – and I'd take a red pen to the script if we had more time – but I prefer a much more natural style than Colin West prescribed. Stand right where you are and read your lines as though this is really happening. Your girlfriend has just discovered that her stepmother is dead. Show me the emotion that's running through you. Let me feel the compassion you have towards her."

Regardless of whether he was an old hand or a total novice, there was something inspirational in the way that Marius spoke to his cast. I felt sure that, had I been acting alongside them, he would have known how to get the best from me.

The actor with the fake moustache – who the programme I had pilfered informed me was called Brian Grimage – cleared his throat and addressed his colleague with great tenderness. "I'm sorry, Miriam. I can't imagine how awful you must feel."

Tallulah Alanson was more beautiful every time I saw her. Admittedly, I'd only seen her twice, and I was much closer this time, but she had round cheeks that I picture the woman I one day marry having. Her modern haircut, with its sharply pointed bob, only accentuated them.

"Everyone says they're sorry, but what does it really mean?" She stared into the middle distance and her whole being spoke of sorrow and pain. "The truth is, I never loved my stepmother, and I would be a hypocrite to say otherwise."

He put his arm around her ever so gently, as though he were touching a box of explosives. "That doesn't change the fact that it must have been a shock. I was hardly best friends with Emilia, and it knocked the stuffing out of me to see her so... so... lifeless."

I'd stopped nearby to watch the scene and immediately fallen into it. This really was a significant failing for a detective. The most often repeated "foremost rule" – of the many that my grandfather liked to repeat – was that a detective must be observant at all times. That was hard to do when there was something so exquisite and captivating as a fragment of a new play being performed right in front of me.

The important thing that I hadn't noticed, however, was that my grandfather had run down the aisle and was up on the stage. I was reluctant to follow him and kept peering over my shoulder to watch Tallulah's performance. She was a truly wonderful actress, and I could have listened to her all afternoon and longer.

"Please do hurry, Christopher," Grandfather muttered without turning around when he heard my footsteps behind him. "Dawdling is one of my least favourite things, after green tea and blue cheese."

Dancing Denny and his colleagues were busy checking over every piece of equipment on the stage to ensure that no more 'accidents' could occur. My lofty forebear, meanwhile, was staring at the plain wooden stage beneath his feet. Well, there was a tiny black smudge there, but that was hardly going to lead us to the killer.

"You don't like blue cheese?" I said with some surprise. "Not even Stilton?"

"No, I do not. Now perhaps you could explain why you would pay more attention to my taste in dairy produce than the other essential pointers I offered you."

I could have, but I didn't. "I believe you were going to look for evidence to show that Peter Canning was murdered."

He spun around and, with a jaunty step, sallied over to the offending armour.

"Were I to wish to murder someone – which seems rather unlikely…" He let out a truly phoney laugh. "Were I to wish to murder someone on this stage, the axes that were already here would be the obvious weapon to use. However, making an axe fall without handling it is more complicated."

"Then how would you go about it?" I was waiting to be impressed by his massive brain.

"You would need a way of freeing the blade but delaying its descent. Can you imagine how that might have been achieved?"

He was very good at answering questions without actually answering them, and I considered the potential solutions. "A rusty old bucket like this would have needed oiling."

He ran one finger over the metal bolt that was secured halfway up the hollow armour. Though the axes had been removed, the device that had secured them was still there. He raised his hand to show me that his white cotton glove was now greasy.

"Very good, my boy. Someone lubricated the bolt that held the axes in place. That ensured a more dramatic chop and helped the axe to fall. Now, what could have triggered it?"

"Marmaduke said that the great crescendo of the orchestra was to blame."

"Is that a likely scenario? There were actors tramping about the stage and the orchestra would have already played at the beginning of the performance. Most plays start with music."

I was fairly sure that he was testing me and, knowing Grandfather, could assume that he had already provided me with all the information I needed.

"If – as you suggested – the killer could have slowed the descent of the blade until the drum roll shook the stage, I believe it would have been possible. So what we need to find is some… thing that he used to hold the axe in place."

He looked faintly impressed that I had got this far. "So you're suggesting that he attached some sort of putty to the armour."

"Putty?"

"That's right." He looked a little concerned about me. "You do know what putty is, don't you, Christopher? The substance that glaziers and plumbers use to seal holes?"

"Yes, thank you, Grandfather. I wasn't asking what putty was. I've known that for literally months. I was questioning what role it played in this murder." As I made this indignant statement, I realised what he meant... or rather, what I meant. "Yes, putty! If the killer had loosened one of the blades, that stuff might well have held the weapon in place until the most dramatic moment of the opening scene."

"That's some excellent reasoning, Christopher."

I was rather pleased with myself. "Thank you, Grandfather."

"The only problem is that there doesn't appear to be any putty in sight." He stood there expectantly, as if waiting for me to make my move in chess – a game in which I do not excel, along with cricket, football, rugby, tennis and, well... all sports really.

"That's because it would have had to fall off for the blade to swing. If I look around on the floor, I'm sure I'll be able to find it."

He crossed his arms expressively. "Go ahead."

I got down on my hands and knees to scrabble about in front of him. I started by searching around the feet of the metal man who had caused the carnage, but there was no sign of any putty. I found a farthing coin, a bit of old cotton and a black feather from a boa, but nothing else. A little way in front of him, there was a coffee table with a long tablecloth draped over it, but there was nothing under there either. I was not looking forward to admitting that my grand hypothesis was wrong when I noticed something in a dusty patch at the side of the stage. It was barely visible in the darkness and looked much like a small rock. I scrambled over nonetheless and, on prodding it with a finger, found it a little greasy, much like the bolt.

I picked it up, stood up and returned to see Grandfather.

"Oh, you found it." He sounded a little surprised.

"Of course I did. But I also got a splinter in my knee."

Perhaps sensibly, he ignored my sullenness and took the putty from me. "Supposing your hypothesis is correct – and this hasn't simply fallen off another piece of scenery – the killer would have stuck it loosely to the metal of the armour and then rested the lubricated axe on top of it. The question is, though, would the vibrations of the drum roll have been enough to make the putty fall and the weapon tip."

"That must be it!" Marmaduke had sneaked up on us... or, at least, I hadn't heard him until this moment. "I remember thinking that one of the axes looked a little askew. It was leaning out further than it should have been."

"When was that?" Grandfather still sounded terribly dubious about the whole scenario.

"It's like I said, everything must have happened between the first informal practice and the run-through with the audience. I would have noticed if it was in the wrong place before then, as I had to walk past it several times. But as I watched the opening scenes from the wings – totally engrossed by what I saw, I might add – the closest axe had fallen lower than normal."

Grandfather was suddenly more interested in the scenario. "Which means you would have been standing stage left, if I'm not mistaken. Can you tell me where the rest of the cast would have been at the time the axe fell?"

The budding actor thought for a moment. "They were all on the other side of the stage, waiting to come on for the first scene in the hotel which follows the prologue."

"So we still have six suspects then." I looked about the theatre to add some names to this previously undefined grouping.

There were the three established actors, Lillian Bradshaw, her enemy Gabriel Nelson, and his old partner Oliver Hartley. Then there was the new star, Tallulah Alanson, her part-time moustachioed boyfriend in the play, Brian Grimage and little Dancing Denny. Though, now that I thought about it, there was someone else we hadn't counted.

"Wait just a moment. There are seven members of the cast in addition to you, Marmaduke."

"That's right, but Harriet Taft, who plays both of the dead women, is an absolute chimney. She never sticks around between rehearsals. She was outside the stage door, smoking between the two rehearsals and then on stage, of course, when Peter died."

Grandfather looked relieved that we wouldn't have an odd number of suspects after all, but I had a question for him that could still have altered the matter. "Are we certain that we can rule everyone else out? Isn't it possible that someone set the lubricant and putty? The former director, perhaps, or one of the stagehands?"

It was Marmaduke who answered for him. "Not without being

seen. No one could have come from the front of the house, and it must have been done during our fifteen-minute break. Everyone was nervous. We were all running through our lines on our own because it felt like we'd finally made it to opening night."

"There is one thing that still strikes me as odd." Grandfather lowered his voice and we both stepped closer. "Even if the mechanism for the murder had worked perfectly, that doesn't explain the slapdash manner in which the murder was planned. There was no way to know who the axe would hit. Peter wasn't even supposed to stand on that spot. So the question is, what was the killer hoping to achieve?"

CHAPTER TEN

We'd missed elevenses, and I hadn't heard a whisper about any form of refreshment since we'd arrived. It therefore came as a great surprise when Grandfather spoke some words that were more moving to me than any line that had been spoken in the theatre that day.

"I would like to invite the whole cast and everyone working on the play to have lunch with me." There was a short roar of approval, but then his expression turned serious. "I must caution you that I have not brought my own cook with me today, and so I cannot guarantee the quality of the food. However, I imagine that the Café Royal on Oxford street will be able to accommodate us."

I believe that he looked for Todd or one of his footmen at this point to issue the order to reserve a table, but he was quite servant-less. I was about to tell him that he would have to ring the restaurant himself, when his right-hand man appeared at the back of the theatre. Sometimes, it was terribly irritating just how good a job our factotum did.

"I have parked Mr Adelaide's car on Exeter Street, near the Savoy, M'lord. Do you have any further use for me?"

Grandfather rubbed his hands together to appreciate Todd's fine work. "Yes, indeed. We'll need a table for twenty at the Café Royal, and then I'm afraid you'll have to stay here on the stage until a police officer relieves you. For the play to be able to continue, we must ensure that no one interferes with the equipment."

"Very good, sir." Our faithful retainer was already off in search of a phone as the actors raced to their dressing rooms to fetch coats.

For a moment, I felt a little jealous of my grandfather's charmed life, but then I remembered that I wasn't too badly off myself. In fact, I'd been moaning and sniping all day for no reason. So, just like that, I decided to be more cheerful. And that's exactly what I did.

"This is a treat," Marius told me as we waited for the others to return. "I haven't been to the Café Royal in a long time. Not since my book became a success, actually."

"Have you only written one?" I asked, perhaps a touch undiplomatically, and the writer's face fell.

"That's right... just the one. I've tried to pen a second, of course.

I've actually got a story in mind, but every time I sit down in front of a blank piece of paper, my head just reels. After an hour or so with not even a sentence composed, I give up and walk my dog."

I thought I'd offer him a piece of advice. "Do you know what works for me when I have a problem I can't solve or I'm struggling to make a decision?" His face said no, so I told him. "Cake."

"I'm sorry, did you say, 'cake'?"

"That's right. But any old dessert will do the trick. Everything from an apple turnover to zabaglione. You should try it."

"I certainly will." He was an awfully nice person, and I believed him.

"Off we go, everyone," Grandfather sang as the others returned, dressed for bad weather.

We paraded towards the exit, and there was a real sense of camaraderie between us. It would not last long.

"We should have done this from the beginning." Gabriel Nelson was just as flamboyant in person as he was on the stage. He was dressed in an unseasonably thick fur coat and was preparing a pipe to smoke as we traversed the lobby. "There's nothing like breaking bread with another person to make a friend for life."

"Yes, of course." Lillian Bradshaw spoke in the sarcastic voice which she reserved for her enemy. "I've no doubt that would have prevented the murder."

"Will you please stop being so negative, Lillian?" It was their mutual friend Oliver who attempted to broker peace. "There is nothing to say that Peter was murdered."

She did not want to believe him. "Really, Oliver? You were a second away from death yourself a short time ago. Aren't you the tiniest bit afraid that someone has got it in for us?"

"No, I'm not." Oliver Hartley was far more resilient than I would have imagined. He had been the lily-livered butt of every joke when he'd appeared in a double act with Gabriel, and I was surprised to hear him answer back to the formidable Miss Bradshaw. "I don't know what happened, but I'm certain that, now Lord Edgington is here to get to the bottom of everything, we'll have no further problems."

I was tired of their squabbling and so walked a little faster to catch up with my grandfather, who had come to a stop under the hoarding at the front of the theatre. The skies had opened as promised, and the rain was coming down in endless streams.

"Excuse me, M'lord." Dancing Denny appeared from behind me with an umbrella. "Your man gave me this to pass on to ya. Todd says to tell ya that 'e's reserved a table and called the police to send someone to look after the stage."

"That's wonderful, Denny," he replied as the boy ran over to his friends.

Grandfather held the umbrella high in the air so that he, Marius and I could huddle beneath it. At least one of my arms stayed dry all the way to Regent Street.

"Do they always argue like that?" I asked of the chasing group, and their new director nodded.

"Those three have known each other all their lives, and they enjoy nothing more than a good row."

"Imagine that." I gave my grandfather a wink to acknowledge just how childish we had been to one another over the last few weeks.

He had more important matters to consider. "I hope you don't mind my asking directly about Peter Canning's death." Marius did not say anything to the contrary, and so Lord Edgington continued. "I have been observing the six actors who had access to the stage at the time at which the axe must have been set to fall, and I have found it very difficult to tell which elements of their personalities are real and which are pure artifice."

Marius pouted a little as he considered this. "I feel much the same way myself. I had never met a professional actor before I came to work on this play, and I cannot say that the theatre is my natural milieu."

"What did you do before you wrote your book?" I asked in order to fill in a few gaps.

"After the war, I remained in the army for some time. I remained abroad for a few years and eventually realised that I was never going to become a great artist just by living in beautiful cities and talking to interesting people. I've always loved books, of course. There's something quite magical about the images they conjure in my head and the places they can take me. I'd had a friend at school who wanted to be a writer, and the memory of her inspired me to have a go myself. I sat down in Berlin one day to write a novel and it turned into the sort of book my father would have enjoyed. I'd never thought of myself as a mystery writer, but that's what I became."

"There are worse things to write," I told him, but he was already thinking about something else.

"These theatrical types are not the kind of people with whom I grew up." He hesitated and looked for the right, or perhaps the most polite, way to express himself. "To my face, they all act as though they love the play and everything about it. But then I'd hear through the grapevine that Gabriel wanted to change his character or Lillian wasn't happy with one of her speeches. Colin, our former director, ended up changing my script entirely, and I barely recognise my characters anymore."

He was a perceptive fellow and abandoned this topic to make an observation. "I don't think that's what you want to know, though, is it? What you'd really like me to tell you is which of them would be capable of violence."

Grandfather just smiled, and so Marius continued. "I'm afraid to say that I can't begin to imagine what's happening. If you're convinced that Peter was murdered, then I believe you. But I've spent the last month with this lot, and no one showed any hostility to the man. If I'm being honest, it's hard to imagine a killer even noticing the chap. He was a little…" He tried his best not to sound rude. "Well, he was frankly rather dull."

Grandfather shivered as a gust of wind blew across Leicester Square, directing a hundred or so raindrops straight at us. "You are not the first person to tell me that and, as such, I've come to question whether he was even the intended victim."

Marius was the kind of person who was always a few steps ahead of the average man – which would put him ten steps ahead of me and just a few behind Lord Edgington. "If you're wondering whether I was to blame, I can assure you that I had nothing to do with it. For one thing, if this play does not make enough money, I may have to sell my apartment in St James's Square. My publisher is already furious that I haven't written a second novel, and the men at the bank are sniffing after me like pigs in search of truffles. I would never endanger this production by setting traps and causing accidents."

As we already knew that the dashing young writer had an alibi, I had expected Grandfather to be more effusive in his reassurance, but he replied in a guarded manner. "Hmmm, is that so?"

Marius's mind whizzed and I could see just how much he had in common with the detective. "You will know by now that I was occupied in the auditorium for some time before Peter was killed. Of course, being a mystery writer, I'm well aware of the tricks that killers can play to provide themselves with an alibi." Whatever lightness there had previously been in his voice was gone; he presented the case for his innocence in a solemn, earnest tone. "All I can say is that I am not a violent person, had no reason to wish anyone on the cast harm and would have been a fool to try any such thing."

Lord Edgington regarded him from the other side of the umbrella handle as we approached Piccadilly Circus, and a few of the younger members of the cast ran ahead to get out of the rain. To be more precise, Denny danced happily ahead of us, but Tallulah, Brian and a few of the stagehands looked quite miserable as they bolted away.

"To be honest, Mr Quin, I am confident that you were not involved in the murder." As Grandfather spoke, I wondered how true this was. It did occur to me that he was only saying it in order to keep the number of suspects to a nice round six.

"As you said, though," I interjected, "you are a mystery novelist. Doesn't that give you some feeling as to who is responsible and what's been happening on the set of your play?"

He considered this point for a few seconds before shaking his head. "It really doesn't. I'm a dreamer, not a detective. I write down things that I think might entertain people. Investigating a murder is very different from inventing one."

My grandfather evidently approved of this response. "I agree. Starting with the killer and working towards the murder is far easier than the other way around. Which isn't to say that I would make a good writer. You and I, Marius, have had contrasting experiences in our lives, and we have accumulated different sets of abilities."

"It is a great honour to see you at work, Lord Edgington. Whatever form your investigation may take, I am eager to see what you can do." I believe that this was the writer in him talking and not the stakeholder in the play that had almost folded up twice that day. "Having said that, if you could try to avoid interfering with the production, I would be immensely grateful."

"I will do my best." Grandfather swapped the umbrella to his other hand in order to give our new friend an appreciative pat on the back, which meant I got even wetter than before.

The advertisements in Piccadilly Circus were shining brightly through the falling rain and, upon reading them, I instantly wanted to drink Guinness, drive a Wolseley car and wear Burton suits. It was lucky that the rain fell more heavily at that moment, and I put my head down to brace against the cold. If not, I would probably have pledged my spending money for the coming year to the purchase of items I didn't need.

We skirted around the statue of Eros and the Criterion Theatre, which was showing a musical starring the delightful Miss Bella Bonet. Spotting that beautiful young actress's name on the poster made me want to run away from the investigation to see her in all her glory in 'The Mermaid of the Mountains'. Luckily for my grandfather, the pull of lunch was too strong, and I stayed my course. And besides, I'd already seen that thrilling musical three times over the last year.

We soon arrived at the restaurant, which had been a favourite haunt of every literary wit from Oscar Wilde to George Bernard Shaw. I looked up at the impressive entrance with its green marble moulding around its brass doors and felt great excitement to be entering such an establishment. When traipsing from plush theatre to fancy restaurant, it was easy to imagine the West End as one great, luxurious playground.

To cut through my excitement, Grandfather had something shocking to tell our new friend. "Back in 1894, the night porter here was shot twice in the head. His murder was never solved."

"How interesting, I—"

"You did not let me finish. The dead man was forty years old, originally came from France, and his name was Marius."

The Marius who was still very much alive in 1927 did not know how to respond to this but ushered Lord Edgington through the door in front of him. When he thought no one was looking, he allowed himself a nervous gulp.

CHAPTER ELEVEN

Except for his impressive car collection, his fondness for expensive hotels and the fact he employed nearly two dozen people to look after his immense home, my grandfather was not a man of exorbitant tastes.

Wait just one moment! That doesn't sound right. Thinking about it again, my grandfather was very much a man of exorbitant tastes, as signified by the restaurant he had chosen for lunch. Nelson, Bradshaw and Hartley, the three big stars of the play, showed no amazement as we were led through the bright lobby by a porter in a crimson livery. There were eight chandeliers on the ceiling for no other reason I could detect than to impress people as they entered. They certainly did the trick, and several of us had to pick our jaws up off the floor.

Dancing Denny was particularly in awe of that pretty sight. He can't have been much more than fifteen, and I didn't blame him for being so easily moved by such things. Of course, I'd lived a lot more than an adolescent stagehand from the East End, and it would take something rather impressive to make me—

"Oh, my sainted aunt!" I practically yelped as I entered the Grill Room restaurant. To be quite frank, it made the dining room at the Ritz look rather plain. "This must be where the Gods of Olympus dine when they're visiting London."

I've spent time in luxurious places before. Gold leaf is *de rigueur* in the stately homes I've visited, but there was something special about the Grill Room. The ceilings and walls were dripping with gilding, but what made it so impressive was the way the mirrors around it seemed to make the space almost infinite. If the waiter had come to tell me that the meal he was about to serve would be my last, I'd have shaken his hand and thanked him for the privilege.

It was simply exquisite, and I felt a little underdressed. Admittedly, in their drab work clothes, several of our companions would never have been allowed inside if they hadn't had Lord Edgington to open doors for them – not literally, of course, there were people to do that sort of thing for him – but I regretted not wearing something more glamorous than my plain blue suit.

We were shown to a long table in the far corner, and I noticed that my grandfather divided the group and surreptitiously herded the main players to where he wanted them to sit. Marius, with whom he'd been chatting happily until now, was pushed to one side, and Marmaduke looked very sorry to be left out of the action at the other end of the table. I could tell that he was about to make a fuss, and so I shot him a hard stare. For the second time that day, someone failed to understand one of my hard stares. It was clear that I'd have to practise them in the mirror sometime. To make sure that he understood me, I bared my teeth a little.

He apparently made sense of the gesture. "I'll be just fine, sitting over here with the makeup lady and the man who points the spotlight." For a good actor, he was a terrible actor. "Don't worry about me."

I wouldn't worry about him, not least because Tallulah Alanson had sat down opposite me, and I could think of little else. It's not often that I'm left entirely speechless by a woman's beauty.

Wait, wait, wait. It's happened again. Let me rephrase that; I'm often left entirely speechless by a woman's beauty, and this was one of those times. The pretty young actress looked at me as though I was supposed to say something to break the ice and, when I physically couldn't, she shyly turned away. I'd never been so grateful for my grandfather's garrulous tendencies.

"As it happens, I've always wanted to try my hand at acting," he announced. "People tell me that I have a voice for the stage."

"You're certainly loud enough." Oliver Hartley was presumably trying to pay him a compliment, but it didn't come across that way. "By which I mean…" He looked to his friend to save him, and Gabriel Nelson was only too happy to help.

"Indubitably, Lord Edgington, you have an enigmatic presence which young actors would do well to study. Such experience as you have accrued in your life makes you a natural to tread the boards."

For once, Lillian Bradshaw did not disagree with him. She closed her eyes and nodded like an Indian sage who had taken a vow of silence.

I knew better than anyone that Grandfather was acting even now. He was the master of manipulation, and I felt that he would have their secrets from them before the meal was over.

"I'm curious," he said as the waiter laid menus before each of us. "What was it that attracted you all to the profession?"

He was seated at the head of the long table with three suspects to his left and three to his right. Amongst all that glittering gold, only Brian Grimage – sans fake moustache – and Dancing Denny – also sans fake moustache, as he never had one in the first place – looked out of place.

"I never meant to become an actor," Denny replied in a small voice. "I was just moving some furniture around and had to wait for someone to get out of my way. I did a little dance. The director saw it, and the rest is history. That's all my dance was originally gonna be, you see. I was supposed to change scenes with a little jig to lighten the mood."

I doubt that the young lad's career had been at the forefront of my grandfather's mind when he posed this question, but he nodded gratefully and turned to Tallulah.

"Well, I wasn't very good at school." There was a hint of nervousness in what she said, but she soon grew into the topic. "My teachers were always telling me that I didn't concentrate, despite the fact I loved any stories they told. Even when I was a tiny thing, I just adored reading books and, the first time my parents took me to the theatre, I fell in love."

She was not nearly so well spoken in real life as on the stage, and I realised just how much I'd believed in the character I'd caught a glimpse of her playing earlier that day. I was moved by her speech and watched her intently. Afraid she would suddenly turn to me and demand I stop staring, I eventually looked at the others to see their reactions instead.

Blank-as-paper Oliver seemed just as taken by her as I was and smiled a little more with each word she spoke. Lillian had a rather maternal look on her face as she gazed at the young actress, whereas Gabriel wore an expression that suggested he would much rather we were talking about him.

"That's lovely," Grandfather said when she'd finished the charming account of her path to theatrical stardom. "I approve of anyone who finds his calling. My parents never supported my decision to join the Metropolitan Police, but it was the right choice for me, and I've never regretted it."

"A calling!" It had been a few minutes since Gabriel had said anything, and it was about time he had a platform for his thoughts.

"You know, that is very nicely put. Just like priests or monks, we actors must listen to the call of the stage, the ringing of a bell, or the voices inside our heads which say, *leap, commit, be excellent!*"

I had a strange sense of *déjà vu* about this scene, and I had to wonder whether all actors sounded so pretentious when talking of their craft.

"I really cannot say that I chose my occupation." He was a great artist on the stage, but something of a ham in person. However, the other actors seemed eager to hear what he had to say. "I was ever so young when it found me. Do you remember our first act, Ollie?"

Oliver Hartley looked wistfully up at the elaborate lamps on the wall. Between each mirror, a disrobed golden woman held a glowing crystal globe over her head. "I'll never forget it." His tone immediately changed. "I had to stand there while you and Malcolm Delaney threw shaving foam at me."

The well-dressed histrion laughed awkwardly at his friend's painful memory. "Oliver and I were in a comedy trio back when we were young." He positively exploded with mirth at this moment. "That act was the funniest thing I've ever done."

Hartley's dour expression hadn't faded. "I would prefer to be remembered for my serious acting than my time as a feeder for your jokes."

Lillian put her hand on her colleague's shoulder. "You take everything so seriously, Ollie. Don't forget that I saw your act back then. I remember laughing until there were tears in my eyes."

"Gosh! That feels like a hundred years ago," Gabriel murmured, before his neighbour took up the discussion.

"I only went into the theatre 'cos I thought women would like me if I was on the stage." Brian Grimage was a less than savoury character and this comment did little to change the impression I had of him.

"Did it work?" Tallulah asked.

"Nah. It turns out that most women know how poor us actors are. Still, it kept me off the streets, and the police've never given me no trouble since. Easiest job in the world, too. Anyone with half a brain can remember a few lines and shout a bit."

While they were speaking, someone had apparently ordered wine, and the waiters now came to serve everyone. With our glasses full, Gabriel proposed a toast. "To the theatre, and Marius Quin's thrilling new play."

Marius was on the other side of me and raised his glass when he heard his name. "Here's to opening night, if we ever get there."

I stopped paying much attention to the main suspects then and allowed my ears to wander the length of the table. I tried to listen in to the various conversations that were taking place among the stage crew. It was amazing how little discussion there was of the accidents or Peter Canning's death. All anyone was talking about was the menu, the décor and the shininess of the cutlery. Oh, and Marmaduke was still glaring at me for not including him with the other actors.

It took me a moment to realise that someone was talking. I turned my attention to the young woman in front of me and tried to make sense of what she had asked.

"Cakes, bird watching and failing to form full sentences," I replied, as several common questions about me can be answered in such a manner.

She covered her mouth as she laughed. "I don't think you heard me properly. I asked whether your grandfather placed you under his tutelage from a young age."

"Oh… ummm… yes, but also, no."

"Yes and no?" she asked with a note of amusement.

"Well, more yes than no. I remember when I was five or six years old, I went into his library one day when he was reading over a case. He had already retired by that point, but he would still help out the police when he could. I thought he would shout at me and tell me to clear off, but instead he invited me inside and asked what I thought of a gruesome murder."

"How sweet." There was more than a touch of irony in this.

"Not really, but I remember sitting on his knee as he took me through the details of the crime, and I found it really very fascinating."

She waited for me to continue and, as I didn't, she prompted me for more information. "So…? What happened after that?"

"After that, my grandmother was murdered, and Grandfather went missing for ten years." I hadn't meant to sound so dramatic.

I'd wiped the lovely smile from her face. "My goodness! I don't remember hearing anything about that in the newspapers."

I turned to look at my grandfather as he played puppet master with the other actors. "Oh, you wouldn't have. They don't know anything about it. When Granny Katherine died, Grandfather shut himself away from the world for a decade and my training was put on hold."

"Yes, I can see that." From her tone, I could tell that the old police officer wasn't the only one who had suffered. There was a sadness to Tallulah that I hadn't spotted at first. She seemed out of place among the other actors. She was less loud and exuberant than her colleagues, and I liked her all the more for it.

"May I ask you something, Miss Alanson?" I dared propose and, with that same cautiousness running through her, she nodded. "I rather wonder what you think of this whole thing. A week ago, you were rehearsing a play like always. Now, one of your number is dead and the possibility of further violence hangs over the production. Doesn't that frighten you?"

She looked down at her hands and rubbed one thumb across her fingertips for a few moments. "I don't suppose it matters either way. I'm playing a part here just as I will be on that stage. There's really nothing genuine about me."

To hear one of our suspects say such a thing was intriguing. I was desperate to hear more, but an argument was about to break out beside my grandfather. I had no doubt he was to blame – not that anyone would have realised it.

Lillian Bradshaw tutted loudly, and I wasn't the only one to hear. Everyone at that end of the table turned to look at her, and she felt it necessary to defend herself.

"I love acting, I do, but must we really be so pretentious?"

I don't know what had caused her to say such a thing, but the others did not like her response. Oddly, it was roguish Brian Grimage who first took exception.

"You're one to talk, Missus. You swan about the place like you're Marie Antoinette, and yet you're throwing long words about at other people? That's a fine tale, that is!"

Lillian bit back a reply, as though she was afraid how the greasy character might respond.

Seizing the opportunity, Oliver jumped into the fray. "I've fought my whole career for some recognition of my talents beyond the ability to receive a custard pie to the face. Now that I'm about to receive some attention for my versatility as an actor, I'm accused of pretentiousness. I thought better of you, Lillian. And I would certainly never have put you forward for this part if I'd known that you would think such things."

"You put her forward for the part?" His old friend Gabriel was incredulous. "You recommended my sworn enemy for a part in my play, knowing that we can't stand to be in the same room as one another?"

Oliver pulled at his shirt cuff and looked from face to face. "I… I didn't mean any harm by it, Gabe. I only wanted the production to be a success, and I knew…"

Gabriel's voice dropped to a crisp whisper, but this only made his words more intelligible. "I won't forget this, pal."

"I'm still not happy about being called portentous!" Brian Grimage stood up from the table to declare with a grimace. Marmaduke fought off a smile. Lillian quivered, and I was afraid that a fight might start.

Grandfather picked his moment to intervene. "What do you all think of the menu? Perhaps we should take a moment to order lunch."

CHAPTER TWELVE

After everyone had calmed down, we ate our meal and wandered back to—

No. Stop, stop. I can't just skip over our meal, it's practically immoral. There's no need for me to write a eulogy to the dishes we consumed, but at least let me tell you what was on offer.

To sum it up in one word, meat! The Grill Room was well named. They had French quail, German sausages, beef all the way from Argentina and – less exotic but delicious nonetheless – Welsh lamb. My mother once told me that there are people in some countries called *vegetarians* who eat nothing but greens. I can tell you this, those poor folk would have starved at the Café Royal. Even the dessert had gelatine in it, so does that count as pork?

I had chicken soup to start, the lamb covered in mint sauce to continue, and venison skewers to continue continuing. But once lunch was eaten, and the fault lines that Lillian Bradshaw denied existing had been exposed, we wandered back to the theatre. The heaviest of the rain had moved on, leaving nothing but fine drizzle that somehow made me wetter than the downpour. Storms are exciting; they make you want to run from building to building and, when you arrive at your destination, you gleefully look at your friends to see how drenched everyone is. Drizzle, on the other hand, is just depressing. We Brits surely know more about it than anyone else on Earth.

When it was time to return to work, we had to wait in the auditorium as the stagehands finished checking that all the lights, props and scenery were well secured. The cast exchanged frosty looks as they lounged in the front rows of the stalls. Lillian never stopped staring at Gabriel, and Oliver Hartley looked as though he was suffering from a lifelong stomach ache. I had to wonder whether any of them had an inkling of who was to blame for Peter's death.

The younger actors were harder to assess, somehow. Denny peppered his work with dance steps, and I must say he was very good. He could even do somersaults, and the only unusual thing about this display was the reaction from his audience. It was quite uncanny to see the cheery little chap so full of energy in the face of such discord.

He barely raised a smile, which meant that I had to clap all the harder, and that caused even more frowns to break out around me.

I stayed quiet after that but turned to my grandfather to discuss his findings from the restaurant.

"What did you think of lunch?" I asked him.

"Delicious, thank you. Did you enjoy your lamb?"

"Yes, of course. It was as tender as a spoonful of cream. But I was referring to the discussion, not the food."

He sighed but managed to resist criticising my vaguely phrased question. "The discussion was certainly lively."

"And what did it tell you?" I hoped this would be direct enough to prompt an answer but, when it didn't, I tried again. "You had all of our suspects around you. They were there in the palm of your hand. You must have extracted something from the experience."

"Oh, yes. I certainly did." He seemed determined not to tell me.

"Is there one suspect in particular who has emerged as a likely candidate?"

He looked even more shocked than before. "A likely candidate? Christopher, we're talking about an innocent man's murderer, not a vacancy for a post in a bank."

"Please, Grandfather, just tell me what you uncovered." I was frankly exhausted by now. "I apologise wholeheartedly if my choice of vocabulary does not meet your approval, but please stop avoiding my questions."

"No, it's not that, dear boy." He looked as though he felt a little sorry for me. "It's not your fault that I can't tell you who the killer is. I really should be more forthcoming with— Ooh, they're starting."

He turned to the front of the theatre just as the house lights were extinguished. With the stage apparently secure, it was time to rehearse another scene from 'A Killer in the Wings'. There was a moment of silence as the three main actors took their places. After the tumultuous morning, the tension between them was palpable.

"Very good, everybody. We're going to run through as much of the second half of the play as we can," Marius announced from the darkness of the stalls. "Start with the final scene of Act Two. This is a key moment in Edward Buxton's story, and I'd like to see you give your all."

The stage was still laid out like the courtyard of a hotel, and I wondered whether they'd borrowed some of the palms there from the lobby of the theatre. In his guise as Rupert L'Estrange – complete with Homburg hat and camel-coloured mackintosh – Gabriel Nelson was on his feet in the centre of the stage. Sitting in the big man's shadow, Lillian and Oliver were on a pair of deckchairs nearby.

"I put it to you that Emilia had to die," the fictional detective began. "I put it to you that your illicit love affair left no room for any other solution."

"You're wrong." Lillian's character, Marjorie Whitstable, was evidently the mistress of Oliver's character, Edward. "That's not what happened. Emilia knew about us."

Edward eyed the detective but said nothing.

Inspector L'Estrange strolled over to stand between them. He looked a little surprised by Marjorie's revelation but persevered with the same line of investigation. "Oh, yes, it's very easy to deny it. You can say that you bore her no ill will – even though she was keeping you apart – but that doesn't make it true. The way I see it, she was the ultimate obstacle to your love." With a melodramatic pivot, he directed his ire at Edward. "Much as your first wife stood in your way when you met Emilia."

Edward shot to his feet. "Don't you dare speak that way of Carolina! I've spent my life trying to recover from her death. Can't you imagine how she haunts me? Can't you see that she was everything to me and she died in my arms? She bled to death from a bullet wound that I caused. I suffered, I have suffered, and I will continue to suffer that moment until my dying day. And now my dear Emilia has been taken from me, too."

I got the feeling that he was referring to the scene at the beginning of the play that Marmaduke had described to us. I was starting to regret not listening to him.

The detective on stage narrowed his eyes in such a manner as to tell the audience that he doubted the version of events that Edward Buxton had presented.

"I'm talking about the present. I'm talking about the fact that your second wife was murdered in the middle of the night, and you were engaged in an affair with another woman."

Edward bit his fist to stop himself shouting. "So just because I was having an affair, I must be a killer? My first wife died accidentally by my hand and so the second death must be my fault, too? Have a heart, man."

L'Estrange didn't respond. Instead, he went for a brief pace in a circle. I'd certainly never seen my grandfather do this exact same thing time after time on every case we'd ever investigated. (Oh, yes, I had!)

"Really, Inspector," Lillian Bradshaw... or rather, Marjorie Whitstable pleaded. "We know nothing about Emilia's death. You must understand that she was my friend. I would never have hurt her."

"A friend whose husband you had stolen?" the detective's question froze the scene. This was the first point upon which I noted a difference between my old sleuth and the one on the stage. I very much doubted Grandfather would have phrased the question quite so salaciously.

"I didn't steal him. Emilia knew about my feelings for Edward and understood. We'd been friends for too long to fight over such things."

This was a surprisingly modern arrangement, and I was a little shocked by the theme. I'd always thought that the Lord Chamberlain was required to approve plays for public viewing. He clearly had a more relaxed attitude to censorship than in the past.

L'Estrange was prowling across the stage, perhaps waiting to see whether Edward would reveal anything. When no one spoke, he took it upon himself to continue. "It's all very easy to say these things now that she's dead. Were there any witnesses to the conversation?"

Edward was standing beside a small fountain in the middle of the stage and peered across at his lover, the anguish clear in his eyes. I must say that Oliver Hartley wasn't nearly so bad an actor as I'd first assumed. I really believed he was suffering at this moment, and it was most effective.

"Why would we have invited anyone else to listen to a private discussion?" Marjorie Whitstable held Edward's gaze even as she replied to L'Estrange's question. "You're making no sense whatsoever."

"Forgive me, madam." The detective leant casually against the edge of the stone fountain. "But you must see how shallow the story you've presented is. Without proof, it doesn't help you. In fact, any killer could make up such a tale. I investigated a case once where a man's wife was shot dead, and he insisted that she had told him to do it. He said that she was tired of life – tired of the very fact of existing – and she begged him to end her misery."

He had employed an interesting technique. Rather than tearing apart their defence, L'Estrange had introduced precedent into the proceedings. It was just the kind of thing that my grandfather would have done, and yet this imaginary detective had his own unique style.

It clearly did the trick; even Edward Buxton was interested. "So, what happened? Did he go to prison?"

"Of course he went to prison," L'Estrange's voice became a growl. "The police might have felt bad for him, but then another woman came forward who claimed to have three children by him, and his argument fell apart." His sour expression remained as he finished the tale. "My point is that, in other circumstances, his story might have been impossible to disprove, but that wouldn't have made him innocent, and there's nothing to say that you are."

This was too much for Edward to accept. He marched around the fountain to tell the meddling detective what he really thought. "I've had enough of this, L'Estrange. You clearly have some kind of personal vendetta against me." He balled his fists up and, for a moment, I thought he might throw a punch. "You've had it in for me ever since we arrived here."

The inspector would not yield. "There's no vendetta, Buxton. The only thing that strikes me is how unlucky you've been to lose two wives in a similarly violent fashion."

"Precisely!" Spittle flew from the man's mouth as his paramour looked on in silent dismay. "I'm unlucky, deeply unlucky, and you should try your best to summon some sympathy for me." He turned to walk away but stopped dead when he heard the policeman's response.

"You say that this is all a vendetta, but what you don't realise is that I saw you."

I was so caught up in the scene that only the faint echo of L'Estrange's words reminded me where I was. I was not on the English riviera, enjoying the comforts of a fine hotel. I was sitting in a dark hall in one corner of Leicester Square.

"I saw you, Buxton," he continued. "I saw you late last night. I was standing on the balcony of my room smoking my favourite Gauloises cigarettes and watching the stars perform their twinkling dance when you walked through the courtyard, not moments after your wife had gone off that way, crying."

"You conniving—" Edward couldn't finish that sentence as it was presumably too rude to pass the censors. Instead, he turned back to his accuser, and his beloved Marjorie came to comfort him.

"That's right." L'Estrange was enjoying his big moment. "I saw the anger on your face as you thundered past. I saw the fury that was in you, and I said to myself, this is a man with the capacity to kill."

It took Edward Buxton a few moments to recover, but he eventually fashioned a response. "You're right. I went after Emilia, but if you were standing on your balcony, then you would have seen me return a few minutes later. You see, try as I might, I couldn't find her. It was as though she'd simply vanished."

"Only to turn up once more this morning, strangled with a gold chain that you had given her."

Edward's mouth hung open. "How did you know that I gave it to her?"

"The inscription on the back, of course. My assistant, P.C. Dunts, may not have noticed the letters, but I certainly did. N and M, I believe they were. Tell me; what was Emilia's nickname for you?"

"Nice Man." Marjorie had her hand on her lover's shoulder but removed it one finger at a time. "She called you Nice Man. Wasn't that it, darling?"

L'Estrange didn't take his eyes off the suspect, and I didn't dare blink for fear of missing even a moment of the intrigue that was stirring before us.

"That's right," Edward finally replied. "She called me Nice Man. It was to remind me that I was not evil, and that Carolina's death was not my fault. On the first anniversary of our marriage, I bought her that heart-shaped locket on a golden chain with the initials N.M. inscribed upon it."

He stared across the heads of the audience, – well, my grandfather, Marius and me – and tears appeared in his eyes. Real tears sprang forth as readily as water from a hose. "Do you actually think that I would murder her with it? Even if I didn't love her – which I very much did – do you think I would be so stupid as to garotte her with something that could be connected to me?"

Silence fell. It was not just audible, but tangible. I could feel it on my skin like drops of rain, and it seemed to push the three actors apart.

"It's an easy defence, Buxton." Inspector L'Estrange was not about to believe the word of this thorny suspect so readily. "But I know what kind of man you are. I've dealt with hundreds just like you – thousands, even." He took a few steps closer, and his eyes were afire as he finally put the accusation against him into words. "You found Emilia in the woods and saw red. You were furious that she'd made a scene over dinner, and you decided to punish her."

"No." The first time he said it, this word was little more than a whisper.

"That's it, isn't it? She walked away from you and so you took hold of her necklace and you just pulled." There was such anger in L'Estrange's speech, and this marked him as different from my grandfather. Lord Edgington had seen so much suffering throughout his career, but he rarely allowed his emotions to take control in the way that L'Estrange clearly had.

"No. It wasn't like that!" Edward looked at his girlfriend, but she had moved further away from him and finally seemed to doubt what he was saying.

"I bet it was so easy," L'Estrange continued as he drew himself up to his full height like a bear standing over its prey. "So easy to choke the life out of the woman you'd been married to for two decades."

"No!" It was a shout now. A shout that would not convince his accuser, but a shout, nonetheless. "You aren't listening to me. I didn't kill her. I didn't kill my Emilia."

L'Estrange was walking closer. Step by step he bore down on the suspect and something in the way he spoke told me that this was more than an act. For both the fake inspector and the real actor, there was a lot invested in this moment. "You betrayed the person who had given you so much. Someone who had built you up from nothing."

"That's not quite the line, Gabriel," Marius called from the third row, but the star wasn't listening.

"You are a traitor. I knew it from the first moment I saw you. You're not to be trusted, and anyone who does so is a fool."

From the look in Oliver Hartley's eyes, it was obvious that this wasn't how the scene was supposed to progress. He'd lost the sense of his character and peered around the theatre in search of help. Instead of the denial I might have expected from the defiant character of Edward Buxton, the actor playing him could only issue a weak, "Come along, old man. Steady on."

"All those years of dedication and loyalty. You threw them away, and for what?"

Marius stood up and waved his hands above his head to get Gabriel Nelson's attention. "You've moved far away from the script now, Mr Nelson. We'll stop the scene there, please."

The star of 'A Killer in the Wings' was right beside his old comedy partner, and he was staring down at him with fury in his eyes. I thought he might utter one last furious statement but, when he opened his mouth to speak, it turned into a whisper that only Oliver could hear.

The poor fellow was trembling, but then Gabriel pulled back, smiled at his audience and strolled calmly from the stage.

FIRST INTERVAL

A Killer in the Wings by Marius Quin – Reflections on the play from the case notes of former Superintendent Edgington, once of Scotland Yard.

N.B. I was lucky enough to be one of the few people to see a special performance of the play on the very day it was due to open. My thoughts, as set out below, were compiled on that occasion.

Act One
A prologue introduces us to a married couple by the names of Carolina and Edward Buxton, who are approximately in their thirties. There are some signs in the large, well-appointed sitting room in which we meet them of there being children in the family, though no names are mentioned.

As an opening scene to a play, it is quite effective. From the off, Carolina is in tears, a pistol in her hand and a look on her face that she is very much determined to use it on her husband. For his part, Edward does his best to reason with her, but Carolina is evidently convinced that the man has been having an affair behind her back – presumably with a mutual friend or acquaintance, to whom they both refer as Emilia.

There is a struggle in which Edward disarms his wife and takes the pistol for himself. If anything, poor Carolina loses her composure even more at this point and is unable to respond when her husband demands that she sit down. Seemingly accidentally, the gun goes off and Carolina falls to the floor, a red stain visible on her breast and, a moment later, she dies.

At first distraught at the terrible scene, Edward Buxton mutters what amounts to a confession that he had always intended to kill his wife. It simply shouldn't have happened then or there.

For some reason I couldn't quite understand, the stage falls black at this point and a boy with an oversized newspaper dances across it as unseen members of the cast shout comments on the case. The headline reads "Wife-Killer Found Innocent" and the young gentleman spinning it looks most animated about the fact. I really didn't understand why they needed a dance routine in the middle of a serious play, but I suppose that's the sort of thing that pulls the hoi polloi into the theatre these days.

The scene changes to a rather nice hotel somewhere on the south coast. The stage is lit as though the sun is shining brightly and there are a number of actors cavorting about the place in suitably long bathing costumes or sportswear. We are reintroduced to Edward, played by an older actor and now in his fifties. Lying next to him on a canvas chair is his wife of some years, Emilia Buxton.

It does not take a master detective to infer that she is the same woman with whom Edward had been having an affair three decades prior. A little jarringly, however, she is played by the actress who portrayed the dead woman in the first scene, though now in a grey wig. I had to wonder if this was a stylistic choice, and the same woman had been cast for each role to prove the motto that the past repeats itself, or whether it was simply down to budgetary constraints.

The couple seem happy but, when the famous police inspector Rupert L'Estrange coincidentally appears at the hotel bar, Edward becomes nervous, and Emilia tries to comfort him. They speak of the trial that followed his wife's death and his experiences with police officers. Evidently unaware of what a monster her husband is, she promises that the earlier part of his life is now behind him.

Soon after this, more characters are introduced. First comes Edward's daughter Miriam, who is in her twenties and appears to enjoy a happy relationship with her father and stepmother. She is accompanied by her much older boyfriend, Clive McCormack, who we soon discover is an acting colleague of Edward's. The group is completed by another actor, a rather glamorous woman by the name of Marjorie Whitstable. She makes no attempt to hide her affection for Edward, which upsets Emilia.

The actors have come together to discuss the possibility of putting on a play by a new playwright. None of them had heard the author's name before, and the script turned up in the post at Edward and Emilia's house. Most imprudently, if you ask me, they decide to go ahead with the production, despite Edward's daughter's misgivings. She takes him aside to tell him that there is something about the play that she finds suspicious. The main character in particular reminds her of her father, and she feels as though they are being manipulated by an unseen hand.

Somewhat irritatingly, the play within the play is called 'A Killer in the Wings', which is confusing as it was also the name of the play I was watching, and I find such trickiness perplexing. The only thing worse than that would have been if the play within the play within the play was also called 'A Killer in the Wings' and the actors within that play were putting on a play of their own with the same title.

That night at dinner, the group are reunited once more. Edward's wife Emilia shows her discomfort at the scene and, for some reason, all five of the characters sit on one side of a round table, as though attempting to re-enact the Last Supper of Christ. The play's director had presumably never been to a restaurant. People simply don't sit like that in real life, and I found it quite unrealistic.

As the meal continues, Emilia becomes drunk and belligerent and shows great hostility to her husband and his female colleague, Marjorie. Ever the peacemaker, her stepdaughter tries to calm her but to no avail. Emilia rises unsteadily from her seat, knocking a glass to the floor as she does so and blaming Edward for the mishap, her sorry state and various other problems in their life together. With tears in her eyes, she runs from the scene and the table is plunged into silence.

Edward eventually makes his excuses and pursues his wife off the stage. Without his knowledge, he is observed by the watchful eye of Inspector L'Estrange who glooms down from his balcony.

The next morning, Miriam and her boyfriend Clive look for her stepmother in the courtyard of the hotel. After a brief, slightly unconvincing search – as I could already see a body at the front of the stage – the woman is found dead.

Regardless of the minor quibbles I have mentioned, the opening act of the play was quite engaging and, as we reached this key scene, I was enjoying myself immensely. First and foremost, the audience was now in the unique position of having to decide whether the man we know to be a murderer has killed again – repeating the act of uxoricide which he had committed twenty years earlier – or whether a sinister third party is to blame.

CHAPTER THIRTEEN

"What do you make of it all, Grandfather?" I asked as we left the theatre, without too much hope that he would actually answer the question.

"I don't know, I really don't." He stood on the steps looking up at the sky as he puzzled this over.

We didn't need his umbrella anymore. It had stopped raining and there was even a patch of blue sky over towards Buckingham Palace. Perhaps there is always blue sky for the king, though. Do monarchs have the authority to control such matters?

"The whole thing was truly odd, wouldn't you say?" I tried to animate him.

"Yes, indeed. Odd. That's the very word for it. The day itself has been thoroughly odd."

We were interrupted at this moment by several of the actors who emerged through the doors behind us. I turned to look at them and noticed Gabriel Nelson marching off ahead of the others without a word of farewell. Lillian looked the most put out by his behaviour, which was no surprise.

"Don't worry about him," Oliver said and put his arm through hers. "We'll go to the Ivy for a drink and let the old misery wallow in whatever he's upset about now."

Lillian looked less sure than her friend, but the pair wandered away along Cranbourn Street as Brian Grimage and young Denny sped off in opposite directions. There was no sign of Marius, Marmaduke or Tallulah, nor could I see my grandfather, who had evidently vanished across the square without me.

By the time I caught up with him, he had at least come to some conclusions about the spectacle we had witnessed, not on the stage but off it. "…which proves what I've always said about actors. However, I do concur that the chances of anyone inventing a machine to remove prawn shells without making a terrible mess are extremely low."

I couldn't begin to imagine the cause of all this rambling but, as he hadn't noticed that I'd missed the beginning, I grunted my agreement and said, "Oh, absolutely."

He came to a stop in front of the bust of Isaac Newton in the corner of the garden square. I thought for a moment that he might consult the great scientist, but instead he directed his question to me.

"Tell me, Christopher. Why did I take the cast and stage crew to lunch this afternoon?"

This seemed a deceptively easy question, but I answered it all the same. "To put them at ease, remove any sense that you were considering their capacity as murderers and eavesdrop as much as possible on any interesting conversations they might have."

He gave a second quiet clap of the day. "That's an exceptional and accurate answer… almost." We moved off again towards the Strand. "You forgot one key element of our visit to the Café Royal."

"The food?" I tried, knowing full well that I'd be wrong.

At least he smiled at me. "No. I was rather thinking of the drink. The Café Royal is known for having one of the finest wine cellars in Europe. Nay! The world."

"At least I was close." I made sure to say this quietly enough that he didn't hear me.

"In vino veritas, as every yokel knows," he continued with a wink.

"And in fine vino very veritas!"

He looked at me through the side of his vision. "That doesn't make any sense… in either language. But the Beaujolais at lunch was excellent. It takes a lot to break through the no doubt numerous layers of artifice with which actors protect themselves, but I believe we did a good job of it."

"That's wonderful." I was so tired of not having the information I wished to know that I decided not to repeat the question I had already asked so many times. To my shock, he came out and answered it all the same.

"Their tongues certainly wagged. Tempers flared, and the fissures of which Lillian had denied the existence were laid bare. But what interested me most was not the fact that a group of people who work in close proximity for months on end might argue, but that Lillian Bradshaw sought to hide the possibility." He looked ever so pleased and posed a question of his own. "Let me ask you this, Christopher. Why do you think she lied?"

"Perhaps…" I gave it a go, even though I knew I should have

94

remained silent. "Perhaps she didn't want us to think badly of her friends."

He nodded to himself as we walked down Green Street. "Yes, that is a possibility." I breathed a sigh of relief just a moment too soon. "It does not help us with our investigation, but it is a possibility."

I pretended that I hadn't heard but, by not saying anything, I managed to work some kind of magic spell on him, and he told me just what I wanted to hear.

"I think it more likely that Lillian wishes us to believe everything is perfect in the company so that we don't dig deeper in a certain area."

I looked at him, showed that I was listening, but said not a word. And what do you think happened? He just kept talking!

"It's hard to say exactly what her secret might be. Perhaps she is simply a private person who does not wish the glare of public attention to be directed upon her outside of her work, but her contradictory behaviour certainly gives us pause for thought."

I emitted a short, *hmmm,* but said nothing more. This was my greatest discovery since I'd started investigating cases with the old marvel. I was not about to ruin everything now by speaking. In fact, it was becoming increasingly apparent that I should have adopted such a silent state some years earlier. From now on, I would learn from my mistakes, and he would forever be content with me. Just think! No more grumpy critiques of my foolish comments. No more sighs or shakes of the head. My life from this day forward would be blissful.

"And it wasn't just our lunch that was revealing. The seeds I had planted only grew as the day continued. By the time we got back to the theatre, the actors had become suspicious of one another." He produced a short, celebratory hoot. "Whatever has passed between them is emerging into the light, and I'm certain that we will soon understand what happened to poor, boring Peter Canning, and why anyone set traps in the theatre in the first place."

I couldn't believe how much I was learning by saying nothing, and it suddenly occurred to me that I probably shouldn't be happy after all. As he divulged his every hypothesis and suspicion, I was effectively functioning as a brick wall against which his voice could echo. It was as this doubt entered my mind that he realised something was wrong.

"Christopher, why are you so quiet?"

Quiet? I thought in reply. *I'm not quiet.* But he saw right through this argument.

"You're intentionally not saying anything in order to avoid my proving you wrong, aren't you?"

Little old me? I thought and pointed innocently at my chest.

He sounded terribly unimpressed. "This isn't even the first time you've tried this tactic. It didn't work last time, and it won't work now."

"What do you mean, this isn't the first time?" I certainly had no memory of such a thing.

He opened his mouth to tell me off again, then shrugged, sighed, released a short tut and rolled his eyes before giving up on any form of criticism and putting his hand on my shoulder.

"Christopher, my dear grandson, I very much enjoy your company, and I'd rather hear your voice than chatter away to myself like a drunken sailor... even if you do, just occasionally, make improbable statements that offend one's sensibilities."

"Thank you, Grandfather." We'd skirted the National Gallery to reach Charing Cross Road but had to hold our step to allow a London General double-decker bus to rumble past. "And I accept your apology."

"Apology?" His voice rose before he realised that I was only teasing him. "Come along, you rascal. We have plans for dinner."

We positively skipped back to the hotel and, on the way, I told him all about the last musical I'd seen, 'The Mermaid of the Mountains', and my heartfelt admiration for that stirring production's leading lady. I could tell that he would have preferred me to wax lyrical about one of Wagner's operas or some Russian ballet, but he nodded, mumbled at the appropriate moments, and almost made me believe that he was interested.

This time, when we arrived at the Savoy, the staff were prepared for their famous guest and welcomed us warmly.

"Lord Edgington," the porter cooed. "What a pleasure it is to have you here." He had evidently been told what to say after the prior criss-cross.

"It's very nice to be here, thank you." Grandfather tipped his hat to the man as we entered through the rotating wooden doors.

In the glimmering front hall, a maître d'hôtel was there waiting to greet us on the checkerboard floor. "Lord Edgington, it has been too long. I don't suppose you remember me, but my—"

"Michael Horley," Grandfather replied in a short, succinct burst. "You attended me here on January 12th, 1913." He'd left the man quite stunned, but I was used to such tricks and managed to hide how impressed I was. "I never forget good service."

"That's right!" The bespectacled man with seemingly gigantic eyes was clearly taken aback. "The staff here are well known for remembering guests, but we don't expect you to do the same in return. I hope you and your grandson will have the most wonderful time here at the Savoy."

"I'm certain we will." Grandfather offered the man an approving nod of the head and we were directed towards a lift over to one side of the hotel. We crossed an elegant foyer, which looked like the perfect spot for a spot of tea, and soon found our way to the lift where a slightly doddery attendant in a black jacket with red and gold piping addressed us by name.

"Lord Edgington and young Mr Prentiss, your suite of rooms is on the fifth floor." He kept his eyes closed as he spoke, as though trying to remember his lines. It made me wonder whether everyone in the neighbourhood was an aspiring actor.

The lift moved silently and smoothly up in the world like a spaceship from a book I'd once read. When we arrived at the fifth floor, there was another fellow in black livery waiting for us. I really couldn't make sense of it. Had the hotel stationed various members of staff around the building to await our arrival? Were they so worried about the porter's faux pas earlier in the day that they would go to such lengths to re-obtain Lord Edgington's high opinion?

"The answer is yes, Christopher," Grandfather whispered as we followed the smart employee along the warmly lit corridor.

I didn't even react to his clairvoyance but blinked a few times to make sure I wasn't dreaming. "Gosh, that is impressive."

It was not quite as impressive, however, as the suite that Todd had reserved for us. I didn't spot its name, but it was most definitely fit for a king. We entered through thick double doors of mahogany or perhaps some even more expensive and exotic wood that I'd never seen before. An entrance parlour turned seamlessly into a sitting room and, on either side, doors led off to the other wings of the apartment.

"You may have the largest bedroom, Christopher," Grandfather offered, perhaps to make up for one of his bouts of rudeness that day – I can't say which.

Before he could change his mind, I rushed off in the direction he pointed. I passed through more sets of doors and a lounge filled with cut flowers and small trees, to a large bedroom with a black and gold bed and a view across the Thames towards Waterloo Bridge.

I was tempted to dive headfirst into that monument to sleep in order to enjoy the plump pillows and soft fabrics, but I had one concern. "Grandfather, are you angry with me for some reason?"

There was silence for a few moments, presumably as the place was so big that it took my voice that long to travel to him, but his reply eventually arrived.

"Why would you say that, my boy?"

I wandered back to the entrance to see his face when I told him. "It's just that our bedrooms are so far apart, I wondered if you were sick of the sight of me."

He laughed but, before he could deny any such thing, we heard a noise like a dog barking and followed it. There was a beautiful bathroom beside his suite – which was surely the real reason he'd given me the bigger bedroom. It was complete with a black and white checkerboard floor, to match the downstairs entrance hall, oak pillars, and a freestanding roll-top bath. Oh, and the noise that sounded like a dog? That was a dog.

"What is she doing here?" Grandfather demanded of his factotum, whose hands were covered in foam as he was giving Delilah a good scrubbing.

Todd literally, well, not literally, but I imagine you know what I mean... Todd froze. "Ah, Lord Edgington, my apologies. I didn't think you'd be back so soon."

Grandfather strode across the floor to look at the scene from another angle. It made no difference, and he was still irritated. "You did not answer my question, Todd. What is my dog doing here?"

Delilah did not look upset by her master's behaviour and offered another affectionate woof. Her tail splashed puppyishly in the water.

"I truly am sorry, M'lord. You see, she blocked the path when I tried to drive Mr Adelaide's car off the estate. I picked her up and put her out of the way, but before I could move off again, she went back to where she'd been sitting. I must have tried ten times, but no matter how far I put her from the car, she always outran me. In the end, I gave up and brought her along."

Grandfather needed a deep breath at this moment. "I am sincerely disappointed." I'd never heard him talk to a member of staff so critically before, and I felt terrible for our loyal assistant.

Todd couldn't look at his employer and bowed his head. "Truly, sir, I can't express how terrible I feel. If you wish me to tender my—"

"Not you, man!" the old lord squawked and hurried forward to address the real culprit. "I was talking to my troublesome canine. Really, Delilah, I thought better of you. Stopping a man from going about his duties like that. How were you to know that I wouldn't fire poor Todd on the spot?"

He was kneeling down with his face just inches from her muzzle to show just how serious he was. For the dog's part, she showed no remorse but gave him an affectionate lick.

"You cannot get around me so easily, my dear girl. You may not believe it, but I am quite furious."

"I'm sorry, Todd," I said in the hope of calming the situation. "You've explained what Delilah is doing here, but not why she's in the bath."

He still looked a little anxious. "We got caught in the rain. I was originally planning to drive her straight back to Cranley, but then you needed me to guard the stage at the theatre and, when I took her from one car to the other, she got all muddy. I couldn't just put her in the Daimler in such a state so I—"

"I completely understand, Todd." Grandfather spoke in the same stern voice as before. "It is not your fault that you were manipulated." He whistled out a stream of air and looked at the soapy beast before him. "Really Delilah, what did you think we were going to do with you? Take you for a drink in the bar? Enjoy some music in the ballroom?"

Half an hour later, once we'd washed and dressed for the evening, we headed to the American Bar beside the Front Hall to enjoy a drink or two.

"I really can't believe this," Grandfather grumbled as we entered the chic enclave which was renowned for its exquisite cocktails and fine service. "I really can't."

The American Bar was everything I'd imagined it to be, and yet nothing like the rest of the palace in which we would be spending the night. The lighting was low, people sat smoking at marble-topped tables, and the whole place was framed in dark wood, from the curving bar to the walls all around. It was exactly how I pictured a prohibition bar in America and, though I didn't have much fondness for spirits, I was thrilled to be here.

"This is ridiculous, quite ridiculous." Grandfather was shaking his head so much I was surprised he hadn't sprained his neck.

Oh, yes! And one more thing that The American Bar had was a surprisingly tolerant attitude towards guests' dogs. Having persuaded her owner that her presence that evening was essential, Delilah walked ahead to our table and sat waiting for us to attend her.

CHAPTER FOURTEEN

"Todd, you have two tasks for this evening," Lord Edgington explained as he settled down at our comfortable alcove in one corner of the bar. "First you must make friends with the barman – I'm sure that won't be difficult for you. And then you must learn everything you can from him on the art of making cocktails. You're second to none in my book, but people said the same about my detective work, and I still learnt a lot from experienced police officers."

Todd looked even more in shock now than he had when Grandfather had lost his temper in the bathroom. I had thought it strange that the old lord had told his employee to go incognito to the bar, but I now understood his plan.

"Lord Edgington, that's Harry Craddock!" He seemed to think this should mean something to us, but I'd never heard the name before. "He's the best-known barman in London."

"That's right, though I hear that the woman who preceded him was even more talented." Grandfather looked quite relaxed on the matter. "Make sure you watch him carefully. Oh, and find out what the Astaires drank when they came here. I'm rather an admirer of the pair of them."

In something of a daze, Todd stumbled to the bar to carry out his task for the night. It had been a good half hour at least since anyone had mentioned murder, falling axes or dead bodies, and I was about to raise the topic when we were joined by a guest.

It turned out that the person whom Grandfather had arranged to meet was that man of mystery (novels) Marius Quin. He was dressed more chicly than last we'd seen him, in full black tie and tails – though he later told me he'd had to borrow the outfit from a neighbour as he hadn't anything else to wear. I can't say he looked particularly comfortable, but he certainly fitted in at the hotel. He had a rather glamorous look about him, and I could just imagine him sitting there surrounded by the fashionable London set, enjoying a Manhattan.

"Marius, I'm glad you could join us." Grandfather did not maintain this level of charm for very long. "We have a lot of work to do."

"Yes, of course." He did not seem perturbed by the limited welcome but sat down beside me, and Delilah immediately took to him.

"Please forgive the presence of that animal," the old policeman told him. "I didn't want to bring her, but she threatened to bark the place down if I didn't. She's become increasingly obstinate recently, and I'm not happy about it."

Delilah looked at her master and emitted a brief but deeply melancholy moan.

"Don't worry at all," Marius replied as he scratched her behind the ears. "I love dogs. I have a Basset hound myself and he never listens to a word I say. Although I have a sneaking suspicion it's because Percy doesn't understand me."

"Murder!" I interrupted, more than a little rudely. "Sorry, I didn't mean to say that so dramatically, but can we please concentrate on the goings on at Daly's theatre?"

"Yes, indeed, Christopher." Grandfather straightened his already perfectly straight cravat. "Why don't you begin?"

He'd routed me there. I hadn't formed any significant conclusions on the case. I couldn't say who the likely culprit was, and I still wasn't certain that Peter Canning had been murdered. "Well, I thought it might be a good idea to… perhaps…"

Marius interrupted, and I liked him even more. "I have a question for you, Lord Edgington."

Before he could tell us what it was, a nimble-footed, middle-aged man in white overalls arrived with a tray of pale cocktails in wide-brimmed glasses. "The man sitting at the bar thought you might like these, M'lord."

I turned to look at Todd, who had raised his own glass in a silent toast.

"Three White Ladies," the waiter explained and placed one in front of each of us before retreating to his usual haunt.

There was something slightly luminescent about the drink, and I instantly feared what it would contain.

"My question is, why did you trust me to come here tonight over any of the others?" Perhaps he foresaw my grandfather's tricky non-answer, as he added some extra information. "To be quite frank, I'm uncertain whether you really do trust me. Am I actually here because you suspect my involvement in the accidents and wish to keep a close eye on me?"

Grandfather had set his drink back down on the table and had two hands free to clap together. "You are clearly an intelligent young man."

Aware that Lord Edgington would take some convincing, he continued to defend himself against a theoretical accusation. "I don't know if it will do much good, but I can tell you once again that I am not to blame for any of the terrible things that have happened. I really will be close to bankrupt if the play closes."

"Yes, you said that."

As Grandfather examined our witness, I risked a sip of my drink. I really hadn't prepared myself for how tart it would be. It felt as though I'd just been shot in the tongue with a bullet made out of... Well, it contained lemons, that's for certain and, judging by the burning sensation in my mouth, there was presumably a dash of gunpowder in it, too. I pretended to drink a few more sips and waited for the conversation to start in earnest.

"You are a mystery writer." The detective spoke as though he had uncovered a major secret. In reply, Marius just nodded and his competitor in whatever game they were playing continued. "There can be few people better suited to planning a perfect murder than someone in your line of work."

"Grandfather, I thought that—" I tried to interrupt, but he merely did the same back to me.

"I can only imagine that you spent months of your life plotting the murders in your first novel. Furthermore, you will have read countless detective stories in order to write your own and learnt myriad ways to avoid detection and provide yourself with an alibi. Were I to rule you out of our investigation, I would have to be a true and unmitigated ignoramus."

Marius did not react to this. In fact, he fell silent for a moment, his dark eyebrows flexing uncertainly as he replied in a resigned voice. "I see. So I am a suspect after all."

I looked at my grandfather and knew what he was thinking for once.

I gave him a not-so-gentle kick under the table and decided to put Marius out of his misery. "No, you're not. Not more than anyone else, anyway. My mentor here was just seeing how you would react.

From what he's told me, there's no way you could have set the axe that killed Peter to fall. Marmaduke told us you were in the auditorium when it happened."

I thought my grandfather might object to me giving the game away, or kick me back, but he retained his superior look and explained further. "Not only that, but the fact you are a novelist, in actuality, is moot. As much as I admire certain writers in the genre, for the large part, they are noted tricksters. Few of the alibis that their killers use would save them for any length of time and, as I've already mentioned, starting with the killer and working towards the murder is far easier than the other way around."

"So you're saying I couldn't be a killer?" Marius appeared confused by this contradictory message.

"Not quite. I'm saying that there is no reason to think that mystery writers must automatically possess great minds. Your job is much simpler than that of a police officer who must reconstruct a crime without knowing the identity of the criminal in advance."

Marius needed a long sip before replying. "Then why *did* you invite me here?"

Delilah looked at her master. Perhaps she thought someone had finally flummoxed him.

He took his time before answering. "I asked you here despite all of that. I asked you here because I happen to believe you have a sound head on your shoulders, and I would like your opinion on the other suspects."

Now that he knew where he stood, Marius grew in confidence. "Of course, I might have been working with an accomplice. Or perhaps I set a mechanism that would trigger the axe at the right moment and then I removed it later."

"Are you saying you'd like me to change my mind and search for evidence against you?" Grandfather interrupted.

"No, no. Not at all. I just don't think that I've done enough to prove my innocence beyond any doubt."

Grandfather said something then that really surprised me. "In which case, Marius, I'll tell you the truth. When I met you at the theatre today, I noticed something interesting and, in the deepest recesses of whatever part of my brain informs such decisions, I felt that you cared about the people with whom you work. Rarely in my life have I had such cast-iron intuition, but I'm certain that you bear no responsibility for the attacks at the theatre."

"Wonderful!" I said when they'd grinned at one another for long enough. "Now perhaps we can rule out the other six names on our list."

CHAPTER FIFTEEN

"I very much doubt that Dancing Denny will turn out to be our culprit," I stated quite confidently after we'd been talking in circles for half an hour.

Grandfather did not agree on this particular point (or anything else I'd said). "On what basis?"

"A feeling."

He huffed and spread his hands out on the table in front of us as though he were about to hold a séance. "I evidently haven't taught you well if you think you can use non-existent evidence to decide the guilt of a man."

"You just did the very same thing with Marius."

He shook his head. "Don't be naïve, Christopher. A feeling is quite different from the capacity for intuition that I have honed over decades."

I was surely about to obliterate his argument when Marius intervened. "Perhaps we can say that, due to his youth, upbeat demeanour and lack of connection to anyone else on the cast, Denny is a less likely suspect than the other five actors." Neither of us replied and so he took this as a sign of begrudging acceptance. "In which case, what do we think of the biggest names involved? Oliver, Lillian and Gabriel, in particular, have staked their reputations on the success of the play. Would they wish to harm its chances?"

"Perhaps not," Grandfather conceded.

"Which proves what I've been saying from the beginning," I tried once more. "Brian Grimage is the obvious culprit. He even mentioned the fact he'd had trouble with the police when we spoke to him. He's just the kind of person to stage several accidents over the course of a week with one of them eventually leading to the death of a fellow actor." Now that I said this out loud, I was no longer so certain.

"Thank you for your passionately expressed theory, Christopher." Grandfather knew when to be diplomatic. "But I'd like to hear what Mr Quin thinks on the matter."

After the heated squabbling that Marius had just witnessed, I think it came as a surprise that Lord Edgington and I had fallen quiet for long enough to listen to his point of view.

"Well," he began tentatively, just in case one of us should want to seize the conversation again, "on the surface, the older generation would be less likely to risk their livelihoods than their young colleagues. But before we consider murder, isn't it possible that a silly trick got out of hand?"

Grandfather took his time to answer. He sipped his drink, then carefully returned the glass to its coaster and turned it around so that it was at the angle he considered best. It was understood that he would be the one to answer the question; he simply had the air of authority which could dictate such a fact.

I was tired of waiting, though, so I replied on his behalf.

"I've no doubt that Grandfather considered that very point," I said with deference, even as I barged my way back into the conversation. "However, for that to be true, the tricks would surely have stopped after Peter died."

"Why do you say that?" Grandfather looked down his nose at me rather haughtily.

"Because if it was an innocent prank that led to a man's violent demise, who in his right mind would have continued playing them?"

The old detective tapped his hand on the table three times. "Yes, I would say that is fair reasoning. Had the killer unwittingly caused a death, he would be distraught. It is far more likely, therefore, that we are dealing with a premeditated murder. Which brings us back to the very first question we had when Marmaduke came to see us at Cranley Hall. Why were there dangerous weapons on stage in the first place?"

We both turned to Marius, and he looked more uncomfortable than he had since we'd first met him. "Ahh, yes... that is a good question. From what I understand, it was far cheaper to purchase a dusty old suit of armour from some crumbling pile than to create a new one. Evidently, no one considered the possibility of a killer adapting it for his own ends."

I laughed then, as I imagined that such macabre outcomes were continuously flowing through my grandfather's brain. "That solves one mystery, at least. What about the question of who set the axe to fall?"

The writer bit his lip for a moment and held my gaze. "I keep coming back to the three original actors that the director hired. Hartley,

Nelson and Bradshaw."

"Were they contracted in that order?" Grandfather asked.

"That's right. Oliver Hartley helped the play get off the ground. It was presumably through him that Gabriel Nelson heard about it and then, as you discovered earlier, Oliver asked Lillian Bradshaw whether she would join the cast, too."

"That is surely the most taxing problem in all of this." The real sleuth picked up his drink to run his finger around the frosty rim. "Though we spoke to Miss Bradshaw on the roof of the theatre, just after the lamp almost killed Oliver Hartley, we did not discover why she took a part in a play opposite her sworn enemy."

The three of us considered this for a few seconds and, rather improbably, we all came to the answer at the same time. "Money!?" Admittedly, the others put an exclamation mark on this comment, whereas mine sounded a lot more like a question.

"That would seem a likely motivation," Grandfather concluded. "The prospect of seeing two actors who have played out a very public grudge over the last few decades together on stage would be a great incentive for people to buy tickets."

"That's all true, of course, and it was one of the reasons we were so keen to have them both." Marius took his time to consider this. "In fact, we could hardly believe our luck when Gabriel contacted us."

"It was Gabriel Nelson who got in touch with you, not the other way around?" Grandfather clearly considered this a significant point... I couldn't say why.

"That's right. Everyone was over the moon," Marius said. "I must admit that I know little of their relationship. I don't read the kind of newspapers that describe the lives of the rich and famous. Do either of you know the root of the falling-out between Gabriel and Lillian?"

They both looked at me for some reason. It was hard not to take offence. It was as if they were saying, *you are young and trivial, you would know about such nonsense.* As it happened, I did have some idea, but I did not appreciate their aspersion.

"No one knows for certain, but it started before I was born. I believe that, along with Oliver Hartley and another comic, they worked together at the beginning of their careers. Lillian Bradshaw became famous sooner than the others. The other man in their ranks couldn't take the disappointment and disappeared from the limelight, and Gabriel and Lillian never spoke again. I've always assumed that's what caused the fracture."

"You see, this is why today has been so frustrating," Grandfather confessed. "This really isn't my world, and I don't feel I have grasped the exact nature of the relationships between our suspects. Much like you, Mr Quin, I have no time for such tittle-tattle. That is not to say I don't admire certain players on the London stage, but my interest in them concludes with the falling curtain at the end of the night."

Marius brought his hands down on the table in exasperation. "But at least you have all the wits of a great detective. I'm just a writer, and I'm quite lost in the whole affair. In fact, by the rules of a mystery novel, I'd say that I am the most likely killer, as there is absolutely no way I could have done it."

"You're contradicting yourself," I told him. "If there's no way that you can be the killer, you can't possibly be the killer."

Grandfather's moustache bristled at this. It was hard to tell whether he was upset by my comment or interested in the suggestion Marius had made. Luckily, he soon clarified his position using more than just his facial hair.

"And yet, that is the task of a truly talented murderer." He often spoke of criminals as though they were artists, or master craftsmen. "Much like a novelist, he must go about his task in such a way as to trick and confound the detective. A truly perfect crime is the one which the culprit could never have committed."

"Precisely." Marius raised his chin to show his appreciation. "And that is what I try to create in any novel. I strive to bamboozle the reader into thinking that we can rule out one particular suspect, but the truth is that you should never dismiss a possibility until the real killer is behind bars."

Lord Edgington leaned back in his chair. "That is a very wise approach, Mr Quin. Now, perhaps we can return to the group of six potential killers we have already established. From what I've seen, Miss Alanson's star is on the rise. Perhaps she will be the actress for whom this production is best remembered."

"It's interesting that you should mention Tallulah Alanson," I replied, which provoked a raised eyebrow from my grandfather.

"Oh yes, and why's that?"

I pointed to the door into the bar. "Because she's standing just over there."

CHAPTER SIXTEEN

Miss Alanson had evidently changed before coming to find us at the hotel. She was dressed in a slinking, silvery gown that was suitable for that refined establishment. The employee who had greeted us when we'd entered the hotel was hovering behind her to ensure that Lord Edgington wished to receive such a person, but grandfather gave him a nod and he scuttled back to reception.

"Gentlemen, I'm truly sorry to disturb you," she said a little breathlessly as she reached our table. Before she continued, she noticed our companion and had to stop herself. "Oh, Mr Quin. I didn't expect to see you here."

Grandfather appeared to welcome her presence. "There is no need to apologise, my dear, but I'm afraid that we have an appointment to keep in the restaurant."

I looked around the smoky bar just then and realised that she was the only woman in sight. Something in Grandfather's tone told me that this was no place for a lady, and it was time we left. He drank the remainder of his cocktail, so I was faced with the decision of whether to leave mine and look like a child or do the same. For some silly reason, I plumped for the latter. I rose to my feet and immediately felt lightheaded.

He'd said nothing to me about an appointment in the restaurant, but it was no surprise to Delilah, who confidently led the way. I must say that it was a little incongruous to see that fluffy beast stroll through one of the most luxurious hotels in London. I could only wonder whether the staff tolerated her presence to retain the patronage and high opinion of Lord Edgington, or because he had paid them a good sum for the trouble. I recall from Sarah Bernhardt's obituary that the beloved actress had regularly stayed there with her Irish setter, but that's because I tend to waste my time reading of such trivialities in unsophisticated newspapers.

The Savoy was far more modern than the other grand hotels we'd visited in the capital, but it was no less sleek and chic for it. Everything was just so. I know that might sound like a small claim to make of such a place, but as the five of us trooped through the establishment, I was impressed by the way that even the tiniest detail was maintained.

Wherever we walked, there were potted plants and cut flowers – and surely more palms than could fit on a desert island. The décor was rich and dramatic, and each space through which we passed made me want to spend more time there.

"You know," Grandfather said to interrupt my thoughts, "in 1923, an Egyptian prince was murdered here by his wife Marguerite. It was the scandal of the day but, when the case went to trial, the jury decided that Prince Ali had been such a brute to the poor woman that she was cleared of the crime. It was really quite extraordinary."

I looked at the hotel through a slightly different lens after that. "Really, Grandfather, I don't need to hear about every murder that happened in the history of the country. I think I would prefer it if some places could retain their innocent charm."

His moustache evidently didn't approve of my comment, and he quickened his step after his courageous canine. The four and a half of us soon arrived at the Savoy Restaurant, by which I was instantly charmed. It was not just the grandeur of the place, surrounded as it was by Corinthian marble columns with scrolling volutes and acanthus leaves on the capitals atop each one. Nor was it the banks of mirrors on the walls, which reflected back the dining area and dance floor. No, what immediately won me over was the eleven-piece band seated in front of a floor-to-ceiling, black silk curtain with the letters S and O repeated over and over as a motif.

"The Savoy Orpheans!" Marius exclaimed with no lack of excitement in his voice. "I can't tell you how many times I've heard them play on the wireless. The BBC has been camped out here ever since 1923 to capture the best music around."

The band hadn't started their performance but, dressed in formal black suits, they were as smart as many of the gentlemen in the gathering audience and were getting everything ready on the low stage.

The head waiter rushed over as soon as he spotted my grandfather and, with a stooping bow, led us to the best table in the house. We were in one of the mirrored alcoves at the side of the room, but with nothing to obstruct our view of the dance floor or the band beyond. I had to wonder whether there was a telephone system in the hotel – or perhaps a pack of pageboys who ran about secret corridors to relay messages – as the waiters had clearly been informed of our change in party size.

Not only was there a chair for Tallulah Alanson, they'd placed a bowl of water and a plate of biscuits beneath the table for our spoilt dog.

"I truly am sorry to come here uninvited," the actress told us once we were all seated. "I didn't know what else to do. You left the theatre before I could talk to you and, to be quite frank, I'm not sure I would have had the courage to do so even then."

I thought that it would be my grandfather's job to put her mind at ease, but Marius provided that service. "You can speak quite openly, Tallulah. Although I haven't known him long, I have no doubt that Lord Edgington is a fair man and will hear whatever you have to tell us."

"Thank you, Marius." She had previously addressed him more formally, but he was not the type to require any such unnecessary propriety.

"Yes, Miss Alanson." Grandfather, on the other hand was very much the type to require such unnecessary propriety. "You must express yourself freely. If there is anything I can do to help, I am at your disposal."

She looked at me then, and I thought perhaps she required unanimous agreement before she could tell us what the matter was. I nodded, and it sparked her into life.

"You see, I came here…" That spark briefly faded out again but was soon revived. "I came because I do not agree with what I've heard from my fellow actors. They all hold to the idea that Peter was a soulless automaton with no passions or thoughts of his own."

"And that was not the case?" the subtle sleuth enquired.

"No, it certainly wasn't."

She would not provide any further explanation until a waiter had come by with water for the table. This was not all he brought, and I was now certain that, somewhere in the hotel, there existed a file all about my grandfather's tastes and preferences. A trolley had arrived with a bottle of Veuve Clicquot champagne (the old lord's favourite tipple) and two trays of oysters on a bed of ice (the old lord's favourite smelly snack from the sea). He was most appreciative of the refreshments and, once the oysters were distributed and the champagne had been poured, he set to work sipping both. I, meanwhile, had a glass of water. If only they'd had a file at the hotel on The Marquess of Edgington's grandson's tastes; I could have been dining on pork pies and ice cream all evening!

115

Tallulah had quenched her thirst and was able to continue. "Peter Canning was a man of great intensity and creative ambition."

No one knew what to say to this, as it was the opposite of everything we'd heard about our victim. When she said no more, Grandfather urged her to speak. "Go on, child. I'm very interested to hear your thoughts on the matter."

"The only reason that anyone had any other impression of him is because he wasn't a swanking, peacocky show-off. Peter's only failing was that he chose the wrong profession. He loved the theatre and could talk about it for hours, but he wasn't the kind who fitted in with all the rivalry and two-facedness."

Grandfather turned his head to look at her through just one eye, and I wondered whether he had problems with his vision. "Do you take this to mean that someone might have wanted him dead?"

She moved her bottom lip back and forth against the tips of her teeth. "I don't know. I just want you to have the whole picture. Peter was special. He might not have been particularly famous, and he would never be cast as the leading man, but he was good through and through. What I loved about him most, though, was that he was nothing like Gabriel Nelson or Lillian Bradshaw. They're all smiles and sweetness to your face, but I've always thought there is something very false about them."

Marius was the first to respond once more. "I must say that I've had similar thoughts myself. I know I do not have a theatrical background, Tallulah, and so perhaps I'm not as accustomed to the way actors interact, but I find it hard to know where I stand when people behave in such a contradictory fashion."

Grandfather had been occupied by the oysters and had to dry his mouth with a white cotton napkin before speaking. "This is very interesting, Miss Alanson. Very interesting indeed, and it certainly shows a side to Mr Canning that we hadn't seen before. However, I don't believe that it helps explain why he died."

"Unless you really do believe there is a ghost at Daly's," I said with a laugh in my voice and a shudder down my spine.

Tallulah closed her eyes for a few moments as though she were tired of hearing this. "That was just something that Brian started saying. The stage crew all went along with it, but I imagine he wanted to scare everyone. Little Denny's terrified to be alone there, and I'm sure you know how superstitious we actors can be."

"Yes, it's very silly," I said casually. I'd once come face to face with what I thought was a ghost, and not a night had passed since without me lying in bed, remembering that terrifying moment. Incidentally, if you happen to be afraid of such otherworldly visitors, I would not recommend living in an ancient stately home that has more creaks, whispers and scratchings on a daily basis than there are passengers passing through Waterloo Station.

Grandfather would not be distracted by talk of the supernatural. He never was. "The fact is, nothing you have told me has changed my perspective on Peter Canning's death. Either it was an accident, and the falling axe was never supposed to make contact with a living person, or – and I feel this is more likely – the axe fell at the wrong moment and Peter was not the intended target."

Tallulah's voice became more insistent. "I disagree. What if someone told him to stand on that spot? What if one of the more established actors suggested that the scene would work better if he moved a few steps to his right?"

"That still wouldn't explain why he was murdered."

There was a moment of silence at our table that was soon interrupted by the crunch, crunch, crunch of biscuits being munched beneath the table. Don't worry. It wasn't me! Delilah was enjoying her supper.

"Isn't that your job?" The young woman's deadly straight fringe trembled as she spoke. "Don't you have to find out the reason? I'm telling you that the story you've heard is untrue. You'll have to use your famous skills to discover what really happened."

"I'm sorry, Miss Alanson." Grandfather tried to console her with a sympathetic smile. "It's not that simple. We must follow the evidence that we find, and I've seen nothing to suggest that someone held a grudge against the victim. I'm very much open to the idea, of course. But unless you have something to tell me which sheds new light on the death, I will have to continue with the investigation as it presents itself."

She turned to Marius in search of help, but before he could say anything, the bandleader stepped up to the microphone to address the audience.

"Good evening, ladies and gentlemen." He had a clipped, lively voice, much as the presenters on the radio did. "We're privileged to be here tonight to play a number of wonderful modern pieces that I hope will meet with your approval. Welcome to an evening with the Orpheans."

He waved his white baton, and a pair of saxophonists stood up from a row of chairs at the back of the group and released a barrage of sound. They were soon joined by trumpet, tuba and trombone before a double bass player lent some low notes to the sound. It was quite exhilarating, and Grandfather's fingers had already started tapping the white tablecloth. This surprised me, as he occasionally bemoaned more recent musical trends. I'd always assumed he would take exception to American jazz music, much as he did novelty songs and romantic crooning.

The drummer was the last to strike up his instrument, but he paused after a bar or two to wave to the crowd and encourage the fashionable young couples to take to the floor. The bandleader did the same, and the song picked up pace just as one of the trumpeters lowered his instrument and began to sing.

> "Somebody stole my gal.
> Somebody stole my pal.
> Somebody came and took her away.
> She didn't even
> Say she was leavin'."

It didn't take long for the audience to desert the round tables that filled one side of the restaurant. As the women in their brightly patterned dresses pulled their partners to the dance floor, it looked like a flood of different-coloured paints spilling across the room. In seconds, the couples had taken up their poses and were dancing a speedy foxtrot around one another.

A muted cornet took up the melody, and the singer sang once more.

> "The kisses I loved so
> He's getting now I know.
> And Gee! I know that she
> Would come to me, if she could see,
> Her broken-hearted lonesome pal.
> Somebody stole my gal!"

118

I watched the spinning pairs and wondered how they knew how to dance so well. It seemed to me that dancing is one of those things that I should have learnt how to do, but no one had taken the time to teach me. I had to assume that – much like picking up certain languages or being good at chess – it is almost impossible to learn past the age of fifteen or so. As a result, I could only choose between life as an eternal wallflower or stumbling about the place, stepping on toes.

Different musicians would occasionally pull back from their instruments to shout encouragement to the dancers, but the song continued at full pace until a round of applause marked the end. Grandfather looked so thrilled by the scene that I thought he might get up himself for the next number, but he stayed where he was, with one hand on the top of his disobedient dog's head and the other on the table.

"You young people should be up there enjoying yourselves," he said, though I could tell that he was not concerned with my happiness so much as that of our companions.

Marius glanced across at the painfully exquisite actress. He finally found his voice, which is good, as, if he'd waited any longer, I think my grandfather would have prodded him until he spat out the words.

"Miss Alanson?" He had slipped back into a more formal mode. "Would you care to dance?"

She smiled ever so sweetly, and I don't know if she really wanted to accept the offer, but with the Marquess of Edgington looking at them so expectantly, it was hard to decline.

"Of course."

Marius gave her his hand, and they glided between the tables towards the other dancers.

120

CHAPTER SEVENTEEN

A slower piece of music without any lyrics animated the room, and I recognised it as 'Fascinating Rhythm' by George Gershwin, which is odd, as I rarely ever remember the names of records I've heard.

"Christopher, there are more important things to occupy your mind than music just now."

"Why? What's got your goat?"

"No one has 'got my goat', thank you. My goat is mine and mine alone." He made a snooty noise that was a cross between a humpf and a pfff. I suppose you might call it a pffhumpf. "However, I am rather interested in Miss Alanson. Don't you think it's curious that she should change into her finest clothes and rush over here, desperate to talk to us, then fail entirely to impart anything useful?"

"Ummm..." I hadn't thought about this until now and would need a few seconds to look vacuous. "I suppose you're right. But I think she means well. She clearly just feels bad for a man who, even in death, has been overlooked. I'm sure I'd feel the same if someone murdered dear old Halfpenny or one of our gardeners and no one made a fuss about it."

Something was clearly weighing on his mind and my explanation hadn't done enough to answer his concerns.

"It's a possibility." His gently tapping fingers matched the tempo of the drummer's snare. "And yet..."

He broke off what he was saying, and we watched Marius and Tallulah disappear amongst the spinning couples, only to reemerge a few moments later, several feet away. They were both good dancers, and I wondered once again how everyone knew how to shimmy, foxtrot and tango but me. They stared into one another's eyes as they moved, almost as if they were unaware of anyone else around them.

"Shadow boxing!" Grandfather declared in an unexpected bark. "That's what we've been doing today. This isn't a case so much as the hint of one. All we can say is that someone at that theatre caused an innocent man's death. I don't know what the killer was thinking or why anyone would go to such trouble to sabotage the play. All day long, we've been fighting shadows without landing a single blow."

For all that we bickered, I still adored the old coot and couldn't stand to see him so downfaced. I searched for something to make him feel better in the hope that some revelation on the case would present itself in my brain at just the right moment. It did not.

"Perhaps we need to go back to the beginning," I tried instead.

"Oh, yes?" He sounded less than eager to do so.

"Yes. Perhaps we need to consider everything from zero. First, we must examine our victim with fresh eyes. Lillian and the other actors told us that Peter Canning was a passionless man of little consequence. Tallulah swears that he was a deeply enthusiastic human being and a spirited conversationalist."

He winced a little, as though this simple statement of facts was giving him indigestion. "Yes, but I've been pondering it for some time, and there's nothing to say those two statements can't both be true. After all, we present ourselves to different people in different ways. Perhaps our victim was shy with the established stars with whom he performed but found a soulmate in a young actress who is just making a name for herself."

Something in his earlier question resounded in my mind. It was not unusual for information to filter through to me several minutes after it should have. I just had one of those brains.

"Grandfather, did you send Marius and Tallulah off to dance in order to see how they would react?"

His eyes followed them around the edges of the dance floor. It was almost as if he was dancing along with them, and I noticed the muscles in his cheeks flexing in time with the music.

"Indeed I did. I may not have focused on your tuition enough recently, Christopher, but this is one thing you can learn. When adequate evidence does not present itself, a detective may have to take measures to tempt it to the surface."

The music came to a sudden, dramatic halt, and Grandfather stood up to applaud our companions as they returned to the table.

"Look lively, my boy, you'll be dancing next."

I was quite lost for words, but he always has plenty for the two of us.

"That was wonderful," he told them, taking Tallulah's hand in his. "My grandson here was just saying how jealous he was of your partner, Miss Alanson. Would you make his night and accompany him for the next dance?"

I thought of staying right where I was and calling him a wily frog just then – as *wily fox* would have been too much of a compliment. Sadly, dear Tallulah smiled so warmly that I didn't have the heart to tell her that the sweet old man who had told this pretty tale was a heartless manipulator.

"I'd love to dance with you, Christopher."

Quite hypnotised by her polite manner and the reflection of a candle flame in her pale green eyes, I rose to my feet. I held my hand out just as gallantly as our writer friend had, and she glided back to the dance floor. The bandleader was addressing the crowd once more, and I had my fingers crossed that he would not announce some terrifying new American dance that I hadn't the first clue how to execute. I watched his lips move, trembling in fear that he was about to say a word that every young boy with two left feet surely fears: Charleston!

Luckily, it was a waltz. What could be easier?

I'll tell you one thing that definitely could be easier; starting a conversation whilst trying to remember in which order I'm supposed to move my legs.

"Have you ever been here before?" It was not the most promising start, and I did not expect her to say, *No, but I do possess the key piece of information that will help us solve Peter Canning's murder.*

"No, but it is lovely." See, it wasn't even close. "I didn't grow up with a lot of money…" She looked away for a moment and her expression turned pensive. "In fact, I still don't have a lot of money, but since becoming an actress, I do occasionally have the opportunity to go to nice places with the owners of the theatres and such like."

This wasn't as bad as I'd imagined. Perhaps she had connections to the money men behind her play. Perhaps the accidents and the murder and our whole reason for being in London was a simple insurance swindle, as Grandfather had initially posited.

Regrettably, instead of asking her about that, I kept rabbiting on about the pretty hotel. "It's all so shiny, isn't it? Shiny and bright and beautiful. If I ever own a house one day, I want it to look just like this… only smaller and also somehow rustic. In fact, it wouldn't look much like this at all."

She laughed at me but, even in this seemingly joyful reaction, there was something sad about her. "I'm sure that wherever you live will be wonderful."

I stumbled but managed to avoid crushing her dainty tootsicums with my massive stampers. All sorts of ridiculous questions flowed through my brain. *Would you like to live in a house? Do actors prefer caravans so that they can go from place to place? What do you think of profiteroles?* But none of them would have helped me understand what had been happening at Daly's Theatre, so it was lucky that she had something more relevant to tell me.

"I'm very sorry, Christopher. I'm not normally this grim. Even last week I was so greatly looking forward to the premiere of the play that I felt as though, wherever I went, I was walking in the clouds. When Peter died, everything changed, and I haven't recovered my normal positivity."

I found it interesting that, of all the actors, she was the most affected by events. "Then you should tell us exactly what you think must have happened. Perhaps you spotted something that didn't originally seem significant but now takes on added meaning." She shook her head slowly as we whirled, and so I spoke again. "Is there anyone in particular who you could imagine killing Peter and sabotaging the play?"

"That's just it," she said with a little more urgency. "I've got to the point where any one of them seems capable of it. I'd enjoyed my time working with such popular actors, but now I see them for the sniping, self-important characters they are. And, as for Brian Grimage, I've always found him an odious sort, but he's been especially shifty since the full run-through last week." A sound caught in her throat then and it became a moan. "I've even imagined Denny having some evil plan, and he's the sweetest little chap in London."

Perhaps *too* sweet, I thought but didn't say. "We've been considering similar questions, but it hasn't got us very far."

Suddenly, I was the one being interviewed. "Are you so certain it couldn't have been someone from outside the theatre? Or what about our beloved director who deserted us? Don't you think it's possible that the killer hid his tracks and things are not as simple as they appear?"

"Oh… ummm. Maybe?" I didn't know what else to say except, "Grandfather is quite certain of his suspect list. Normally when there's even the chance that the truth of a killing has been obscured, he's a lot more circumspect. He's told me several times already that one of the six actors – excluding Marmaduke and your colleague who plays the two victims – must be to blame."

She looked over at our table just as the music rose and the couples around us began to twirl with greater finesse. The women's dresses fanned out like whirligigs, but I only had one level of finesse and could not dance any better than I already wasn't.

"I think that Lord Edgington is something of a stirrer." She had a wry smile on her face, and I wondered what she had noticed. "He evidently wanted Marius and me to dance together, and I believe I know why."

I wondered whether she had concluded that Grandfather suspected the pair of them of murder, but I had quite misread her meaning.

"He evidently thinks two sad, lonely people would be better off together, but I'm afraid he's wasting his time. For one thing, Marius Quin carries any number of wounds and perhaps even a broken heart. He hasn't spoken of his past, but I sensed it from the first audition I had for the play, and nothing here this evening has changed that impression."

"That can't be pleasant," I said, as such adult concerns still didn't make a lot of sense to me. While I had been in something approaching love on several occasions, I hadn't actually got to the broken-hearted stage. It was a state through which I would have to pass at some point but was still on the list of experiences I had yet to enjoy or endure.

I noticed, of course, that she had described herself as lonely, but before I could ask after the cause of her sadness, the band played the final note of the merry melody and we bowed to one another to finish the song. She certainly looked distant as I escorted her back to the table and, imagining myself a potential knight errant for every woman I meet, I wished there was something I could say to make her smile again.

"That was not terrible, Christopher," my rarely effusive forebear commented, "not terrible at all."

"Thank you, Grandfather," I replied, happy to have garnered even this faint praise. "I did what I could."

"You dance very nicely," Tallulah told me, but the smile on her lips was fleeting.

We sat back down just as there was a commotion by the entrance to the room, and a young gentleman with scruffy red hair rushed through it to dart between the tables over to our own. He was pursued by a butler, the maître d'hôtel and several porters.

Grandfather put his hand in the air to wave off the pursuant pack, and Marmaduke practically collided with our table before landing in a chair that he'd stolen from our neighbours. He was quite out of breath.

"What is it, boy?" Grandfather asked, full of interest for whatever he might have to tell us. "Have you discovered something important? Has there been another accident?"

My old school chum assumed a bewildered expression. "No, not at all. I just thought I'd get a free meal out of you. I've never dined at the Savoy before, and it doesn't look half bad."

CHAPTER EIGHTEEN

It was a frustrating day all round, and the crime we were investigating was harder to fathom now than when we'd first learnt of it. The fact remained that Peter Canning's death had endangered the success of the play, and its failure would only harm the suspects. Were the production to close before it had even opened, the actors would be out of work, Marius Quin's investment would be for naught, and the already faltering theatre might even have to close.

I went to bed searching for a solution to this riddle. Wait a moment… that's not quite true. The mattress in our suite at the Savoy was so supple, supportive, yet soft, that it was like floating weightless in the very air. I tried to think about falling theatrical equipment and a man with an axe in his head, but, within a few seconds, I was fast asleep.

I'm not going to tell you about breakfast the next day. Oh, fine. Yes, I am.

"Morning, Master Christopher," Cook sang to me as I stumbled from my bedroom at the end of the suite.

I was a little surprised to see her, as she hadn't been there the night before. There were maids, valets, and waiters stationed on each floor to tend to our every need, but it was no great shock that my grandfather had sent for his favourite domestic. Even the presence of our elderly footman, Halfpenny, who was standing in the corner of one of the many lounges with a newspaper in his hand was to be expected, though I couldn't quite imagine why our gardener Driscoll was there.

"Morning, Master Christopher," he said in his gentle Irish accent as he watered a small palm in the corner. "It's a beautiful day."

"Your wife didn't join you this—" I began, just as our maid emerged from the next room along. "Oh, good morning, Alice."

Grandfather followed her a moment later but stopped a few paces into the room. "Don't look at me in such a rude manner, Christopher."

"I didn't realise that I was." I made sure to use a grammatically complete sentence to avoid offending him further.

From the look of things, Cook had brought up our breakfast from the hotel kitchen, and Todd had laid two places at a dining table for my grandfather and me. We sat down without another word, and

Halfpenny presented his master with *The Times*.

"Grandfather?" I asked when I simply couldn't hold my thoughts in any longer. "Why do you need five members of staff to wait on you?"

He folded his paper and tossed it onto a free spot on the table. "I do not need five people to wait on me, Christopher," he began rather officiously. "I need six. Dorie is making my bed."

"You do realise this is a hotel, don't you?" I was beginning to despair of him. No… my apologies. That's another lie. I was *continuing* to despair of him. "There are people here to do that sort of thing."

He peered out of the window towards the Lambeth leadworks and Shot Tower on the other side of the river. "I didn't want to put anyone out."

"But you made six people drive all this way to wait upon you when there were perfectly good workers here to do the same thing." I paused then and looked at him a little more carefully. "You do know that this suite comes with its own butler?"

"Look at this breakfast!" he cooed to distract me and, would you believe it? It worked!

Cook had evidently been inspired by our cosmopolitan surroundings as our meal that morning had a decidedly international feel.

"There's Ukrainian Palyanytsya bread, Polish faszerowane jajka devilled eggs, and Morcilla from Burgos, which is a Spanish black pudding with crispy rice inside." Todd unloaded dishes off a trolley as he explained what everything was. "Then there are Scottish potato scones, Welsh cockles, Cornish scrowled pilchards and pork sausages."

"What nationality are the sausages?" I felt the need to ask.

"I believe they are English, sir," was Todd's succinct reply before he whistled back to cook's trolley in search of jams and whatnot.

Uncertain whether we would be eating again for the foreseeable future, despite the infinite number of dining options in every square mile of the capital, I filled my plate, then my mouth, then my stomach as Grandfather looked on disapprovingly. It was delicious, and I suggested to Cook that she should make such international feasts more often.

"You're very welcome, sir," she replied most formally. "Now, if you'll excuse me, I must get back to the kitchens. The staff weren't very happy with me taking up space down there."

Grandfather raised a devilled egg in salute to her talents and she hurried from the room.

After a bath and a change of clothes, I was ready to roll out of the hotel and across London to the theatre. By the time we reached Daly's, the cast was already amassing, and Marius was in place in the stalls to issue commands.

"Good morning, everyone. Tonight is the night. We have our full dress rehearsal with an audience ahead, and so I want to run through as much of the play as we can this morning. We'll start where we left off yesterday, at the beginning of Act Three."

"I'm afraid we have a problem there," Gabriel Nelson announced in his deep, resonating voice.

"What's that?"

"There's no sign of Brian Grimage."

Marius looked a little breathless, as though he'd only just managed to make the speech he'd delivered and was not prepared for this proverbial monkey wrench in the machinery.

"Very well." He bowed his head to think. "What we'll have to do is... Yes, we'll skip back a couple of scenes to L'Estrange's interview with Miriam Buxton that we didn't practice on stage yesterday. Once Brian arrives, we'll run through the whole of Act Three."

I believe that Nelson was about to reveal another problem when Tallulah rushed into the theatre from the front entrance. "I'm sorry I'm late, everyone." She was flustered and looked as though she'd been running. "I stayed out past my bedtime and overslept."

Marius offered a forgiving smile. "Don't worry, Miss Alanson. We're about to rehearse Act Two, Scene Three. Could you please take your position when you're ready?"

The actors who were required came to the centre of the stage, whereas the others disappeared into the wings. Grandfather and I were about to sit down to watch this scene when we were interrupted by a police officer who was sitting in the back row of the stalls.

"Lord Edgington, sir," he said, in a short, sharp burst of words. "I was told to report directly to you. I have been on duty since midnight. I relieved one of my colleagues at that hour, and I can report that neither of us witnessed anything untoward. I stayed on that stage for half the night and did not fall asleep for one moment. I can solemnly attest that there was no funny business of any kind."

"Jolly good, constable." The self-appointed commanding officer pursed his lips together in steely admiration of the man's work. "Then I am relieving you of your duty. Go home and get some sleep. I will report back to Chief Inspector Darrington on your behalf."

As the junior officer marched towards the public exit, Grandfather issued some orders to me.

"I would appreciate it if you could find Brian Grimage's dressing room and check that he hasn't arrived."

"Of course, Superintendent Edgington," I replied in an imitation of the man who had just left. "However, I'd appreciate it if you spoke to me as your blood kin rather than a subordinate."

With a cheeky grin on my face, I sped away through the theatre before he could tut at me. There were stairs up to the stage on either side, and I hurried up them and around the scenery so as not to disturb Tallulah Alanson's interrogation by the fake detective.

"I put it to you, Miriam, that you hated your stepmother," Gabriel practically roared as he stood over the suspect. "I suggest that you blamed her for your real mother's untimely death and would have done whatever it took to exact your revenge upon her." If anything, he sounded more like Lord Edgington than he had the day before. He had evidently taken some notes during the time the two men spent together.

"No. That's not what happened!" Tallulah uttered, and I really believed her pain. "I appreciated dear Emilia. She raised me as her own daughter, and I would never have hurt her. I simply couldn't do such a thing!"

Inspector L'Estrange was quick to cut through her argument. "You appreciated her, and yet you didn't love her. Is that how the land lies?"

I watched the scene for a moment, then cut through the backstage area where a woman in a thick cardigan was sitting in case the actors forgot their lines. She was approximately ninety, and the lenses on her glasses were as thick as Bibles. Even if she had been there on the day that Peter Canning was killed, it seemed unlikely that she would have seen much.

Marmaduke was waiting to come on as P.C. Dunts – the role that Canning himself would have played. He looked a little nervous, and I couldn't quite remember why he wasn't considered a suspect. Perhaps Grandfather had grown tired of my friend being implicated in our murder investigations and, as this was the fourth now, he had given him a bye.

I was about to ask Marmaduke where the dressing rooms were when he marched onto the stage. There was only one door on that side of the theatre and, upon taking it, I found myself in a storage room filled with scenery from old productions. There was no sign of life, and so I returned to the shadowy backstage area once more. At the rear of the stage, there was a thick curtain and then a few steps leading down to a bright corridor. I was about to descend them when I heard two voices in hushed colloquy and froze.

"We mustn't let anyone know," a woman said, and I had a good idea who was speaking.

"That goes without saying," a man responded. "This really isn't the sort of thing you walk around telling people."

It was Lillian Bradshaw and Oliver Hartley, the same pair who had wandered off to a bar together the night before. I had to wonder what had brought about this clandestine meeting.

"I'm sorry," she said, and I could hear the rustle of fabric as though they were standing very close to one another. "Really, I'm terribly sorry, but this isn't easy for me. I'm haunted by the idea that someone will find out, and then everything between us will be over."

"I'll make sure that doesn't happen," Oliver replied, and there was a determination to his voice that wasn't usually present. "It could never come between us."

For a few moments, silence fell between them, and I wished I could have seen what they were doing. They couldn't have been more than a few feet below me and perhaps I moved my feet or bumped against something as, all of a sudden, Lillian said, "Hush, I think I can hear someone. We'd better go before we get caught."

I heard the definite sound of lips against lips then and prayed that they wouldn't come up the steps to catch me. Luckily enough, they moved in the opposite direction, mumbling happily between themselves as they went, and I could breathe once more. I tiptoed down the stairs and poked my head around the corner to make sure no one was there. I have no idea why I was being so secretive. I hadn't done anything wrong, and it wasn't as though I was expecting the ghost of Daly's Theatre to jump out on me.

Nevertheless, I tiptoed along the dim passageway, listening at each door I passed. The first I came to was ajar and gave on to a space where the actors could wait before they came on stage. It was large, had plenty of furniture and a few old newspapers and scripts discarded on a table in the middle. It looked rather like the waiting room in a doctor's office.

The second door I reached had Gabriel Nelson's name on it and, judging by the gap between this one and the next, he had been awarded the largest space. There was no sound coming from inside, and so I kept moving. If the rooms were arranged by order of importance, I would have expected Lillian's to be next. Instead, I found Oliver's, (which I decided not to enter after what I'd just heard) then Tallulah's (who was being interrogated on stage). I came to Brian's but spotted Lillian's name, two doors along, right at the end of the corridor. She'd clearly chosen the room as far from Gabriel as possible.

I put my hand out to open greasy Brian Grimage's door but didn't have the courage to do so. Surely the reason he hadn't appeared for the rehearsal was that Lillian and Oliver had just murdered him out of some deranged secret love pact. As soon as I pushed the door open, there'd be no doubt about it. The man was dead and—

Oops, I ended up leaning against the door so that it creaked dramatically ajar. My mind had got away from me and there was no dead body inside. It was just a normal dressing room. There was a mirror and a sink and a rack for hanging up costumes. There weren't even any significant clues. I'd hoped to at least find a mysterious note or perhaps a lock of hair, but no.

Just as Grandfather said, it was one of those cases. We had no definite motive or particular theories about what happened, and it was becoming increasingly likely that the whole thing was an accident after all. Perhaps… Perhaps the putty we'd found had been placed on the suit of armour by the stage crew to stop the axe from falling, but it hadn't dried properly because of the grease that someone put on the bolt because… because…. Well, I'm not really sure why, but whatever the reason, I was fairly certain that we were chasing after a killer who didn't exist.

These reassuring thoughts were interrupted by the sound of a scream. At first, I thought it had to be the actors on stage, but then I heard the pounding of feet, and I ran back up there to see what was happening.

"Tallulah?" Marius shouted from the auditorium. "Miss Alanson, where are you going?"

I could hear sighs and gasps coming from a door on the opposite side of the stage. Running behind the back curtain, I reached a similar room to the one I had previously visited. It was full of props and scenery for the play, but there was one important difference. Brian Grimage was hanging from a rope with his feet just inches off the ground.

His eyes were open, but his body was limp. The dubious fellow had breathed his last breath.

CHAPTER NINETEEN

From the way the stage crew and a couple of the actors moved to comfort him, I could tell that Dancing Denny had found the body. It must have been his scream that I'd heard.

"He was like that when I got here," the poor lad moaned, apparently desperate to prove that he had not contributed to the man's death. "I swear I had nothing to do with it."

"Of course you didn't, Denny," Gabriel spoke for everyone there. "The man's clearly been dead for some time, and we would never suspect you anyway."

"I don't understand. Do you think he killed himself?" Tallulah murmured, just as Grandfather and Marius arrived to see what had caused the commotion.

The playwright caught sight of the dead man and would not say a word for some time. He'd mentioned his service in the Great War, and I wondered whether the sight of a body would be difficult for an ex-soldier to bear. I counted myself lucky not to have experienced the horrors men like Marius had gone through for our country.

"Why did you leave the stage like that?" Grandfather asked the young actress.

"I heard a scream." Tallulah's eyes were stuck to the dead man as she made sense of what she saw there.

"It was a shout, not a scream." Denny rolled his shoulders as he tried to calm himself. "It's not every day I find a dead body."

"Has anyone touched him?" Grandfather made his way through the line of onlookers.

Denny shook his head, and the other stagehands took a few steps back towards the door.

"It seems not," Gabriel replied on their behalf. Even now he had a dramatic tone of voice, as though he was imagining himself playing out this scene one day in an even bigger theatre.

"I'll call the police." Denny turned to leave, and there was a flash of fear in his eyes that would be hard to forget.

"Ask for Chief Inspector Darrington," Grandfather told him. "He'll want to see this."

I had to wonder what Brian Grimage had done in life to deserve such a violent death. The room where he'd died was essentially a large cupboard, with all-black walls and no natural light. A strange thought entered my mind, and I decided that this was how I imagined purgatory. A blank, featureless space, perhaps befitting of the roguish actor who had met his Maker there.

Of course, I was only considering the existence of a third realm between heaven and earth because I didn't want to have to solve the sad, violent puzzle in front of us. With little other option, I finally looked more closely at the dangling corpse. There was a rope hanging over a low metal beam that was three quarters of the way to the ceiling. The dead man's feet could almost touch the ground and there was an overturned stool nearby from which he had presumably jumped.

Rather than accept the evidence as it appeared on the surface, Grandfather pushed a wooden crate over from the side of the room and climbed atop. Without touching the body, he inspected it carefully.

"He didn't commit suicide," he said with great assuredness. "Well, not unless he was so distraught about the great gaping wound on the back of his head that he decided to end his life."

I moved around to see what he meant and, sure enough, there was a bloody hole at the back of his skull. His khaki jacket was covered in rusty red stains, but the killer had presumably hoped that, by placing the stool there, he could make us think that Grimage had done this to himself.

Oliver and Lillian came to inspect the killer's handiwork. I suppose there was nothing strange about this as they would have been due on stage before long, but I hadn't forgotten the conversation I'd overheard, and I watched them closely. I tried to signal to my grandfather that he should do the same thing, but he was too busy looking over Brian's clothes for stray hairs or threads of cotton from the killer's clothing or other useful evidence we never seemed lucky enough to find.

"What happened?" the great lady of the London stage asked. Her voice was unusually restrained, but it was impossible for me to say whether she was acting.

No one answered her question, as we didn't know any more than she did. Oliver Hartley stood beside her, his arms hanging limply at his side in an unintentional approximation of the hanged man's pose.

136

I followed the rope to work out how it had been secured and found that it was tied to a metal bar on the nearest wall. Of course, even if he'd killed himself, he would have had to secure the cord somehow.

"I'd like you all to leave this room and sit several seats apart in the front rows of the theatre," Grandfather said, and I wasn't so stupid that I thought he was talking to me. Or rather, I wasn't so stupid that I thought this for long.

There was always going to be one person who objected, and it didn't surprise me that the person in question had his name in the biggest letters on the poster at the front of the building. "But the play... We still need to practise."

"There is no play, Gabriel," Marius told him in short order. He was finally back with us, but his voice was cold. "This is the end; can't you see that?"

"I'm afraid that Marius is right," Lillian added in her softest voice. "One dead actor might be considered bad luck, but two means we are finished."

Gabriel didn't disagree with her for once but cast a desperate look in her direction.

"I'm not so sure," Oliver commented. "It's a terrible situation, but this might be just the thing to sell tickets."

Tallulah groaned at the very thought, but it did not dissuade her co-star from explaining his position.

"Just listen for one moment. Everyone loves a murder; that's why the Snyder case over in New York has become so famous. Imagine what people will think when they hear that—"

"That's enough." Marius turned to look at the man and his jaw trembled. "It's too horrible. I'd rather die a pauper than make a fortune from such opportunistic cruelty."

Oliver showed that same innocence I had witnessed several times the day before. I felt that he truly regretted offending anyone. "I'm sorry, Marius. I didn't mean to..." His words got quieter and quieter and eventually faded to nothing.

The writer was a forgiving sort, though, and put his arm around the man he'd had to barrack before they joined the human tide that flowed from the room. "So am I, Oliver. Truly, I am."

In a moment or two, I was alone with my grandfather and the body.

"I feel this could have been prevented," he told me in a hushed tone. "And yet, I don't know how." He circled the victim several times, as though trying to solve the conundrum before us. "I'd say he's been dead about an hour judging from the blood I can see and the colour of his skin. It could be longer, but I doubt it."

"Do you think this makes the case any clearer, Grandfather?" I asked him, as, personally, I couldn't think what connection there was between shifty Brian Grimage and the picture the others had painted of nice, friendly Peter Canning.

"It's too soon to say," he eventually replied, and I could see how anxious he was. "This may well be the most protean case we have faced together. There is nothing upon which we can build our investigation, nothing even to spark a hypothesis. Had Gabriel Nelson or Lillian Bradshaw been murdered, I might have known where to start, but it is hard to say what anyone hoped to achieve through this strange series of events."

I couldn't stand to see him so glum and spoke to fill the silence. "Grandfather, I know you don't like it when I ask such questions, but would it now be possible to rule out our lady suspects?"

"If you know I don't like it, why do you insist on asking?" He sighed then, and his voice turned apologetic. "No, Christopher, we cannot dismiss Tallulah or Lillian from the inquiry. No matter what most mystery writers would have us believe, most women do have some strength in their arms. Furthermore, Grimage was either unconscious or dead by that point and would not have put up a fight."

A constable arrived just in time to hear this explanation. I had to assume that Marius or one of the others had found him patrolling the square outside.

"Oh, my goodness." In his dark blue police cape and high helmet, the young officer turned quite pale. "Oh, my great goodness," was all he could say, and I almost offered him a chair, but Grandfather had something important to tell him.

"My name is Lord Edgington." He was already putting on his trademark white gloves as he spoke. "Do I have your permission to search the body for clues?"

The constable looked uncertain, but managed a silent nod and was happy to stand back from the scene.

Grandfather moved the crate around to face dead Brian. He mounted it once more and set to work looking inside his jacket and in his trouser pockets. It seemed to me that he worked from the inside out, which, as it happened, was not the best policy that day as the most useful evidence there was located in the outer pockets of the actor's khaki pea coat. It occurred to me that officers in the army would have worn such items, but, as most men over twenty-seven years of age had served in the war, I doubted this would be of much relevance.

"Ah ha!" Lord Edgington proclaimed rather dramatically as he delved into the man's left-hand pocket and pulled out two long envelopes. "Look, Chrissy."

He held the first one up to me, and I saw that it was addressed to Gabriel Nelson at his address at number thirty, Maida Avenue. Though it did not state the postal district, I had to assume it would be in the area of Maida Hill in the north of the city. He was about to hand it to me to inspect when he pulled the envelope away and passed me his spare pair of gloves. They were the greasy ones he'd used to inspect the bolt the day before. He really should carry three pairs for just such instances.

"And the other letter?" I asked.

"It's addressed to Lillian Bradshaw, as I expected."

He gave it to me as he needed his hands free to check the last pocket. I didn't notice anything unusual about the envelope, but made a note of the address, in case it turned out to be significant at a later stage of the investigation.

The Red Houseboat

Moored opposite Park Place Villas

W2

"What about the weapon, Grandfather? The killer must have used something to knock out Brian before the noose was placed around his neck, but there's no sign of a piece of lead piping, or a candle stick, for example." I searched between the discarded scenery of plays gone by. "Even a spanner would have done the job, but I can't see anything of the sort."

He wasn't listening and, when I returned to the open space in the centre of the cluttered room, I discovered why.

"Is it a picture of the killer?" the still shocked bobby at the door asked. This was too hopeful a proposition, even by my standards.

"Not the killer," Grandfather responded with none of the tetchiness he reserved for me. "The first victim."

He held up the postcard-sized photo, which he'd found in Brian Grimage's other pocket. It was a sepia capture of a smiling Peter Canning. He was wearing a trilby hat and winking. I imagined it had been taken for one of his previous acting roles. More interestingly, there was an inscription on the back, which Grandfather now kindly showed me.

"To a special friend," I read aloud, and my mentor helped me draw some conclusions before I could express just how little any of these findings meant to me.

"It's unusual, don't you think? It's definitely not the kind of message you would write to a fan."

Well, I didn't say it was a particularly dramatic discovery, but he'd understood its significance better than I had.

"In which case, why would Brian have been carrying it in his pocket? Were the two men friends?"

He thought for a moment and then hummed to himself. I've no idea why.

"That is a very good question and one which we must put to our other suspects." He came to take the envelopes off me and held them in the air next to one another. "They were clearly written by the same hand, and I've no reason to think that Brian was not the man who penned them."

"Do you know what they say?"

He shook his head before replying. "Alas, I do not have the power to see through opaque objects, Christopher. We will have to wait until Chief Inspector Darrington arrives. I will not open them until I have his permission."

And with that, he gave an infinitesimal bow to the constable in the doorway and swept from the room.

SEC⦵ND INTERVAL

A Killer in the Wings by Marius Quin

Reflections on the play from the case notes of former Superintendent Edgington, once of Scotland Yard.

Act Two

The investigation now begins into the death of Emilia Buxton and, from the off, Inspector Rupert L'Estrange – a rather pompous character who has nothing in common with the detectives I have known – expresses his distaste for the dead woman's husband. I must say that I found myself siding with Edward Buxton, a man I knew to have already killed once, as L'Estrange's manipulative techniques were far too brutish.

He was forever leaving dramatic pauses, as though his suspects would fall into his trap and reveal whatever he wished to know. Furthermore, with his faux-aristocratic delivery, the man was a born snob. He loomed menacingly over witnesses and believed he had the right to frighten and intimidate each of them to further the investigation. If Christopher had behaved in such a fashion on one of our cases, I would have taken him to task! I really do despair for this country if police officers like L'Estrange go about with so little care for good manners.

Of course, it was Christopher himself who put forward the frankly ludicrous idea that L'Estrange's voice and mannerisms were based on my own. I gave the suggestion the short shrift it deserved and would hear no more about it.

Regardless of my opinion of L'Estrange's methods, I concede that they produce results in the play. With the help of his blank canvas of a police constable assistant, he quickly divines that there are at most five suspects. This was a little disappointing to me, as I greatly prefer an even number. As it was merely a two-hour play and not an investigation that would take up a longer period of my life, I was happy to overlook what some people would regard as a minor issue.

To be clear, the suspects in question were…

Edward Buxton – known wife-killer and husband of the deceased who was seen arguing with her a short time before she was slain.

Marjorie Whitstable – actress, close friend of the deceased and, it has already been suggested and will soon be confirmed, Edward's secret lover.

Clive McCormack – another actor and long-time friend of Edward Buxton. He is also the boyfriend of Edward's daughter.

Miriam Buxton – the aforementioned daughter who is perhaps the most distraught of everyone in the group and shows her sorrow more than her largely unpleasant companions.

The suspicious-looking waiter – a nervous adolescent who lurks around the main cast throughout much of the first act. As identified by L'Estrange, this interloper might well have been eavesdropping on their conversation and gleaned some important piece of information with which he confronted Emilia Buxton, thus leading to her death. This did not turn out to be the case; however, I found L'Estrange's attention to detail admirable. Just because the waiter being the culprit would have added little dramatic tension to the play, such possibilities should never be dismissed out of hand.

Thanks to an interview with the deceased woman's stepdaughter, the trickle of facts that will lead us to the killer begins. Had I been interviewing her, I would have shown compassion and tried to win her confidence with a soft, considerate approach. L'Estrange, meanwhile, screams and shouts like a pettish child. The poor witness is so terrified she will end up in prison that she inadvertently reveals that her boyfriend was not with her at the time of the murder.

L'Estrange moves from one suspect to the next. This approach was a little prosaic for my liking, and we suffered through five scenes in a row of interview, interview, interview, interview, interview. There was surely something in the hotel he could have investigated to break up all the talking. He could have at least sent his assistant to poke about in the suspects' bedrooms but, perhaps due to the constraints of the theatre or the cost of producing extra sets, the drama was largely confined to the courtyard of the hotel.

I don't mind telling you that my first suspicions fell on Edward Buxton's friend, Clive McCormack. First and foremost, I have never thought it proper for men of a certain age to throw themselves at much younger women; there must have been twenty years or more between

142

Mr McCormack and Miriam Buxton. Of course, this in itself was not enough to condemn the man as a killer, but it was clear from these initial stages that he was concealing some sordid secret and, sure enough, his streak of darkness is soon revealed.

Before L'Estrange can uncover any such corruption, we witness the characters of Edward and Marjorie engaged in heated debate. Edward confesses to his lover – and the third cerebrally challenged woman in the play to fall in love with him – that although the gun that killed his first wife had gone off accidentally, he had planned to murder her in order to be with Emilia. As a result, he believes that his past has come back to haunt him.

Being of limited intelligence, Marjorie tells him that he had been in a terrible, loveless marriage and only murdered Carolina because he absolutely had no other option. Happy with this bizarre logic, she concludes that he is innocent of his second wife's murder, even though the cases are almost identical. Perhaps I should have had more sympathy for the people he had so horrifically manipulated, but I did find this section of the play difficult to digest.

They swear one another to secrecy, but part of the conversation is overheard by L'Estrange's constable, who relays to his boss that the pair are keeping secrets. So ensues a torrid confrontation between detective and suspect as the wise inspector confronts Edward Buxton with the possibility that he himself was to blame for both wives' deaths. He denies it, as he would, and says that the secret that the constable overheard them discussing was his love for Marjorie, about which they had already told his wife.

Clever old Rupert L'Estrange spots a flaw in his argument and repeats the words back to them that the constable had heard.

"You said that you were worried the secret would come between you. How would your love come between you?" This rather well delivered blow certainly silences the pair of them for a few moments. That smug philanderer Buxton is just about to make up an explanation when his lover speaks for him. The secret they are hiding is not the affair, but the pressure that Edward has been under since someone started blackmailing him.

CHAPTER TWENTY

"Grandfather, do we have any way of knowing when Brian was killed?" I asked as we navigated the dark space back onto the stage.

"Rephrase the question, Christopher. I know you can do better than that."

I considered its grammatical construction, but that seemed all right. It had a subject, a verb and a complement, at least, and I'd even thrown in an auxiliary verb for good measure. It had to be the content to which he objected, and so I tried again.

"Very well. Judging from his skin tone and the fact that rigor mortis is yet to take hold, it seems to me that the victim has not been dead for long."

"That is an excellent observation. Of course, to give a more accurate picture of what happened, I would have had to take his temperature. But we are in London. The Metropolitan Police will not let us do as much as we might in the countryside."

He stopped in the middle of the stage and glanced down at the floor before toeing a dirty mark with his foot. I was not so short of brain cells that I hadn't realised by this point that the black dot had been put there to show actors where to stand, but Grandfather offered no further explanation.

Instead, his expression became a fraction sterner. "Of course, as you managed to answer your own question without my help, it does make me wonder why you felt the need to ask it in the first place."

I might well have stuttered over an answer or ummed and ahhed for a while, but we had reached the front of the stage and the company was waiting for my grandfather to tell them what had happened.

He cleared his throat and began. "As you will all know, Brian Grimage is dead. We found him hanging in the stage-right storage room. Though the killer may have wished us to think otherwise, his victim did not commit suicide. He was knocked about the head with a blunt object which was removed from the scene. A rope was tied around his neck and thrown over a beam to muddle the evidence."

He maintained a clinical attitude throughout, as though he were presenting the findings of a scientific study. "Although I cannot say for certain who killed him or whether the death is linked to that of Peter Canning's, I very much believe that the culprit is here amongst us."

He allowed our audience to absorb this message, but no one reacted. I felt they were most likely resigned to the situation. They'd already lived through one nasty death and were busy coming to terms with the idea that the play to which they'd devoted so much time would never open. The presence of a killer, so long as there were plenty of police officers in the vicinity, no longer frightened them.

"What happens next?" Marius stood up from his red velvet seat to ask.

Before either of us… Fine, it would have been my grandfather's job to reply, but before he could, there was the sound of stomping boots at the back of the theatre and several caped constables rushed along the aisles. They were followed by a distinguished, grey-haired gentleman whom I recognised from previous cases.

"I imagine this man will tell you," Grandfather murmured, and everyone turned to the back of the theatre to watch the senior officer's approach.

"Ladies and gentlemen," he began, "my name is Chief Inspector Darrington. I will be in charge of this case henceforth." He took the closest set of steps to climb onto the stage and then came to shake his former colleague's hand. "Lord Edgington, I appreciate your informing me. Since the Gutteridge case last week, the press have been hounding my men. They're saying that our standards are slipping, and London is becoming a hotbed of violent crime. I need this murder to be kept quiet for as long as possible and solved even quicker."

"Of course, Chief Inspector." Grandfather showed our capable acquaintance the respect he deserved.

Darrington turned from us to speak to the scattered crowd once more. "My officers will be taking statements in time, but before that happens, I would like to ask whether you are in possession of any solid evidence that could explain why this man was killed?"

He cast his gaze around the few occupied rows at the front of the house. When no one spoke, he nodded in his usual efficient manner. "I thought as much." He clicked his fingers at his subordinates, who were standing in a line at the side of the theatre. "Constables, two of you must guard the dead body. The rest of you must find out what you can from these good people. Should you need me, I will be discussing the case with Lord Edgington."

The two men turned to talk in private, but I stayed where I was to watch the suspects in case the killer would give himself away. Each of them must have been nervous, and I thought that just by standing there staring at them, the pressure would get to be too much, and someone would yell out a piercing confession.

"It was me!" nobody there said, and so the investigation continued.

Marmaduke had his feet up on the seat in front of him, and I felt rather sorry for whichever officer would have to interview my insolent friend. His demeanour was in stark contrast to that of his fellow actors.

Oliver Hartley was staring at the floor with his head bowed, while Gabriel Nelson – who might have done a good impersonation of a detective on stage but was clearly out of sorts in real life – stared up at the ceiling as though to ensure that he wouldn't catch anyone's gaze.

Just below me, Lillian was a little more controlled and her nerves only manifested themselves in the regular pulsation of a vein on the side of her neck. Denny was being comforted by his friends and, much like in the hotel restaurant the night before, it was Tallulah who appeared most fearful. She sat right in the corner of the theatre, as far as possible from the line of officers, and her knee jogged up and down as her fingers tapped out a rhythm on the armrest of her seat.

I considered remaining in that very spot to observe them all, but then I remembered what my grandfather had found and rushed over to see him.

"Chief Inspector, I didn't want to open them without having you here." He had removed the two letters from his pocket and held them by the tips of his gloved fingers.

"That's very good of you to wait," Darrington told him, "but I would have understood if you had bowed to curiosity."

Grandfather examined the envelope addressed to Gabriel Nelson under the bright electric stage lights. "I don't just mean that I waited in order to be polite. I wondered whether the scientists at Scotland Yard could uncover anything from the envelope itself. Things advance so rapidly these days, I half hoped that your experts might discover something on the gummed seal of the envelope."

Darrington smiled at the idea. "I can honestly say that I have not heard of any such method, and these are not the first letters I have encountered at the scene of a crime." He whistled to a nearby officer who was carrying a small bag. "We'll check them for fingerprints before opening them, of course."

Once the man had poured a vial of black filings all over the envelope and found nothing to report, Grandfather needed a few seconds to finish his examination. Content that there were no identifying marks on the envelope that he might disturb, he took a small, folding penknife from inside his coat and cut the first letter carefully open. The attendant constable went through the process once more, before ruling out the presence of fingerprints.

The stage was laid out for the hotel scenes, and so Grandfather walked over to an occasional table beside one of the deckchairs and spread out the letter. He motioned to me to read it aloud.

"Lillian Bradshaw," it began. "I know the secret you've been keeping all this time. Place a bundle of ten five-pound notes in a paper bag between the wall and the public bench at the junction where Bowling Green Lane meets Corporation Row. If the money isn't there by the end of this week, I'm sure that Lord Beaverbrook at *The Daily Express* would like to hear what I've discovered."

"It says nothing more than that?" Grandfather sounded surprised, and I wondered for a moment whether he was expecting to discover something else when he'd opened the letter.

"Blackmail!" Darrington proclaimed with great disdain in his voice. "And a particularly unsophisticated case at that."

Grandfather quickly read the contents of the other letter. "It says much the same thing."

It was Darrington's turn to ask a question. "Do you think it could be a ploy? Perhaps the blackmailer didn't know anything about the two actors but was trying to extract some money from them."

"No, I don't think so." Lord Edgington leaned closer to peer down his nose at the first letter, then pointed at one key phrase. "Look there. He says, 'I know the secret you've been keeping all this time.' Why would he say, 'all this time'? It's too specific to be a guess. If he was trying his luck, he would have kept the message as vague as possible."

"Are we to assume that Brian Grimage himself wrote these letters?" I put to the two more experienced detectives and, rather than

148

hazard a guess, Chief Inspector Darrington waited to hear what Lord Edgington had to say.

My grandfather apparently did not know the answer and so turned to call down the stage to Marius. "Mr Quin, would you happen to know where Brian Grimage lived?"

"I'm afraid not. I rarely saw him outside of the theatre."

Tallulah was still sitting in her trance, but the question stirred her. "He was from Clerkenwell, I believe. He talked to me about Spa Fields once, as he still lived with his mother somewhere nearby."

"Thank you, Miss Alanson." Grandfather's resultant bow was florid, even for him. He turned back to us and struck the letter once more. "The bench where he told them to leave the money was on his way home from here. We'll have to compare a sample of his handwriting to be sure, but it certainly looks as though he penned these letters."

"So that solves it," Darrington replied, far too optimistically. "This Grimage fellow was blackmailing the two actors, and they worked together to silence him."

"It's a theory." Grandfather was remarkably restrained in his response. If I'd been the one to make such a statement, you can be sure he'd have put an adjective in front of that noun, and it would not have been a complimentary one. "But the two actors from whom he planned to demand money are known adversaries. Yet more tellingly, though, as the letters had not yet been sent, it does not appear that they knew anything of his scheme."

A possibility occurred to me, and so I seized one of the empty envelopes and compared the handwriting on it to that of the letters. To my untrained eye, at least, it was a good match and I let out a soft, "Blast!" My superiors (in so many ways) looked at me and I explained my thinking. "It seemed feasible for a moment that, if Nelson and Bradshaw had made a truce and worked together, they could have placed these letters in fresh envelopes – in order to suggest they had never received them – then killed Grimage and placed them in his pockets."

"What quick thinking, Christopher." I'd always liked the chief inspector. "You really are taking after your grandfather. I'm impressed."

Grandfather was…. less impressed. "He is a very bright boy indeed, but I'm afraid that my grandson's thinking is only half correct. While everything he said is true, it would have made more sense to kill the man and not leave anything in his pockets that would connect him to the killers."

He was right. That made a lot more sense and, though I tried to conceive of another explanation, I couldn't.

"We must still interview them as possible suspects," Darrington affirmed.

"I agree." Grandfather looked back over his shoulder to spy on them. "You should take the lead."

Gabriel and Lillian were a few rows apart on the same side of the theatre, and I felt that, had they known what we were discussing, they would at least have sneaked a suspicious glance at one another. They would not remain oblivious for very much longer, though, and with a quick signal to one of his men, Chief Inspector Darrington called them up to the stage.

CHAPTER TWENTY-ONE

From what I've seen of such places, the backstage area of a theatre is not so very different from the cells of a police station. On the floor above the corridor I'd previously visited, there was a row of rehearsal spaces and a few offices. Darrington put the quivering suspects into two separate rooms, and I held my grandfather back for a moment to talk.

"Grandfather, in all the confusion, I haven't had time to tell you something important." I looked along the corridor to make certain that no one was listening. "I overheard Lillian Bradshaw and Oliver Hartley whispering to one another before we found the body. I think they may be…"

"Sweethearts?" He surprised me then by laughing.

"Well, yes. And I heard them plotting something. They said they were afraid of being discovered, but they must have heard me moving about as they suddenly cut off their conversation."

He was still laughing! "Oh, Christopher. You are funny sometimes." Shaking his head, he entered the room where Gabriel Nelson was sitting at a desk as though he was the one who would interview us. Darrington was on his feet, ready to put the potential culprit to the sword, and there was a sofa on one side of the room from which Grandfather and I would watch the proceedings.

"I imagine you know why we've brought you in here," the serving officer said.

Gabriel showed none of the fear he'd exhibited in the auditorium. "I honestly haven't the first idea why you'd drag me to such a gloomy spot." He had quick eyes that darted about as he spoke. "I certainly had nothing to do with poor Brian's death, if that's what you're thinking."

"Then you've already contradicted yourself." Darrington always made me think of an old soldier. There was something wonderfully precise and correct about him. "You do have an idea why you're here. We're investigating Brian Grimage's death, and we believe you had a reason to kill him."

"Me?" To say that Nelson acted surprised then would be an understatement. In fact, he was overacting surprised. "You do know who I am, don't you?"

I'd rarely met a man to whom this phrase came so naturally to the tongue.

"Yes, we know who you are. You're a star of the London stage – a man who would do anything to protect his reputation."

The suspect became a little more defensive at this point, and I wondered whether his innocent façade would slip. "Now listen here. I may have a reputation to maintain, but there is a limit to what I would do to guard it. I'm simply not the type to go around murdering people." He huffed out his indignation as another thought occurred to him. "I suppose you're suggesting that I had something to do with Peter's death, too?"

Darrington stepped closer to lean over the desk. "You tell me."

Grandfather watched the brief staring contest which the chief inspector was bound to win. For the first time since I'd met him, Gabriel's attitude had become a touch muted. The theatre was a realm that was stuffed with big personalities whom the public loved to see at their worst on stage and their best off it. We were not in a play now, though, and the actor looked smaller and less invincible.

He hesitated, opened his mouth, then paused and started again. "I did not mean to appear so hostile. I really don't know anything about either of my colleague's deaths. In fact, I barely knew them. I'd been in a play with Peter once before, but he was a very discreet sort of person and, as for Brian, he was quite the opposite. His murder, if that's what it was, surprises me far less than Peter Canning's, as Brian Grimage was not the kind of man who people loved."

"In what way?" Darrington straightened up again and seemed content to let the suspect talk.

"In that he was a jackdaw. He never knew when to keep his mouth shut and loved nothing more than poking his nose in other people's business."

"So you didn't like him?" The officer leading the interview had evidently learnt a thing or two from the days when my grandfather was his superior. He was very good at deflecting our suspect's responses back to him.

"I didn't say that." Gabriel's expression only became more severe. "Brian may not have been my kind of person, but he was entertaining in his own way and, on the odd occasion that the cast went for a drink

152

after rehearsals, he could be a lot of fun. In fact, he had a rather nice voice and wasn't too bad on the piano when we wanted a—"

"I don't think his musical abilities will be relevant to the case, thank you, Mr Nelson." Darrington decided it was time to make the man sweat. He stood back from the discussion to consult my grandfather, and they whispered for a minute or two in voices that were too low for me to hear.

When Grandfather had finished speaking, Darrington nodded and turned back to our suspect. "The reason we have called you in here this morning is that, in the course of our investigation, we have discovered your dirty little secret."

Gabriel had already looked uncertain as to why he was facing this probing and now lost another degree of confidence. "My dirty little secret? But I don't have any dirty secrets. I'm as clean as a newborn baby after a soapy bath."

"That's not what your fellow actors believe." Darrington did his best to pretend that he knew more than he really did but, if this was Grandfather's strategy, it would only backfire.

"Oh, yes? And what have they said about me?" Gabriel was too smart and would not fall into their trap. "If you have an allegation to make, then you had better do so."

Had I been found out like this in an interview, I would have become self-conscious and blathered out an apology, but not Darrington. He may not have had the endless creativity that my grandfather possessed, but he was an experienced officer.

He showed no sign of regret and simply moved the discussion on to the next point. "We found a letter address to you in Brian Grimage's pocket. It demanded a fee in exchange for his silence on that very secret. Did you know anything about it?"

Nelson sucked in both cheeks as he considered the question. "Brian was a blackmailer?"

"It certainly looks that way."

"It really is impossible to know a person these days." He sighed and displayed the most innocent expression he could summon. "Although now that I think about it, he certainly seemed to have some unsavoury acquaintances."

"Oh, yes?"

The flamboyant thespian passed one hand in front of his face as though it were a fan. He was dressed in the long cream mackintosh of his character in the play but had managed to make this simple rigout more extravagant by adding a spotted silk neckerchief and matching blue pocket square.

"You know, I'm not one to gossip. However, I got the impression that Brian mixed with the wrong people. On the night that Peter was killed, we all went to a pub in the East End to drink to his life and commemorate his death." He leaned closer, as though he wished to take us into his confidence. "Before we'd even had time to order, two huge chaps with pork chop sideburns, flat caps and beige raincoats got their hands on him."

"What did they want?" I didn't mean to ask this out loud, but I had fallen into his story and found myself speaking without thinking.

Gabriel looked at me as though he didn't feel it was his place to reveal the facts of the world. Grandfather urged him to answer with a hard stare, and he did just that.

"I didn't hang around to hear the conversation, but it was clear that he owed them money. Do you think that was the reason he was killed?"

He was so smooth, so capable of making us believe that his only desire was to help, that I was left wondering whether he'd invented this story to throw us off the trail.

"That does sound plausible," Darrington conceded, as he looked in my grandfather's direction. "However, the chances are slim of two colleagues being murdered in the same building such a short time apart without the crimes being connected."

Gabriel was totally relaxed by this point. He was actually enjoying himself and displayed a patronising grin. "In my experience, life is full of such quirks. Have you ever noticed how improbable the world is? I'm constantly amazed by the coincidences and idiosyncrasies I come across. For example, I might not see a friend for ten years, but then his name will cross my mind one morning, and I'll bump into him that very same day. I don't see any reason to believe that two separate killers couldn't be connected to this theatre. In fact, it makes more sense to me than one person having a bone to pick with both Peter and Brian."

I had to wonder why my grandfather wasn't saying anything. This was the perfect moment for him to lunge from his chair with an unexpected accusation, but instead he sat listening.

Darrington did his best to scare our witness. "Back to the little matter of the brutally murdered blackmailer…" He pulled himself up to his full height. "Perhaps you would now care to inform us what sort of information the man held over you?"

The actor put one hand to his chin to consider the question. "My life is an open book." He retained his silky tone, but it was undercut by something else. It was not fear – he was too cocky for that – but a touch of trepidation, and I knew then that there really was something he wished to keep from us.

The letter talked of a long-held secret, and my mind ran with ideas for what it might be. Before I could express any of these no doubt worthless theories, Darrington presented the final piece of evidence.

"There was something else in the pocket of Grimage's coat when we found him hanging from a beam with a hole in his head." There was a hint of dark humour in the inspector's words. "He had a picture of his fellow victim, Peter Canning. Did the two men know one another well?"

Gabriel studied the copper's face for a moment, as though trying to identify the precise motive behind the question. I thought he might bend and finally buckle under the sheer weight of suspicion, but he was stronger than that.

When his answer finally came, it arrived with a patient smile. "I'm afraid I cannot tell you, Chief Inspector. As we've already established, I didn't know either of the men particularly well."

Darrington looked at his former boss, and the two exchanged a harried glance. It was clear the interview was getting us nowhere. Even if Gabriel Nelson was our man, he was clever enough to hide anything incriminating from us.

He held all the cards, and we were yet to discover the rules of the game.

With an obsequious expression, he excused himself. "Now, I'm terribly sorry that I can't be more helpful, but this has been a stressful morning for me." He sounded increasingly smug, and I wanted to point out that it was surely more stressful for Brian himself or poor Denny, who'd found the dead man. "If you don't have anything more to ask me, perhaps you should move on to my distinguished colleague."

Darrington looked from his honorary boss to their suspect and gave a curt nod for the star to rise. "You may leave."

Gabriel Nelson made a big show of tying his coat, then strutted proudly to the door as though he was off to collect an award for his performance. Grandfather finally seized the opportunity to cut him down a notch.

"Mr Nelson?" These two words stopped our suspect in his tracks, and he peered cautiously over his shoulder. "We'll be seeing you again very soon."

It was in that moment that I saw the man behind his public mask. Nelson's face fell for just a moment, but it was enough to tell me that his relief was short lived.

CHAPTER TWENTY-TWO

"That sneak jolly well foxed us!" Grandfather declared once the door had shut, and we were on our own.

"Don't you mean he outfoxed us?" I responded.

"Come along, boy. That's going too far!" He shot a puff of air in the direction of his fringe. "I don't believe I've ever been outfoxed in my life, though I'm not too big a man to admit when I've been foxed."

"Don't be so hard on yourself, Edgington," his near-namesake Darrington told him in a firm voice. "The interview went exactly as you said it would."

Grandfather was up on his feet and went for a pace about the small room. It was tricky as, every time he went around the table, he had to breathe in to get through the gap against the wall. "That's very true, but I still hoped for more. I really do not approve of people like Nelson whose whole life is one great pretence. He could be the perfect killer, as there is no way of knowing whether anything he says is true."

"You got him in the end, though, just as you said you would." Darrington looked rather impressed by the old fox, even if he had been foxed.

"What were you hoping to achieve?" I had to ask.

"In all honesty, very little." Grandfather frowned indifferently. "I wished him to know that we suspect him, and I rather like the idea that he will underestimate us. But he certainly didn't reveal anything useful in the time we were interviewing him."

"You're speaking as though you think that Nelson is the likely killer."

"That is exactly what I think, my boy." I don't believe he'd ever stated such a suspicion so openly before. "Of all the suspects we have considered, there is something in Gabriel Nelson's character which makes him the obvious murderer. Call it ego, or self-preservation, but there's something under the surface. I just know it."

This didn't sound particularly scientific to me, and so I pushed him for more. "But what proof have you found?"

He stopped his nervous movement, and his eyes locked onto mine. It almost felt as if there was a force weighing me down in my chair as he looked at me. "Surely you have noticed certain points that speak to his guilt? Think of the way he acted yesterday evening in the rehearsal. Think of his interactions with the group."

My head swam with possibilities, but none of them seemed realistic. "I suppose he is an odd character."

He gazed at me for a few moments longer before making an exasperated sort of chirping sound. It was an odd reaction, but then he was an odd man.

"What should we do next, Lord Edgington?" his colleague enquired. "Lillian Bradshaw is waiting for us in the adjoining room."

"Good. Let's see her right away. We'll use the exact same technique as before, but you should send a couple of plain-clothed detectives to follow Nelson. Oh, and Bradshaw too when we finish here."

"Excellent." Darrington rubbed his hands together like a pantomime rogue as he went off to issue the appropriate instructions.

By the time he came back, Grandfather had returned to his cheerful best. He practically shimmied from the room to a melody that only he could hear. For the span of approximately three-fifths of a second, I considered whether he had finally lost his mind. This was not the first time I had questioned this very thing, and I soon realised that I was getting ahead of myself.

The next room along the corridor was a close copy of the one we'd just left, much as the interview that took place there followed a near identical script to the last. The only difference was that, in place of a preening thespian in love with the sound of his own voice, Lillian was quiet, cold and restrained. It rather reminded me of her performance in one of the scenes I'd witnessed in the play.

It was quite jarring to hear Darrington and my grandfather react to her responses in the same slightly artificial manner as they had to Gabriel's. There was evidently a fair amount of acting involved in being a police officer and, should I ever attend university, perhaps I could read dual honours in criminology and theatricality... Now that I think about it, I'm not sure that either of those degrees actually exist in British universities. If they don't, they certainly should.

As I was pondering the possibility, Lillian denied any knowledge of the blackmail or who might have wanted Brian dead. "Which isn't to say that the man was a saint, mind you. He clearly had his flaws, and I always found it odd that he'd taken up acting in the first place."

"Had your paths crossed before, then?" Darrington was exceptionally good at extracting such information from our suspects. Well, he was better than me, at least.

"We'd been in several plays together." She chose her words carefully, as though to distance herself from the man. "He was forever entangled in some form of mayhem. Either he was sleeping with the wrong woman, or some thugs were angry with him over a debt, or some thugs were angry with him for sleeping with the wrong woman."

"Do you know to whom he owed money?" This would be the one question I asked in this particular interview. Again, I hadn't meant to, but my mind has a mind of its own.

The corners of her mouth turned down as she answered. "One bookie or another, I can't say which. But I do know that he was not only a regular gambler on any sport which involved animals racing against one another, he was also an exceedingly unlucky one. Brian Grimage was simply born to lose."

"What about Peter Canning?" Darrington fired off one question after another in quick succession.

"What about him?"

"Did he have any connection to Brian Grimage?"

She turned her head at a slight angle, and I knew that she was considering the question for the first time. "Not outside of the theatre. Peter was a dear, sweet man. As actors go, he was no twitterer. He knew when to keep his mouth shut and was the opposite of Brian in many ways."

"Such as?"

In my head, I thought, *full sentences, Darrington.* And I realised that Grandfather had infiltrated my very brain!

"Such as the patience, kindness and empathy he showed those around him."

I spotted a contradiction. "The last time we talked to you, you told us he was boring."

She reflected on this for all of five seconds, then explained away the seeming discrepancy. "Can't that also be true? To some people, men who don't walk into a room and immediately illuminate it are considered terribly dull."

"There was a photograph of Peter in Brian's pocket when his body was found," Darrington explained.

"How very odd." Lillian's restraint was impressive. Much as Gabriel Nelson was a master of melodrama, she was an expert at hiding her true emotions. On the stage, it was this very sense of control which had won her so many fans.

The conversation continued in much the same unproductive way, yielding little of interest and giving the actress the impression that we had nothing to link her to the case. And yet, from what Lord Edgington had proclaimed just minutes earlier, he must have suspected her involvement in the crime. Why else would he have told Darrington to set a detective to follow her?

We reached the end of the little drama, and our suspect was granted leave to... ummm... leave.

"I appreciate everything that you do," she said rather wistfully as she put her hand against the door. "I really do think it's wonderful that you are so dedicated to your profession. It's just a pity that yours and mine are not compatible. 'A Killer in the Wings' will never have its opening night, and you mustn't tell Marius, but I very much doubt any theatre will touch his work after this. We are a superstitious lot at the best of times."

She froze for a second, then, with a mournful look, moved to go.

"Miss Bradshaw," Grandfather began, and I was certain that he was about to issue the same ominous warning that he had to Gabriel. "We will..." His words died, and he changed his mind. "I hope the loss of this role has no great impact upon you."

Her emotions once more hidden behind a blank mask, she disappeared through the door.

The three of us who remained looked at one another, and I imagine that we were all pondering the same pair of questions. Was Gabriel's apparent duplicity proof of his guilt? And did the fact that Lillian seemed so calm in the interview show that she had nothing to hide? Together, they made for quite a conundrum.

"I regret not formally interviewing Grimage yesterday." Grandfather stared at the wall as though he couldn't bring himself to look at us. "Who knows what I might have discovered that could tie this forever-shifting case together."

I had an inkling of what the two officers had been trying to achieve, but things hadn't gone to plan. "You hoped that they would provide contradictory statements, didn't you?"

"That would have been helpful," my grandfather admitted as he rose to return to the back-stage corridor. "If I'd detected that Gabriel had told a clear falsehood, I would have asked his colleague next door to confirm it, but he was too clever for that. He gave us nothing."

Darrington had a question of his own. "By sitting back from the interview and leaving me to interrogate our suspects, had you hoped they would feel intimidated and give themselves away?"

Lord Edgington's moustache wiggled like a pensive worm. "It was something along those lines. Alas, it came to nothing. Except…" I think he paused then in the hope I would ask a typically over-eager question. I was not in the mood to play his puppy dog and, when I said nothing, he continued. "At the moment he was about to leave, Nelson showed that he was not quite so sure of himself as he wished to pretend."

"I noticed the same thing," I said. "He evidently thought that he'd beaten us, but then a look of despair came across him when you told him that we'd be seeing him soon. It was neatly done, Grandfather."

"Thank you, Chrissy. And you were smart to have observed such a thing."

We were having such a nice time patting one another on the proverbial backs that Chief Inspector Darrington decided to participate. "You're both incredibly quick-witted. I don't know how you manage it. I really don't."

Grandfather's smile became a straight line and then sank into a frown. "For the little good it does us. The fact is that, even if I think Nelson is our culprit, we have no way of proving it."

He descended the stairs ahead of us, and we followed him to the stage.

"Grandfather, you normally won't tell me who you think is guilty, and now you won't tell me why you think your choice of killer is to blame. Couldn't you be a good chap for once and reveal the whole story?"

I didn't need to see his face to know that he disagreed. "I am 'a good chap', Christopher, whether you think it or not. However, I won't simply tell you all the answers. You'll never learn if I do the work for you."

"But couldn't you…?" I began. "Don't you think you should…?" I sighed and abandoned the challenge. "Chief Inspector, was it so infuriating to work with Superintendent Edgington when he was your boss?"

As we reached the area behind the rear curtain on the stage, Darrington looked at me through the corner of his eye and struggled to think of a diplomatic answer. "Your grandfather was always very good at his job and a truly fair superior officer."

"However…" the man in question prompted him.

"However, he did have his moments."

"My moments!" Grandfather was incredulous. "What 'moments' did I have?"

Darrington cleared his throat. "You expected a lot from your subordinates."

We stopped walking and the thin-skinned former policeman turned to look at us. I couldn't make much out in the darkness there, but he was clearly offended. "You're accusing me of being demanding? I was as soft as a cotton boll to my men, and they greatly appreciated it."

"Of course you were, sir." The chief inspector reverted to an earlier stage of being when the old lord held sway over him. "We admired you more than any other officer. It was merely that…"

"Go ahead, man. Say what you're thinking."

"Well…" Darrington looked at me in the hope I might be able to answer. I could not. "You see… you would never give young officers the answers. You made them guess things that they really didn't have the experience to divine for themselves. It could make learning from you quite difficult."

Grandfather crossed his arms. "Who said this?"

I had to wonder whether he would take note of their names and issue a stern reprimand.

"No one in particular. But then they didn't have to; for one thing it was obvious, and for another I experienced it myself."

Grandfather's eyes widened as he moved out of the wings onto the stage. "I'm flabbergasted. I really am. I've always considered myself an exceedingly fair teacher."

I'd be lying if I said I didn't enjoy his flusterment, but I couldn't help feeling a little sorry for him, too.

"Fair is just the word for you, Grandfather," I said before mumbling a caveat. "Though demanding is another."

I believe he would have thrown his hands in the air in disbelief and stomped about the stage, but he realised we had an audience. Marius Quin and Oliver Hartley were still there in the auditorium. A couple of uniformed constables stood guard on either side, and the whole lot of them were staring silently at the stage with no sign they would ever move again.

Quite suddenly, Marius stood up from his seat in the front row and gave a courteous nod before turning to dash away.

"Mr Quin, wait," Grandfather called after him. "I imagine that you could use a drink to help forget your sorrows."

The author stopped at the top of the stairs and leant against the wall as though he lacked the strength to stay on his feet for much longer. "That would be greatly appreciated."

"I'm sorry to interrupt, Lord Edgington," Hartley told him, "but I was hoping I might speak to you before you leave."

"No, no." Grandfather crossed the stage to walk down the stairs and past the remaining officers. "That won't be possible. You'll simply have to come with us to a bar I know."

He waited for Hartley at the end of his row and, when the forlorn actor reached him, he put one arm around his shoulders and helped him up the stairs.

"You are a kind man, Lord Edgington," he said in a voice so fragile that the slightest breeze might have knocked it to pieces. Of course, I would have added the words, *fair* and *demanding* to this appraisal, but I managed to hold my tongue.

The three of them stopped at the top of the stairs to peer back down at the stage.

"This was supposed to be the play that restored my sorry bank balance and made me a household name," Marius told us and, as actors never like to be outdone, Oliver had something even sadder to impart.

"This was supposed to be the play that wiped the image of me covered in whipped cream from the public's memory and recast me as a serious actor. I'd been looking for a part like this for years... nay, decades."

His eyes traced out a path across the stage. They moved around the stone fountain in the centre and on to the deckchairs and the small bar in the back corner. I hadn't seen the place so empty before then, and it was oddly moving.

Oliver clicked his tongue a few times as he gave a rueful shake of the head. "It's not often that an actor sees so much of himself in a character and knows exactly how the part should be played from the first reading. People expect mysteries to be frothy slices of popular entertainment, but this one was so rich and complex, with such intriguing characters, that, if it had been given the chance it deserved, 'A Killer in the Wings' could have run for years."

There was the definite sense that this was not just an *au revoir*, but a permanent goodbye. Lord Edgington squeezed the solemn thespian's shoulder and led him towards the foyer. Grandfather really was a kind man. I'd made such remarks on any number of occasions, and I would never forget it.

We moved at a funereal pace and crossed the palm lounge towards the vestibule, before stepping outside into the street for perhaps the last time. The sign above the door still promised 'thrills, intrigue and drama' when the play opened the following night, but the lights were all turned off, and the curtains would never rise on Marius's play.

CHAPTER TWENTY-THREE

I'd often noted my grandfather's fairy-tale-esque qualities – he could be as regal as a wise old king, as fearsome as a giant and as infuriating as Rumpelstiltskin – but I had never pictured him as the Pied Piper of Hamelin before. No sooner had he left the theatre with the four of us in tow than he attracted two more followers.

"Can I come with you lot?" Dancing Denny asked from his lonely bench across the square. "I ain't got nowhere else to go."

He didn't wait for an answer but joined the back of our human convoy. He was normally a cheerful little tyke, but the tune he whistled was noticeably gloomier than usual, and he stared at the pavement as we walked along to Charing Cross Road.

"Wait for me, you blisters!" a voice called after us, and I turned to see Marmaduke launch himself from the theatre. "You didn't quite shake me off last night, and you won't manage it now."

He caught up with us and put one arm around me to secure my neck in the crook of his arm. A few minutes later, we entered a public house in Seven Dials. I thought this would be preferable to being manhandled through the West End by my former bully, but I was wrong.

You see, I'd grown fond of such establishments over the last year or two, but this was not the picturesque, oak-beamed pub that I knew and loved. Poked in between a plumber's and a cobbler's, it was surely the least comfortable bar in London. I could only think that my grandfather had taken us there to prove that it wasn't just luxurious establishments that he frequented, and that he was just as home in what might generously be referred to as a 'dive'.

"Grandfather?" I asked, as Marmaduke released me in the entrance. "Have you brought us here because you felt that two murders weren't enough?" I eyed the clientele, who, to a man, were staring at me as though I was a roast chicken dinner.

"You do love to fuss, Christopher," he said to dismiss my concerns. "I've entered more dangerous nurseries than this place. Now, what would everyone like to drink?"

He did not wait for an answer but sallied towards the bar. The others seemed perfectly happy there. Oliver Hartley showed no fear as he ordered a tankard of beer, and the sight of tiny Denny tipping his drink down his neck took me by surprise.

"What d'ya want?" The barman, who had one eye and a scar down his cheek, made me feel that there was no right answer to this question. Instead of enquiring whether he served lemonade – or perhaps a Pimm's Cup to appear more manly – I went with the consensus and ordered some form of lager.

"That's the stuff," Denny said before wiping the froth from his lips with the back of his hand.

"Oh, yes. The stuff!" I dissembled. "That's just what this is."

We gathered around a table in one slightly less gloomy corner of the bar, and I marvelled at the life I led. We had dined at The Savoy the previous night, and now I was drinking in the corner of the roughest bar I'd ever entered. The Skull and Blackguard (or whatever it was called) was quite different from that opulent hotel. The service was hostile. The owner had chosen not to fork out for the luxury of chairs, and the floor didn't seem to have been swept since the pub was first opened. My only relief was that I had a police escort to protect me.

"I'm still struggling to understand what happened." Marius was the first to initiate conversation. "Someone murdered Brian and then hung his body from the beam of the storage room. We all knew he wasn't the most reputable fellow, but I can't imagine why the killer would have gone about it in such a way."

"I would say that was obvious," Grandfather replied. "I don't believe the culprit had any hope of disguising Brian's death as suicide. He was merely indulging in his penchant for theatricality. Sadly, as our six potential killers are all actors, this does not help us one bit."

"Six?" Oliver's eyebrows worked their way up his forehead in short jerks like a climber scaling a mountain.

"Well, six including Brian." Grandfather must have known this didn't make any sense, but he refused to acknowledge that we only had an odd number of suspects for the second killing. "The only people who could have set the trap that killed Peter were you, Gabriel, Lillian, Tallulah, Brian and Denny."

The stagehand took a break from quaffing his beer to shrug. "Fair enough."

Oliver was more distressed by this, and his voice shot higher. "You

166

really think that one of us is to blame for what happened?"

"I'm afraid so. I still haven't discovered why those two men had to die, but the motive is surely within our reach."

"There must be something that connects them," Marius mumbled to himself as much as the rest of us.

I watched Denny as the conversation developed. For a suspect in a murder investigation, he did not seem particularly worried.

"Well, I haven't got a clue." He finished his beer and, from the way he looked back at the bar, seemed keen to buy another one.

Chief Inspector Darrington could be relied upon to keep any such discussion grounded in the facts. "We can talk ourselves hoarse and around in circles, but the key to the whole case will surely come from the items we found in Brian Grimage's pockets this morning."

"Of course," Marius agreed. "No, sorry, I'm not quite following you. What did you find in his pockets?"

Darrington looked at his former colleague, who nodded to confirm that we could talk openly of such things. "He was blackmailing Lillian Bradshaw and Gabriel Nelson."

"What could those two have done that would lead to blackmail?" Marmaduke asked. "I've known more rebellious choirboys than that pair."

Lord Edgington looked at him disapprovingly. For this reason alone, I enjoyed spending time with my old school friend; he drew my dear grandfather's ire away from me.

"I still cannot say, though I did discover one useful fact from the letters." He looked at me then, as though to suggest, *you know what I mean, don't you, boy?* I didn't, of course, but I nodded back all the same.

"My goodness." Hartley sounded surprised to hear of his friends' plight, and he looked oddly afraid.

"Really, I can't believe my bad luck recently..." Marius needed another slug of beer before he could say anything more. "...or for approximately the last decade, for that matter."

"I know just what you mean." Marmaduke was happy to join in with the self-pity convention.

Denny, on the other hand, singularly failed to gauge their mood. "Personally, I've always considered myself a fortunate sorta bloke." He eyed the playwright as though trying to identify a rare species of insect. "Who spat in your porridge?"

Marius had fallen into a blue funk. "Well, I owe my house to the bank and, with the play closing before it even opened, I find myself ten steps closer to foreclosure. I can't find the concentration to write another line of my next book, and my mother, aunt and uncle all live in my house and spend most of their time singing. It's quite infuriating, and I'm at the end of my wick." He was out of breath by the time he'd delivered this lengthy list of complaints.

Denny was still peering up at him, perhaps wondering whether the normally confident author needed professional help. "Fair enough. Though I reckon the best thing you can do is look on the bright side."

"Oh, yes?" Marius looked even glummer to be taking advice from a fifteen-year-old boy. "And what would that be?"

"Think about it, matey." Denny's face was one big smile, and I thought he might start dancing. I'm glad to say that he resisted the temptation. "All that stuff you're worried about; it hasn't happened yet. Things can always be worse."

My grandfather narrowed his eyes in that distrustful manner of his, as though he was adjusting his suspicions and now wondered whether the boy's cheerful demeanour was a cover for more nefarious intents. Standing just next to him, meanwhile, Oliver Hartley still looked lost.

"Denny, why don't you tell us about your background?" Lord Edgington took another small, precise sip of beer. If he kept going at that rate, I feared we would be there for some time. "How did you become involved in the play in the first place?"

"Ah, that's an interesting story. You see, what 'appened was that me mam, she weren't too 'appy wiv me 'angin' round the 'ouse. She told me I 'ad to get a job or she'd turf me out." His thick cockney accent seemed to have become stronger now that he'd had a drink. "I was walkin' round Soho one day and some old gent asked me to carry his bag into the theatre. When I went inside, they just thought I was one o' them, and the producer or what have ya started ordering me about to carry this an' that. Me mam always says it's rude to answer back, so I did as I was told and, at the end of the day, they gave me a few bob. You can be sure I went back the next day and every day since."

"Who was the old gent who you'd first helped?" Grandfather was like a tiger, pouncing on evidence. No, forget that. The metaphor broke down in the middle somewhere.

"It was Gabriel Nelson, of course. Now, I'd better be off. Me mam won't be happy when I tell 'er that the play's closed. I should probably look for work elsewhere before I do."

He wiped his mouth once more and, with a nod to each of us, wandered off whistling 'The Rare Auld Mountain Dew' as he went.

"What a curious little man." Grandfather shook his head in amusement.

My friend Marmaduke suddenly had something more useful to say. "I suppose you've noticed that, if Brian Grimage was blackmailing other actors, he could have got the idea from Marius's play?"

"I'm aware that such a thing is possible." Grandfather replied, and I wondered if this was entirely true. "Still, I'd be happy to hear your perspective on the matter."

"Brian played an unlikable character by the name of Clive McCormack." Marmaduke spoke as though whatever he had to say was obvious. "We learn at the end of Act Two that Clive McCormack has been blackmailing his friend Edward Buxton."

"Played by Oliver," I said to be helpful, though the actor in question was still in a daze.

"In the story, Clive has discovered somehow that Edward really had intended to murder his first wife before she was accidentally killed. He uses the information to extort money from him."

"I don't believe I saw that part of the play." Grandfather gripped his tankard a little tighter. "That may yet prove significant to the case." His sudden optimism only served to show up the others' gloominess.

Even Marmaduke had turned Novemberish. "I really thought I could make a living as an actor, but it seems that's not to be."

"Come, boy. You have your whole life ahead of you," Darrington said, though it might just as well have been his former colleague speaking… or any person over the age of forty, for that matter. "You're too young to be so down in the mouth. Don't give up at the first hurdle."

Marmaduke released a sad breath and drank his beer. If anything, he was the most cheerful of the remaining players. Whatever Grandfather had hoped to achieve by leading us to that grimy den and buying everyone a drink had apparently not been realised.

"Well, gentlemen, I can only offer my heartfelt condolences on the closure of what seemed to be a very promising play, but we must continue with the investigation if we are to have any hope of catching the killer." They began to file away, and, by way of a parting gesture, Grandfather added, "Mr Quin, I can at least promise that you have gained a new reader this week. I will certainly purchase a copy of your book at the first available opportunity."

Marius attempted a smile, but it was too much effort, and so he tramped after Marmaduke towards the exit. The only one of our suspects who did not move was Oliver Hartley. He still wore that shocked expression and, when it was clear that he had no intention of leaving, he mumbled an explanation. "I may be wrong, but I believe I know what the blackmailer holds over Gabriel."

CHAPTER TWENTY-FOUR

In that same slightly dreamy manner, the lean actor glanced around the bar to take in his ill-to-do surroundings. "Perhaps we could get some air before I explain."

The two officers nodded as one and put their arms out to direct Oliver to the door. They could have done well for themselves doing such tricks in a variety performance.

Lord Edgington led us to the garden at the heart of Leicester Square. Oliver sat down on a bench, and Grandfather stood in front of the statue of William Shakespeare, his legs crossed and his hand to his chin in an uncannily close personification of the Bard.

"Take your time," he said to calm down the witness.

"Thank you." The man was clearly shaken by whatever thoughts were flowing through his head, and he would need some time before starting. "When I arrived in London in 1891, I was still a young man. I had the idea of making a name for myself as a serious actor, but the popular entertainment of the day was of the music hall variety, and I took whatever work I was offered. Before long, I found myself in a trio of likely young gents known as the Beaconsfield Three. Now, I'd never been to Beaconsfield – I was born in Newcastle, as it happens – but the name played on the idea that we were country bumpkins. And much to my chagrin, I was the butt of every joke."

"I imagine that another member of your trio was your friend Gabriel Nelson," Darrington suggested and earned a slow nod for his trouble.

"That's right. There was Gabriel, me, and a friend of mine called Malcolm Delaney. We made quite the name for ourselves on the London circuit. We performed sketches mainly, but Malcolm was a bit of an acrobat, too, and Gabriel has always had a melodious set of pipes. We liked to say that we were a variety company in our own right."

"Did you follow the path of so many young stars and fly too close to the sun?" I asked, and I was surprised that Grandfather didn't roll his eyes.

"Don't spoil the ending of the story, boy," he complained instead.

"We had the chance to appear right here at the Alhambra." Oliver peered at the immense palace of entertainment over his shoulder. "The problem was that we couldn't decide what sketches to perform, and Malcolm and Gabriel argued." He sighed for the length of time it took to exhale every molecule of breath from his lungs. "They had been rivals from the start, but we'd managed to rub along together just fine until success came calling."

"And so what happened at the Alhambra?" Darrington was simply the most focused person I'd ever met. He was incapable of straying from the point.

"Their silly feud meant nothing to me, so I told them to sort it out between themselves. I don't know exactly how it happened, but Gabriel agreed to do one of Malcolm's big acts, and Malcolm would do the same in return. I was there, ready and waiting on the night in question. I remember that the duo on before us were The Unicycling Sisters, Betty and Barbara Belgrave. I'd always been a little soppy on Betty – and Barbara, too, if the truth be known. In fact, one of them winked at me as we swapped over. I was full of nerves that night, and I can only think that was a presentiment of what was about to occur."

We remained silent throughout the account, and all three of us hung on his words.

"It all started with me walking onto the stage and doing something idiotic. That was usually what happened in our acts. Gabriel liked to say that it relaxed the audience's laughing muscles and set the tone for what was about to take place. Either way, the setting was a country estate, and we were three gardeners going about our work. I walked to the middle of the stage and immediately fell over, just as Gabriel was passing with a wheelbarrow of mown grass. As you can imagine, I ended up covered in the stuff, but even before I went headfirst into the wheelbarrow, Malcolm swung across the stage from a trapeze with a bowl of cream in his hand to cover my face.

"It was at this point that the audience discovered I had more than a touch of hay fever. I sneezed and went back into the wheelbarrow. I staggered about the stage looking like some kind of monster as Gabriel sang, 'The Green Grass Grew All Round' and Malcolm swung from out of sight beyond the wings to chirp a line of the chorus each time."

He came to a momentary stop then and shook his head. "I suppose it was an amusing sketch, thinking back, but at the time I hated it. I

172

hated being made to look a fool, but that was my job. Like a jester in an ancient court, I was there for the audience to laugh at me."

Darrington did his best to make him concentrate on whatever could have a bearing on our case. "What happened that night? You must have done the act many times. What was different on this occasion?"

"It was terrible." His voice retained a dreamy quality, and he continued staring into space. "When we got to the conclusion of the song, Malcolm was supposed to dangle from his trapeze and fall into a net in the orchestra pit. It always gave the audience a thrill as, from where they were sitting, it looked as though he were falling straight through the stage. We'd practiced it that afternoon and everything was fine, but the rehearsal seemed to have loosened the fixings. When he dropped from the trapeze, he fell thirty feet. The net gave way, and he broke both legs and was knocked out cold."

"Was he... killed?" I asked with some trepidation. I was used to stories of past deaths and ancient wrongs, but the thought of the audience sitting laughing as the man fell to his doom was too much for me.

Oliver looked over and my blood turned to ice in my veins. "No." They soon warmed up again. "But his head was never quite right after that night. Even when his body recovered, he couldn't remember things as he had before. He was a nice man, you know? A good-hearted person who always had a smile for everyone."

"I'm sorry," Grandfather said when this account fell silent. "Are you suggesting that someone intentionally loosened the net that would have protected your friend?"

Oliver peered around at us before turning back to his questioner. "I can't possibly say, but Gabriel has always acted strangely whenever Malcolm's name was mentioned. It was only in the pub just now that I started to question whether Brian found out that Gabriel was responsible for ending a man's career."

"So you don't know for certain that he had anything to do with the accident?" Darrington put to him.

With lips pursed, Oliver could only shrug. "No, of course I don't. But I'm not sure that it actually matters. Regardless of whether there was foul play involved, the incident could be used to blackmail Gabriel. At the time, it was viewed as one of those unfortunate occurrences that can happen in our trade. But Gabriel and Malcolm had been arguing right up to the moment they went on stage, and he would have been the likely culprit."

I watched my grandfather to see his reaction. "What happened to Malcolm Delaney afterwards?"

"He died quite young. He must have been in his thirties when he finally went. After he retired from the stage, he simply drank himself to death."

"So then, who else would have known about that night in the Alhambra?"

Oliver looked around the park again. The weather had improved since the thunderstorm had rolled back out of town, and there were a number of elegantly dressed young gents out for a stroll, suited businessmen chattering in groups, and white-aproned nannies pushing their wards around in frilly blue prams. I doubt he saw any of this, though. He was reliving that scene from decades earlier.

"I mentioned The Unicycling Sisters, Betty and Barbara Belgrave. Well, those weren't their real names. In fact, they weren't even sisters. Barbara gave up on fame and moved to the South Coast, but Betty became a big star." He stopped himself then, as he must have known what we would think. "I'm not suggesting that she was involved in the deaths we've witnessed or even the blackmail, but perhaps Betty told someone what she'd seen, and Brian Grimage found out about it."

It didn't require too much sense to realise who he was describing. Apparently, I had just enough. "You're saying that Lillian Bradshaw was there on the night of Malcolm's accident?"

"That's right." He nodded ever so cautiously to confirm what we must all have realised. "Back then, Lillian Bradshaw was known as Betty Belgrave."

CHAPTER TWENTY-FIVE

"This is a gem of a case," Grandfather declared once we'd made sure that Oliver was in a fit state to get home. "It was rather too simple at first, but there are so many complexities now. As much as I enjoy a good murder in an old house or castle or what have you, there's nowhere like London for investigating a wide-reaching crime – and nowhere like the theatre to find a bunch of ruthless, backstabbing suspects."

As we walked away from Seven Dials, there were two points to this speech I would like to have corrected. First, I'd told him on any number of occasions that he really shouldn't discuss murder investigations in terms of his level of enjoyment. And second, he shouldn't describe actors in such negative and— Wait a moment. From what I'd seen that week, perhaps his criticism of the theatrical world was acceptable, after all.

"Is there anything in particular upon which the police investigation should concentrate?" Darrington asked as we crossed Covent Garden.

"I'm glad you asked," Grandfather replied and came to a stop under the portico of the Actors' Church. "I imagine that you will already have despatched officers to examine the victim's home. In addition, you'll need to send a man to the bench in Clerkenwell where Grimage wanted the swindled money left. It's important to check whether anyone has already fallen for his trick."

"That's smart thinking," the chief inspector replied with a click of his heels.

"It might also be worth leaving a constable on duty at the theatre." Grandfather considered this point for a moment. "We don't know what else the killer has planned, so it's best to keep an eye on things there."

"Quite." Darrington had seemingly forgotten that Lord Edgington was no longer the one who gave orders. "Can I do anything else?"

"Yes, there's one last thing." Grandfather straightened his posture and looked at his friend appreciatively. "I'll need the address of Peter Canning. I heard it mentioned at lunch yesterday that he lived somewhere close to Smithfield. If you could find out his exact address and how I might obtain a key, send the information to Snow Hill Police Station as soon as it's available, and I'll call in there directly."

The distinguished officer was running off to fulfil his orders before this sentence was complete. "I'll see to it right away."

Grandfather looked very pleased with himself. I had no doubt in my mind that, at such moments, he considered re-enrolling in the Metropolitan Police so as to have a troop of minions under his control again. His former employer must have an upper limit for the age of their officers, but he could probably have found a way around it.

He breathed in through his nostrils as we moved across the piazza towards the fruit market. All I could smell were the gutters, but he acted as though we were in a sunny meadow somewhere. "It is a gem of a case, a real gem."

"You said that before."

"Yes, but now I can tell you why. There are two possible reasons for the victims' deaths." He picked up a rather large potato and inspected it as though he had the case there in his hands. "Either the killer went to incredible lengths to conceal his motive, or the pair were killed out of necessity… Or perhaps the first really was an accident."

"That's three reasons, not two!" I complained, not that I expected him to change his tune.

"Well observed, Christopher. We have three definite options to explain this unusual pattern. It is a real—"

Before he could tell me what a gem of a case we were investigating, I interrupted him. "And you're still convinced that Gabriel Nelson is the killer?"

"Of course I am." He squeezed that same potato rather expressively. "I can just feel it. He has the most to lose and the most to gain. He is definitely our man." This didn't sound like my grandfather. He normally prized hard evidence over all other things.

"If you know he's the killer, why don't you have him arrested already? We don't want anyone else to be murdered."

He tossed the starchy tuber back into the pile of vegetables so that a little puff of dried earth took to the air. "There's no fear of that, my boy. I believe that our killer has achieved his objectives and will be happy to step back from the proceedings from this point forward."

"So then, what were his objectives? You just said that we still have several options open to us whilst simultaneously claiming that Nelson is the killer and that he won't commit any more crimes. I hate to say it, but I believe you are contradicting yourself."

He looked quite stunned by the allegation and leant on the edge of the potato cart, before realising that it would tip over and letting go. "I, the Great Lord Edgington, contradict myself? You're talking bosh, twaddle and nonsense!"

Suitably chastened, I scuttled after him. "My apologies, Grandfather, but can you please tell me what you think our main suspect wanted to achieve through the chaos and violence he sowed at the theatre?"

There was a flower stall with a pretty young lady in a bonnet that was almost as bright as her produce. She smiled at the pair of us and might have started in on her patter, but Grandfather was already talking.

"I can, but I will not." He tipped his hat to the flower seller and moved on once more. "I will not, Christopher, because you already have all the information you need and, barring a few small matters which we will investigate this afternoon, you should now have a clear picture of what occurred."

I was becoming more desperate. "I should, but I don't."

Instead of answering, he looked back over his shoulder and winked. It did nothing to lift my spirits.

Covent Garden was as cheerful and bustling as ever, but I felt terribly glum. I thought I'd honed my skills as a detective. I thought I'd actually learnt how to play the game of which Grandfather was so fond, but I'd rarely felt so frustrated.

There was a clown standing in one corner of the piazza, to the rear of the Royal Opera House. He was juggling for the passing crowds, but no one stopped to look at him. His face was painted with both a frown and a smile, and I knew just how he felt.

"Could we at least discuss what's happened today?" I suggested. "Did our conversation with Oliver Hartley convince you that Gabriel Nelson is to blame for the two murders?"

"Oh, yes. Yes, of course. At least two, I'd say. I think we have every reason to believe that their former partner, what was his name… Malcolm Delaney?" He didn't need me to confirm this and continued at the same fast pace. "It seems likely that Gabriel was the one to tamper with the net which would have saved Malcolm from injury. Although his fall from the trapeze might not have killed him directly, it brought about his poor health and early death. Whoever committed that act of sabotage is a killer in my book."

It was my turn to be shocked. His behaviour was so unexpected. He kept making sweeping statements that were quite at odds with his usual meticulous attention to detail. Normally he was like a mathematics teacher who insisted I showed my workings out at all times, but he was suddenly looser, freer and more relaxed. I didn't trust it one bit.

"So you're saying that we can dismiss half of our suspects?" I spoke in a truly astonished tone. "Little Denny, Tallulah Alanson, and Brian Grimage himself are out of the picture now? The killer must have been present all those years ago if the same person who caused Malcolm Delaney's accident killed Peter and Brian."

He stopped beside a fruit stall and frowned. "My dear boy, my beloved grandson, you simply are not listening to me. It's not just those three names you can rule out. You can forget the whole lot of them because Gabriel Nelson is the killer. You often complain that I don't share my theories with you, but now that I have, you won't believe me. We've got our man; all that's left to do is prove his guilt."

"In which case, why are we going to Peter Canning's house?" I thought I had him there. I should have known he'd have an answer prepared.

"I would say that was obvious." He did not hang around to roll his eyes at me but spun on his heels and walked off in the opposite direction. "We are going to find the evidence to prove that everything I believe is true."

My mind was truly reeling by now. My favourite old eccentric was surely contradicting himself… wasn't he? How did any of this make sense? Before I could even attempt to answer these questions, Grandfather had crossed the elegant square. I sped after him, quite bewildered, and we cut along Russell Street towards Drury Lane to commence our zigzagging journey to Snow Hill Police Station.

The sergeant on duty was one of the broadest men I've ever seen, and it was a wonder he could get out from behind his desk at the end of every shift. I questioned for a moment whether he was one of those anchorite hermits of whom I'd read in my history lessons at school. You know the type; they used to wall themselves up in churches and devote their lives to spiritual reflection. Perhaps Sergeant Tolson had a similar approach to fighting crime.

"Number thirty-seven, Cock Lane," he told us, before we could even say hello. "The old lass who owns the place will let you inside. My men had a look around there when Peter Canning died, but there was nothing of interest." He did not appear to need to breathe between sentences, so there was no hope of our interrupting him. "The victim was a reserved, quiet sort of tenant by all accounts. I can't imagine you'll find much there, but don't let me stop you. Good day now."

And with that, he cast his eyes to the papers on his desk and would not utter another word. I believe that Grandfather considered saying something, but instead he just looked perplexed, and we left the muscly officer to his work.

"Do you know of the ghost of Cock Lane?" I asked my grandfather as we searched for the right road. I must say, it was impressive just how well he remembered the layout of the city from his days in the police.

"I can't say that I do, Christopher. But then, as I don't believe in any such entities, that's hardly surprising."

This was a rare moment at which I knew more than he did, and I would not pass up the opportunity. "It was back in the eighteenth century. A woman died of smallpox and her landlord said that a ghostly presence haunted the building. Scratching and strange noises were heard in the flat, and its owner devised a way of communicating with the spirit by suggesting one knock for yes and two for no. Before you knew it, Cock Lane was full of spectators who would pay a penny to commune with the manifestation."

I could see that he was curious about the tale, and so I continued straight on with it. "Seances were held with respected members of society present, and the sounds continued. It was only when the landlord's supposedly possessed daughter was taken from the house for inspection that a small wooden device was discovered about her person, and the mystery was solved. She'd been making the noises herself, and her father and his accomplices were sent to prison for their lies."

His interest had turned to puzzlement. "Christopher? What does any of this have to do with the murders at Daly's Theatre?"

I struggled to answer that. "Oh, ummm…. nothing. I just thought I'd kill time before we found the house." I looked about at the old

179

buildings on the narrow lane where both Peter Canning and the non-haunted family had lived. It was a shabby place, and I was annoyed that he'd interrupted me before I'd reached the story's end. "Do you know what else happened? When the landlord was placed in the pillory, the people of London took pity on him and, instead of throwing stones or rotten vegetables, they gathered up a collection for the poor blighter."

"That's fascinating."

"The case was so famous that the Lord Mayor of London, the Duke of York and Horace Walpole all became embroiled in it."

"Have you quite finished?"

"And Dickens even mentioned the haunting in 'The Pickwick Papers'."

"Thank you, my boy. Now, may we concentrate on the investigation?" He subtly returned us to the matter at hand – not that I minded. I had exhausted every fact I knew on the ghost of Cock Lane. "All we have heard about our first victim is how unexciting he was. Tallulah Alanson is the only person who believes that there was more to him, but even she couldn't explain why he was murdered." He looked at the buildings and eventually spotted the right address. "Peter Canning's house is just over there."

Number thirty-seven was close to the beginning of the road. It had a rather grand shopfront in moulded terracotta on the first floor and a few flats above. I must admit that I was rather distracted by the array of gadgets and timmynoggies in John J. Royle of Manchester's magnificent shop. There were self-pouring teapots, fuelled irons, automatic egg cookers and even a garden engine (whatever that might be).

As I was gawping at the array of thingummies on sale, Grandfather knocked at the door beside the shop.

A woman stuck her head out and squawked at us. "Whaaaaaat?"

"Ah, madam," he began in his smoothest voice, "perhaps you can help us, I'm looking for—"

"Whatever you're selling, I in't interested." With that, she slammed the door, and I realised why the constable at the police station had been so keen to get us out of his office. Peter Canning's landlady was not a woman with whom to trifle.

Grandfather knocked again… and was again dealt with unceremoniously.

"Are you deaf or just stupid?" She didn't wait for an answer. "I told ya that I'm not buying nothing. Now clear off my front step or I'll call the police. There are laws against this sort of thing."

The door crashed closed before Grandfather could answer her. He looked discouraged but decided to have one last try. "Madam, if I may speak. I've just come from the police station, and I'm interested in inspecting Peter Canning's former dwelling."

Her pale forehead was wrinkled in horizontal lines from top to bottom, and the skin now folded together like a closing fan. "Police?" All of a sudden, she was smiling. "Why din't ya say so?"

She turned to go inside. My mentor and I exchanged glances and followed her up to the first floor.

"I always thought there was something a bit funny about that one," she chattered as she went. "You know the kind of thing. He were quiet. Too quiet if you ask me, but then it takes all sorts to make an omelette, don't they say? Or something like that, at least."

We'd arrived in a simple living room with several doors leading off it. The walls were papered with dark paisley patterns and the furniture was threadbare. It was not the sort of place in which I imagined a West End actor living, but then I'd already come to realise that the world of the theatre wasn't all glamour and gaud.

"This is the place." She peered around it dolefully while pulling at a hair on the large wart on her chin. "Terrible what happened, but I suppose that's how it often goes with his type. One day you're king of the world, and the next you're wandering about with an axe in ya head." She groaned like a dying bear. "Ah, well. That's life. I'll be downstairs if ya need anything." She stomped off to the staircase and Grandfather got to work.

"What are we hoping to find?" I asked as he picked through the books on the shelf.

"Evidence, of course. A signed confession from Gabriel Nelson would be nice, but I'll settle for anything that incriminates the killer." He kept his eyes on his work, and so I wandered about the place as I waited for him to spot some vital clue that I would never have noticed.

The dwelling was humble by anyone's standards, but Peter had been a terribly neat sort of person. Every surface was immaculate, and the large shelf that my grandfather was examining was perfectly organised with papers, books and musical scores by name.

Beyond Peter's connection to the theatre, I couldn't say there was much that might be described as personal about the room. It had no photos that I could see, nor diaries or letters. If his home was any reflection, Peter Canning was everything that his colleagues had told us. I peeked into his kitchen, and it was far tidier than any such room in the grand houses I had visited – though, unsurprisingly, also a lot smaller. It made me sad to see that he only owned three sets of plates and utensils. There were three knives, three forks and three spoons in his cutlery drawer and three bowls and mugs in a cupboard beside the sink. I had to assume that he had one set for each meal of the day, and he rarely entertained guests.

"Christopher, come and see this." As I was busy feeling melancholy at the lonely spectacle, Grandfather did something more useful. He'd finished in the living room and gone into the bedroom.

When I arrived there, he was on his knees rummaging between the nightstand and the thick beige quilt that covered the other bedclothes. In fact, the walls, furniture and even the window frames were all that same shade of sickly brown. Is there any colour sadder than beige? As if I wasn't already feeling miserable enough for the dead man, I would now never forget that tragic colour scheme!

"Christopher, stop judging the décor of Canning's bedroom and look at what I've discovered." He held up a small, square photograph of a pretty young woman with the words, *to MY special friend* written on it.

"That's Tallulah Alanson," I said, because I can't resist stating the obvious. "It was her photo we found in Grimage's pocket."

CHAPTER TWENTY-SIX

"Could you at least give me a clue?" I begged once we were back out in the street.

"No."

"Please, Grandfather. I can't begin to dream of imagining how any of this fits together. It's just like when we were tying flies all that time ago."

"That was yesterday morning, Christopher."

This came as a surprise. "Gosh! Was it? It feels as though we've been chasing after this killer for months on end. Either way, you had a perfectly tied work of art, and I had a couple of messy hooks covered in blood. The same thing is happening in my head at this very moment."

The contents of my brain were at sixes and sevens, not least because I'd spotted the price of the self-pouring teapot and was sorely tempted to buy one for the kitchen back at Cranley Hall. That sort of gadget for less than a guinea was a remarkable bargain!

"Christopher, are you considering purchasing that teapot?" my companion asked and, in my already sensitive state, this was one step too far.

"How do you do it, Grandfather? How do you always know what I'm thinking?"

He had wandered a little way ahead, much as a carrot is dangled just out of reach of a donkey, but now returned to check on me.

"I've hardly surpassed myself, boy. You were staring at the teapot through the window with a vacant look on your face. It was either that or you were considering the fact we still haven't had lunch." He considered this point for a moment and then had to concede, "Now that I think about it, the two things may have a bearing on one another. Perhaps some sustenance will empower you to think a little more creatively."

Just the mention of food cheered me up, but I was still sceptical. "I'm sorry, Grandfather, but I won't believe you until we're sitting down to eat."

"Very well. There is a truly excellent establishment that I know not so far from here which has a long tradition of providing fine food to young gentlemen like yourself. And do you know what they sell?" He paused to give me the chance not to remember a recent conversation. "Sandwiches!"

This sounded just perfect but, when we arrived at the address in Soho, it was very different from the sort of restaurant to which my grandfather had previously taken me. From outside at least, it was rather grubby and there were no waistcoated doormen waiting to greet us. We knocked on the door, and an absolute bison of a man slid aside a hatch to see who had come calling.

"Password?" he bellowed, and Grandfather looked up and down the narrow street before whispering the reply.

"The feast of Saint Vitalis of Gaza falls on a Wednesday next year." This seemed to do the trick as the door swung wide and the monster behind it grabbed us both by the collars.

"Nice to see you, Lord Edgington," he declared in a friendly voice. "It's been years."

"Billy?" he was clearly surprised to see the fellow. "Little Billy Pridden? Is it really you?"

The huge animal appeared to blush like a… like a—

"People call me Big Billy Pridden these days." He laughed an amiable sort of laugh and pointed us up a set of stairs.

The room at the top was a jolly place. The walls were a lovely shade of red, there was a bar on one side and joyful young couples sat looking lovingly into one another's eyes. A beautiful lady dressed rather alluringly in what looked like an outfit from a Jane Austen novel rushed over to attend us.

"Lord Edgington." She was most demure and cast her eyes to the floor as she spoke. "Mother Pridden has told us all about you. You used to come here before my time, of course, but some of my older colleagues still talk of the kindness you showed them."

Grandfather laughed and nodded his appreciation as she pointed us in the right direction. We walked over to the bar where an old lady with frizzy hair was standing with both hands on the counter.

"Lord Edgington, will you have your usual?" She asked nothing but this simple question and made no reaction to Grandfather's presence there after so long.

"That's right, madam. And the same for my grandson, please. It is very nice to see you and very nice to be back."

She nodded without betraying the slightest emotion and wandered off to the kitchen to pass our order to the chef. Grandfather clearly wasn't interested in explaining his connection to the place, and so I didn't try to persuade him. To be quite honest, I was more concerned with the case – and also what his 'usual' order might be.

I returned us to the discovery we had made in Canning's flat. "Were Peter and Tallulah in love? Is that what I'm supposed to conclude from the photo we found?"

"I'm sorry?" he replied, as he was busy examining the velvet curtains and lead-backed mirrors of his old haunt.

"Tallulah Alanson and Peter Canning. Were they engaged in some kind of romance?"

"Why do you say that?"

I ruffled my brow to put across my usual state of confusion. "Because he kept a photograph of her beside his bed."

"Yes, but it wasn't in a frame on the night table. It had fallen carelessly. That's hardly a sign that he loved her."

"But they evidently cared for one another," I suggested. "If the photograph in Grimage's pocket was signed by Canning, and the one in his flat was from Tallulah, they must have held each other in high esteem."

He would not let me get away with flimsy assumptions and set out to undermine my theory. "Think about the images in both. The first was a small, professionally taken photograph that actors distribute to theatres when looking for work. There is nothing particularly personal about it except for the inscription. Tallulah's, meanwhile, may have been taken at the seaside or on a nice day out somewhere. They are quite different."

Before I could imagine what this told us, the woman behind the bar returned to pour us both glasses of sweet elderflower tea. It was delicious and made me like the place even more.

"The bigger question, though," I said once the lady was busy polishing glasses, "is how the photographs connect to the wider case. Ever since we found his body this morning, I've been puzzling over the photograph in Grimage's pocket. Did he take it because he hoped to blackmail Tallulah in some way? Does it reveal something that we have missed?"

"Those are sensible questions," he began, and I was hoping he might actually answer them, but then our lunch arrived.

Two large sandwiches were placed on the bar in front of us by a young lad in velvet breeches. They were made up of a hollowed-out loaf with a slab of beef inside. Squashed in the middle were mushrooms, onions and runny melted cheese, which poured out all over. I'd rarely seen such a welcome sight.

"These are the best sandwiches you will find in London, Christopher," my companion told me a little excitedly. "You won't get better at Claridge's or the Ritz, and I very much doubt that Buckingham Palace could serve finer food than Mother Pridden's shooter's sandwich. I first discovered this place when investigating a terrible case twenty years ago, but I kept coming back for the food. They leave them squashed beneath a weight overnight so that the juices of the steak run into the bread. The melted cheese – added just before serving – was Mother Pridden's addition, and I think it improves an already fine recipe a great deal."

To be quite frank, I wasn't paying a lot of attention. I was too busy trying to fit the most substantial sandwich in Christendom into my mouth. It was no mean feat, but I was up to the challenge.

"Christopher?" I could tell that he was frowning even without my looking at him. "There is cutlery just beside your plate."

"Ah, yes." I dabbed my mouth with my napkin to be polite and seized the knife and fork to cut the sandwich into more manageable bites. "Now, about the photograph at the scene of the crime. Don't you think it could have been used in one of Grimage's schemes? In fact, I'm beginning to wonder whether his blackmail was the spark that led to the two murders. Just think, if Grimage was trying to extort money from Peter Canning and he didn't pay, the thug could have murdered him instead." I was rather fond of this idea, and it triggered a further conclusion. "That must be it! And when Grimage tried to blackmail another member of the cast, he got his comeuppance." I was smiling contentedly as I took another slice of sandwich, but Grandfather would only disappoint me.

"I've told you, boy. Gabriel Nelson is to blame for the two deaths and therefore every presumed accident that occurred in the theatre. Don't go looking for other theories. Stick to the one we know is true." He paused to shovel a square of bread, meat, onions, mushrooms and cheese into his mouth. "You must consider exactly how the photographs relate to Gabriel Nelson and why he would have wanted the two men dead."

I was growing a little tired of his certitude. "You clearly have all the answers, so why don't you just tell me?"

He took a bigger bite then, just so that he wouldn't have to answer. Of course, the look in his eyes told me exactly what he would have said. He would have told me that it wasn't his job to fill in the gaps in our cases, and it was down to me to solve the enigma before us. It made me tired just thinking about it.

"Fine, then let's go back to the interview we had with Nelson this morning. You suggested that you learnt nothing from it and yet, once we left the theatre, you were confident he was our killer. That shows me that it was not so much what he said as the way he said it that has persuaded you of his guilt. His attitude throughout was smarmy and evasive. He is surely hiding something from us, but how many times have we investigated such a character only to find out that the secret they were concealing had nothing to do with the crime in question?"

I believe he would have clapped then, but his hands were dirty. "Those are very wise words. I congratulate you."

I was tempted to ask whether this meant my suppositions were correct but decided upon a more productive course of action. "Bearing in mind everything I know and everything you've told me, we simply must probe the two biggest stars of the play more deeply. Though Darrington interviewed Nelson and Bradshaw this morning, you told them both that we would take our own turn before long. I believe that as soon as we finish this sandwich—"

"And order Mother Pridden's phenomenal chocolate cake."

"As soon as we finish this sandwich and Mother Pridden's chocolate cake, we should pay them a visit, starting with Gabriel Nelson in Maida Hill."

He raised his glass to me in celebration. "That is excellent thinking, Christopher. Your conclusions are an unqualified success. Well... Maida Avenue might more accurately be said to be located in Maida Vale than Maida Hill, but otherwise it's an unqualified success."

CHAPTER TWENTY-SEVEN

We finished our delicious and filling refreshments and left that curious restaurant where, for whatever reason, we were the only people eating. This was not the only thing I found odd about the place.

"Grandfather, why did we need a password to get inside?" I asked once we'd left the place behind and were walking towards Piccadilly Circus.

"They wouldn't want everyone finding out what excellent sandwiches they sell now, would they?"

"Oh, I suppose not." I kept thinking for a moment, and the ridiculousness of his statement soon hit me. "Wait just one moment. Surely a restaurant *would* want everyone to find out that they had exceptionally good food. That's their whole purpose."

He scratched his ear but was not discouraged. "Well, that is true. But there are restaurants and there are *restaurants*. Mother Pridden's House definitely falls into the latter category."

I hadn't a clue what he meant, but this was nothing new, and so I didn't say anything again until we were sitting on the Tube, heading north on the Bakerloo line. "Goodness gracious me!" I practically burst when I realised what he'd done. "It was a brothel! You took me for lunch in a brothel!"

The heads of a few of our fellow passengers turned, but no one seemed too surprised that two aristocratic types would admit to such a thing.

"Not just any brothel, Christopher," Grandfather replied unapologetically. "A brothel with the best sandwiches in England. Nay, Great Britain."

"I wasn't criticising the standard of their cooking. It was..." I decided not to go into details. "What if my mother finds out where I've been?"

Sitting in the seat next to mine, he put his arm around my shoulder. "Chrissy, if your mother knew that you'd been to Mother Pridden's, she would only chastise me for not inviting her. She loves those sandwiches even more than I do."

I was without words by now. My very tongue was numb with

shock and would not stir for some time. I knew that my mother had accompanied her father on his cases when she was a young woman, though I had no idea he would have taken her to such insalubrious locales. I would never look at the pair of them in the same way again.

Instead, I glanced along the carriage at the people aboard the train. No one spoke, as was typical on the Underground. Holding onto the leather straps overhead were a few bankers and clerks on their way back to work after lunch. Three well-dressed children stood stock still with their neat, elderly governess, who wore clothes not so dissimilar from a matron in a hospital. Judging by the books on dinosaurs, wild cats and exotic birds that each of them held, I could only imagine they'd been for an educational excursion to the Natural History Museum. Judging by the faint white moustaches on their lips, they must have stopped off for ice cream afterwards.

George Eliot wrote that a "tube-journey can never lend much to picture and narrative", and yet I would have to disagree with the great woman. All life was there in that motorised train. All strata of society were visible in the busy carriage. There was even one young urchin who rather reminded me of Dancing Denny. Though Grandfather insisted that I should focus my efforts on Gabriel Nelson, I couldn't just forget the other suspects. Perhaps he'd singled out Nelson to make me ignore the fact that, in reality, the renowned actor was working with an accomplice.

Denny himself was a puzzling character. Never before had I come across a case in which one suspect had so little to do with the victims. We'd found no evidence to signal that he could be involved, no suggestion that he was in some way related to the other suspects. He was simply a boy who worked in the theatre where a series of strange and violent occurrences had taken place. He'd got a job in the play because he happened to be able to dance and the previous director had approved of his performance. He'd gone up in the world with the death of Peter Canning, though. And yet, had he been killing his way to a more substantial role in the production, the death of Brian Grimage had the opposite effect and 'A Killer in the Wings' had been cancelled before Denny could take his first professional bow.

It seemed most unlikely that the young stagehand was involved in the crime but, as I watched the boy on the train eyeing up his fellow passengers, I knew that this young tyke was up to no good. Grandfather had spotted the same thing and rose as though to consult the list of stations through which we would be passing, just as the boy sidled up to one of the banker types beside the door.

"I don't think that's a good idea." Grandfather lunged forward before he could fish a wallet from the man's pocket.

The train came to a halt at Marylebone Station, and the group of men, the governess and the children alighted to be replaced by a new group of passengers. Grandfather was still holding the pickpocket's wrist but said nothing until the train moved off once more.

"I spent forty years in the Metropolitan Police," he eventually stated. "I saw any number of children start off as you have. *Pickpockets make pocket money*, that's what each of them believed. They thought they could take the odd thing and not get into trouble, then live a full and happy life."

He tipped his head back to look at the terrified child from an even more severe angle. "But let me tell you this. In all the time I worked in London, I can count on one hand the number of children who fulfilled that simple plan."

There was a murmur from the other passengers as they made sense of what was happening. I heard the odd whisper of "Lord Edgington" and "the Bloodhound of the Yard" as the onlookers recognised the distinguished detective.

"The lucky ones ended up in prison. The unlucky ones ended up dead. The really unlucky ones did both and, the last time I saw them, they were swinging from the gallows. So think about what you're doing before you steal again. Think what the future really holds and, if you know what's good for you, you'll go to school tomorrow morning instead of coming out here to try your luck. You'll go to school for as long as you can and learn a trade that won't send you to Pentonville or Wandsworth Prison. Do you understand me, boy?"

The poor cub's teeth were chattering by now, but he nodded all the same. I could see the relief that flooded through him when we came to the next stop and Grandfather released him. As he waited for permission to leave, Lord Edgington removed a one-pound note from his wallet, placed it in his hand and sent the boy packing.

"My goodness, Grandfather." It was hard to disguise just how impressed I was. "You were incredible. Do you really think he'll take your advice?"

"There is a seven in ten chance that he will." This figure was remarkably precise, even for him. "And I would rather he goes on stealing than be deprived of the opportunity to choose the right path."

"How can you be so sure?"

"I know my facts, Christopher. After all, I said that same speech to hundreds of children during the four decades I served in the capital. I soon found out whether they had listened to me or not and, over the years, I got a sense of just how effective my warning was. Seventy per cent of the time, whippersnappers like that one would realise that the extra few bob they were able to obtain through these illicit means were not worth the unhappy existence it would almost guarantee them. The other thirty per cent either had no choice and were made to do such things by people to whom they could not say no, or they were too arrogant to see that I was right."

"And what about that boy just now? Which way do you think he'll turn?"

Grandfather smiled. "You know, there was a belief in the last century that criminals were born, not made. All sorts of intelligent people were keen to make the argument that criminality was a working-class disease that came from breeding, not merely one's situation in life. I never believed such nonsense myself and, were we to follow that boy out of his house tomorrow – based on the look of pure fear that I saw on his face just now – I believe he would prove that both rich and poor alike can make amends for their mistakes."

His case made, he nodded to himself and placed both hands on his knees. I sat quietly admiring him as the train rolled on through the darkness beneath that sprawling city of cities.

CHAPTER TWENTY-EIGHT

We got off at Maida Vale station without any other drama. There were no murders on board that day, no more crimes to witness, which, by my grandfather's standards, is good going indeed.

We took the simply thrilling mechanical stairs to the ticket office and then followed a winding staircase up to street level. I must say that, although I always enjoy travelling on that singular marvel of modern ingenuity, my first breath of fresh air upon exiting the Tube is almost as stimulating as making use of it.

We walked south towards Regent's Canal, and it was lucky that Grandfather knew the route with his eyes closed, as we were both lost in our thoughts. I was still pondering the conundrum before us and, from his pensive expression and fixed stare, I felt quite confident that he was similarly occupied.

When we got to where we were going, it wasn't where I thought we were supposed to be. Perhaps that sounds like a riddle, but what I mean to say is, well… "This is a boat, not a house," I told him as we stood in front of the long red barge.

"It's actually both," he replied. "It's a houseboat. Don't you remember Lillian Bradshaw's address?"

"I didn't honestly think it would turn out to be significant. As you keep insisting that Gabriel is the killer…"

"Which he definitely is."

He didn't break my concentration, and I continued without a pause. "…I didn't see how his greatest foe could be involved in his crime."

"We will have to wait and see."

It was at this moment that a rather greasy individual in a flat cap and braces *psssted* in our direction. "Oi, Guvnor!" He called. "Over 'ere." He looked about him to make sure no one was watching before beckoning the two of us to him with his hand.

Grandfather looked dubious but did as instructed, and we soon reached the corner where the individual stood reading a paper.

"Lord Edgington, my name is Detective Inspector Coleridge," he told us in a far posher accent than the one he'd just used. He was apparently one of these covert officers of which I'd heard Grandfather speak on occasion. The officer that Darrington had sent to watch our suspect made a truly convincing loiterer. "I followed Lillian Bradshaw from the theatre. She did a little shopping in Paddington and got home here a short time ago. I haven't noticed anything suspicious. Should I stick around just in case?"

Grandfather glanced at the boat before shaking his head. "There's no need for that. Go back to Scotland Yard and write up your report. I'll contact your superior should I need you again."

The inspector tugged on his cap and, in character once more, swanned off along the road.

We searched for a gate in the metal fence that divided the pavement from the bank of the canal. Grandfather pushed it open, then stepped over the side of the long boat that was almost at the same level as the bank. Moving carefully, so as not to upset the balance of the craft nor lose his footing, he knocked on the first window he reached, and then we waited for a few moments to see what response this would produce.

Rather than coming out to see us, the owner looked through the window and waved for us to board. The doors were at either end of the boat and, once inside, we had to step down into the long, narrow room which made up at least fifty per cent of her house.

"Welcome," she said in a perfectly cordial tone. "Welcome both. Now, what can I do for you?"

She was standing in the kitchen area and showed us that she was happy to have us there by filling a kettle with water and putting it on the cooker to boil.

She answered her own question. "Tea won't hurt now, will it?"

I don't know how many sides to Bradshaw's personality we'd seen that day, but this version of her was far more relaxed than the woman we'd met in the theatre. She had a colourful handkerchief tied around the top of her head to keep the long grey hair out of her eyes. It made her look more youthful somehow.

It was hard to imagine a well-known actress living in what amounted to a damp wooden box. The fact the old barge floated was the biggest surprise in the case so far, and it only reinforced the idea that an actor's life is rarely luxurious. The room we were in tripled as a kitchen, dining room and, from the look of things, laundry. I noticed her outfit from the play drying on a line that was extended from one wall to the other and served to divide the space in two.

Unlike Canning's flat, one thing that the Red Houseboat did possess was any number of personal belongings. One wall was covered in programmes from the plays in which she'd starred over the years, mixed in with photographs and costume designs. In the centre of everything, there was a framed poster of Betty and Barbara Belgrave, The Unicycling Sisters, and I wondered whether Grandfather would start with that part of the story.

He did not. "I'm sorry to bother you so soon after we last spoke, but the case has developed swiftly," Grandfather claimed though, after an initial flurry of activity, I personally felt that we'd struggled to get a grip on the investigation. "I wanted to know whether anything new might have come to mind."

"I see," she responded vaguely, and they exchanged a meaningful glance that I couldn't understand.

"Is there anything that you know about Brian Grimage that could help to explain his death? Do you believe that Peter Canning was intentionally murdered? Or perhaps Brian was the intended victim from the beginning?"

Lillian perched on a high wooden stool of the sort you get in public houses. She looked directly at us and did not appear nervous to be asked such questions. If anything, she was far calmer than the last time we'd seen her. "Shouldn't that be your job to fill in such gaps?"

Grandfather accepted this point with a bowed head. "You're right, of course, madam. But try as we might, detectives are not clairvoyants. We primarily obtain evidence through the help of the public. Witnesses like you are key to our understanding and resolution of violent cases, and it is not uncommon for people to remember significant facts soon after an interview is complete. I believe that the pressure most officers apply to suspects can sometimes be hindersome rather than helpful. That is why I prefer to speak to you alone here."

I finally understood why he'd been so aloof that morning. He wasn't just being polite by allowing his old colleague to lead the interviews; he'd wanted Darrington to use a heavy hand, knowing that we would come to the suspects' houses and appear more reasonable. And that wasn't all. Our presence there gave us the chance to observe what he insisted were our two key players in their natural habitats. Or to mangle two perfectly good proverbs, we could now kill two birds with one bush.

In the time we had known her, Lillian Bradshaw had been everything from steely and emotionless to outright effusive. For the moment, however, she opted for the former strategy. "Since I left the theatre this morning, I have gone about my tasks with little thought for what happened, I'm afraid. That may make me sound callous, but that is the way of things. I had no affection for Brian Grimage. Unlike Peter, he was a singularly unsympathetic character, and it was easy enough to continue life as normal."

Grandfather moved further into the gloomy boat as the water on the hob began to boil. "That is very interesting... considering how nervous you seemed this morning. To go from such jumpiness to the calm you now convey in such a short time is truly impressive."

She would not be intimidated and answered in the same relaxed tone. "I'm an actress. I'm used to controlling my emotions. I believe we have already discussed this very topic."

She rose from her seat and went to collect some mugs and a teapot from a shelf above one of the few small windows. I have no doubt that her main motivation was to avoid looking at the sly character who was goading her.

"So you've nothing to tell us then?"

"Nothing whatsoever."

Lillian continued to busy herself in the tiny kitchen. In that neat space, all plates and cups were where they should be, but she moved a few piles around to appear occupied.

Grandfather wouldn't let up and asked another probing question, just as a pugilist will land blow after blow until his opponent concedes defeat. "Nor any secret to confess?"

The water on the cooker was really bubbling by now, and she opened a window to let the steam out. "Though my job may suggest otherwise, I'm a simple woman. I've no time for secrets and scandals."

I watched the saucepan on the enamel gas stove as she moved it off the hob and the water calmed down. Little puffs of steam rose into the air like the smoke from a hunter's gun.

"Very well, Miss Bradshaw," Grandfather said when our suspect made no attempt to make the tea she'd offered us. "I will not keep you any longer."

I could see that this surprised her more than anything else he'd said and, as we turned to leave the boat, she followed us.

"Is that all you wanted to ask? You came all this way for nothing?"

He stepped onto dry land and offered his hand to help me do the same. Once he was certain that I was safe, he smiled politely and did what he could to scare her.

"Not at all, madam." He touched the brim of his hat and nodded. "We'll be seeing you again very soon."

CHAPTER TWENTY-NINE

It had been some time since I'd felt as though I were following my grandfather about in place of his dog. On our more recent cases, I'd at least had a sense of his thinking, but I don't mind admitting that I was baffled this time around.

"Grandfather, I'm afraid I'm pondering much the same question as Miss Bradshaw. Why did we come all this way if you weren't expecting to get anything out of her?"

"Have you not stopped to wonder why such a successful and well-regarded an actress as Lillian Bradshaw would live on a small, uncomfortable boat?" He tossed these words over his shoulder as he walked ahead of me along the road.

I clicked my fingers and thought that I'd landed upon a good idea. "She must live there in case she ever needs to make a quick get-away! She was the killer all along."

He came to a stop. "Christopher, why did we come to this part of the city?"

"To interview a suspect," I duly replied.

"And which suspect was that?"

"Lillian Bradshaw," I said without thinking, before remembering the two envelopes in Grimage's pockets and trying again. "No, it was Gabriel Nelson who lived in Maida Vale. Wait! So they both live here, but why would…?"

My words trailed off, and he pointed up at a grand white villa to his left.

"Number thirty Maida Avenue," I said, recalling the address I'd read. "Why would two people who absolutely hate one another live on the same street?"

"Technically, they don't." I may be dim, but Grandfather is a pedant. "He lives on the street. She lives on the canal just in front of it. I had hoped you would make the connection this morning as soon as you saw the two letters."

"But I've never lived in London, Mr Clever," I replied somewhat sarcastically.

"I am a Marquess, Christopher, as you well know." He laughed even before he'd made his joke. "The least you can do is call me Lord Clever."

"Very well, Most Honourable Marquess of Know-it-all. Perhaps you can explain why two people who absolutely hate one another live so close together?" It only took me a few seconds to realise what this seemingly incongruous fact implied, and I answered my own question. "Because they evidently don't hate one another after all."

I was just berating myself for not using my brain when we heard another *pssst*.

"Lord Edgington!" a bush nearby whispered. "It's me, Detective Inspector Lovebrook."

"Oh, Lovebrook," Grandfather said in an amiable voice as the officer stood up from his leafy hiding place. "How wonderful to see you. I heard that you'd made the move to London. I trust that you've settled in well?"

We'd met the inspector on a previous case in the countryside, and Grandfather had taken him under his wing somewhat. He was a cheery, friendly sort of cove, and I was fond of him.

"Perfectly. Thank you, sir." He looked a little awkward then, and I could see that he needed to change the subject. "I was assigned the task of following Gabriel Nelson, but all he did was walk home. I haven't seen him since."

"That's to be expected," Grandfather responded, and I wondered why he'd sent officers after our suspects if he didn't believe it would help. "In which case, you can return to your station now, and I thank you for your assistance."

"Thank you, sir. And hello and goodbye, Christopher." With his usual open-faced charm, Lovebrook picked the leaves from his hair, saluted to my grandfather and hurried off towards the station.

We watched him go before returning to the grand white villa and ringing the bell beside the gate.

I was still contemplating the fact that the two actors lived so close together. While my grandfather's mind was as sharp as a knife thrower's toolkit, mine was not. Still, it was clear even to me that their unlikely proximity in a city of over seven million people was a sign that the animosity between them did not ring true. After all, Lillian Bradshaw could have moored her houseboat practically anywhere else on the canal.

As I was not so deep in thought, the door to the house opened and a strapping young butler with a barrel chest strode down the path. "Good afternoon, gentlemen. Is Mr Nelson expecting you?"

"I did warn him I would be coming." Grandfather wore his shrewdest grin. I doubt it was the servant he wished to unnerve in this manner, but perhaps he thought the man would describe the expression to his master. "My name is Lord Edgington."

"Yes, M'lord. Of course, M'lord." The butler fumbled with the key as he desperately tried to unlock the gate. My grandfather's fame evidently preceded him. "If you could wait in the sitting room, I'm sure that Mr Nelson will join you directly."

Grandfather marched straight past him towards the house, only pausing before the glossy red front door to say, "I have a better idea. I'll tell your master that we've arrived while you run along to his girlfriend's boat and inform Miss Bradshaw that her presence is required."

The poor domestic didn't know what to do. He froze on the cobble path and looked from the house to the canal beyond the gate. "I don't believe that ... I think I should ..."

"Leave the thinking to me. There's a good man." Confident that his wishes would be fulfilled, Lord Edgington marched into the house calling, "Mr Nelson? Oh, Mr Nelson? You have visitors."

Number thirty, Maida Avenue was far closer to how I had imagined the house of a famous actor. Every wall was pure white, to match the exterior of the immense detached villa. The furniture was almost exclusively designed by Charles Rennie Mackintosh and his ilk, and there was a single colourful painting in each room. Most of the art on display was of such a modern strain that it was impossible to tell what the artist had attempted to capture, but I had a feeling that several of them were supposed to be Nelson himself.

Another thought now occurred to me. "That's how you knew that Lillian and Oliver weren't sweethearts."

Grandfather had gone to peer out of the window, presumably awaiting the woman to whom we had so recently spoken. "I beg your pardon."

"The conversation I overheard between Oliver and Lillian before we discovered Brian's body: you knew they weren't romantically involved. You'd already worked out that Lillian and Gabriel were together. But if that's true, what were they discussing?"

He didn't look back at me but replied in an absent-minded murmur. "They were rehearsing the lines of the play, of course. Oliver's character Edward and Lillian's character Marjorie are engaged in an illicit affair."

"Oh, of course." I really was angry at myself for being so slow. "But they sounded so convincing that I had to think they were—"

"The killers?" he glanced back at me, before returning to his watch. "How many times do I have to tell you, Christopher? We know who the killer is. The feeling in my bones would not lie. Gabriel Nelson is our man, and I hope to gain the evidence to prove it before we leave this house today."

He must have caught sight of someone on the path outside as he stepped back from the window to sit in one of the high wooden chairs with the shape of an eye carved into the back. He was flicking through a pamphlet on interior design, which he'd found on the matching coffee table, when Gabriel entered the room.

"What are you doing in my house?" the man who was supposed to play a famous detective said to the famous detective. "Didn't I answer all your questions at the theatre this morning?"

"All but one," Grandfather replied, and he timed his answer to arrive at the very same moment that Lillian stepped into the room.

Nelson didn't know where to look, but his co-star no longer showed the discomfort she'd exhibited a few minutes earlier.

"What are you doing here?" he bellowed in that same irritable voice in which he'd always spoken to her. "Get out of my house, Bradshaw. You and I—" Before he could continue this pretence, the actress interrupted him.

"You and I have been companions and lovers for almost forty years. We might have managed to pull the wool over the eyes of a few prying journalists, but we didn't stand a chance against Lord Edgington."

I could see the fight go out of the actor, and he crashed down onto an uncomfortable wooden bench opposite the man who had defeated him. "I don't suppose there's much sense in denying it then."

"I don't suppose so." Lillian went to stand beside her secret inamorato. "But perhaps we could have a little privacy."

202

The butler had been hovering in the doorway and bowed at this request before disappearing out to the hall through which we'd entered.

"Get it over, would you?" Nelson said, but Grandfather was not in the mood to comply with a suspect's request and merely watched the pair of them with his fingers drumming on one knee.

It took me a few moments longer to realise that he wanted me to speak on his behalf. He evidently believed that the sly couple would be so terrified by the silent treatment he'd already given them once that day that they would fall to their knees and confess.

"We're here because you lied." I thought it would be a good idea to start off with this challenge. "And if you hid the truth once, what else are you hiding the truth... about." It was not the best beginning.

The pompous thespian looked up at his better half and the whole story poured out of him. "We didn't wish to deceive anyone. We were looking out for a friend. That's the only reason we kept our love a secret."

Lillian already had a qualification to add. "...at first."

Gabriel winced. "Right. At first, we were just looking out for the interests of a friend."

"For Oliver Hartley, you mean?" I could work out this much myself. "He told us that he'd always been fond of Betty Belgrave when she was in The Unicycling Sisters."

They looked at one another and I could tell that they were alarmed that we'd discovered so much.

It was Lillian who replied. "That's right. Oliver is a sweet man, and we didn't want to hurt him." She hesitated, and I wondered which version of her personality we would see next. "I knew that he was in love with me when we were young. He'd been through enough when his friend Malcolm died. We weren't going to hurt him more by telling him about us."

"But that was only at first?" I repeated back to her, and she went to sit down on the bench beside Gabriel.

"That's right. We kept things quiet and, whenever we were seen together in public, we'd pretend that we hated one another. What we hadn't realised was how interested people would be in the row between us." She seemed to blush then, and I remembered her contradictory attitude when we'd interviewed her in the roof garden the day before.

"If you compare our careers with many of those with whom we first worked, we've been lucky to do so well, and you have to wonder what the reason was."

"Then you think your feud endeared you to people?" I found the idea a little repulsive.

"Audiences love a villain," Gabriel contributed. "I'm sure our followers were happy to take sides and back one or the other of us. That's just how people are. It's the same with football teams and boxing matches. We all enjoy a dose of clan spirit."

I was struggling to comprehend the lengths to which they'd gone to present a false front to the world. "Let me make sure that I understand what happened. You're saying that you lied to everyone to advance your career. Did you never get bored or tired or lonely?"

Lillian put her hand out to the man she loved. "We did what we had to do. It wasn't perfect, but then nothing is. I would like to have lived every hour here under the same roof as Gabriel."

Nelson leaned forward to echo this sentiment. "And I would just as happily have sailed off around the world with the woman I love. But the thought of leaving behind *the theatre* was too much to bear." He had a far-off, poetic look in his eyes as he discussed his beloved profession, and I remembered the conversation we'd had at the Café Royal. This wasn't all that sprang to mind, either.

"I understand now, Lillian," I said, hoping this was true. "I understand what you were intending when you took us up to the roof garden. We thought you were trying to conceal your involvement in the crime. You said that there were no rivalries between actors in your company, and that there was nothing to explain Peter's death, but it was almost immediately apparent that wasn't true."

Grandfather stood back by the wall as I continued my probing. "You were clearly lying, but it is only now that I can say why. You were frightened that my grandfather would see what was really happening and uncover the truth. But it was not poor, timid Oliver Hartley for whom you were concerned; it was your own continuing good fortune."

I thought they would at least deny my claims, but they just sat there.

"You didn't want your admirers to turn against you. If the truth was discovered, your careers would have been ruined, and so Gabriel played down the possibility that Peter had been murdered. You said that it was an unfortunate accident because you did not wish to fall under the gaze of a great detective and his occasionally competent grandson."

"This is nonsense." Gabriel had been silent until now. "We've done nothing wrong. We may have tried to distract your attention, but we were not involved in the crimes, and so we were hardly lying."

"We're only just beginning." I gave him a few moments to reflect upon this, as I began to trace a path through the evidence that might conceivably incriminate him. "I'm curious how you came to have your parts in the play."

Gabriel had fallen quite still, but his paramour kept looking at him with quick, nervous glances.

"You can ask us whatever you like," he said, far more nervously than his words would imply. "I have nothing to hide…" I was about to correct him when he did it himself. "Or rather, you have already discovered all of my secrets."

"I'm not so sure." I paused to get my thoughts in order. "It strikes me as interesting that three actors who haven't worked together since the beginning of their careers should end up in the same play. We know that Oliver Hartley was the first to accept his part, and what a part it is. As he expressed to us earlier today, it is a complex and dramatic role. I wonder, Gabriel, did you pursue the part on this play to show your old friend Oliver that you were a superior craftsman to him?"

"Of course not, I—"

I was feeling more confident now. "Yes, that must be it. You'd enjoyed great success in dramatic roles, and you didn't want silly old Ollie doing the same, so you took the only part that could outshine his."

"I love Oliver," he blustered. "I would never do anything to—"

I wouldn't let him finish his denial. "Then why did you display such anger towards him during the rehearsal yesterday? You lost your temper at your oldest friend."

He was so vexed by my approach that I was surprised he didn't jump from his chair and throttle me.

"You were angry with Oliver as soon as you discovered how Lillian got her part in 'A Killer in the Wings'."

He huffed and puffed, but I would not fall down.

"You said it yourself; he invited your sworn enemy to audition for the role of his mistress. Oliver saw the gravitas that having an actress of Lillian's calibre would add to what might otherwise be dismissed as a ten-a-penny mystery play. All you could see was the slight it caused. Never mind the fact that Lillian isn't even your enemy. It bothered you so much that you lost your temper on stage with the cast and stage crew in attendance. The emotions of your character melded with your true feelings, and you couldn't contain yourself."

Lillian put her hand on her beloved's arm. "It's my fault for not telling you how I obtained my part in the play. I didn't want you to be angry with Oliver for recommending me."

Gabriel's response, when it came, was surprisingly muted. "I'm not proud of myself. I should have apologised to him immediately, but I'm only human and felt a little betrayed by what he'd done." He stretched his fingers out in his lap as though to steady himself. "If you're saying that any of this implicates me in the murders, however, I'm afraid I'll have to disappoint you."

He had me there. All I'd proven was that he was highly strung and oversensitive; none of that could be used as evidence of his guilt. I turned to my grandfather for help – or preferably for him to take control of the conversation, which was something he hadn't done for some time. Sadly, all he would do was nod encouragingly.

I tried once more to make sense of Grandfather's conviction that the man before us was a heartless assassin. If it was true, and Nelson had killed the two dead players, did that mean Lillian Bradshaw was also involved? O, to have possessed a brain like Lord Edgington's at that moment. I hadn't even been able to work out what it was that Brian Grimage had discovered that could be used to blackmail the pair of them.

Botheration! The blackmail!

I stood beside my grandfather and launched one final accusation. "Nothing we have discussed proves that you were involved in the two killings, but the letters in Brian Grimage's pocket just might. He was demanding money from the pair of you."

"We never got the letters, you foolish boy." Spittle flew from Nelson's mouth as he spoke.

"That doesn't mean you didn't know what they would say. Perhaps

Grimage confronted you and demanded money. That would explain why he doesn't mention your secret in writing."

"What poppycock." He closed his eyes and shook his head as though he were dealing with an imbecile.

The thing is, though, I'm not an imbecile. I'm not even an idiot. I open my mouth without thinking sometimes and, next to my grandfather, I may seem a little slow. But even in the time I'd spent in that elegant living room, I'd become more sure of myself.

"You've already admitted how keen you were to stop anyone finding out about the two of you. It's no stretch of the imagination to conclude that you took things a step further. Perhaps you set the mechanism that killed Peter—"

"Knowing that Brian Grimage would eventually stand in that very spot." This was the one morsel of help Grandfather provided, and I was only too happy to accept it.

"That's right, there are black marks on the floor near the suit of armour, so someone must have stood there later in the play. But your poorly conceived trap fell too early and killed poor Peter Canning. You arranged to meet your blackmailer at the theatre instead, then killed him before you could give him the money you'd promised." I pointed at Gabriel Nelson across the room. "Grimage wasn't a good man, but he did not deserve to die."

I rather hoped that I'd left him speechless, but he managed to summon a response. "I don't think I should say any more until I have a solicitor present."

"What a good idea," Grandfather told him. He seized me by the arm and pulled me back towards the door as Lillian looked on, quite horrified by the scene. "We'll be seeing you again very soon."

THIRD INTERVAL

A Killer in the Wings by Marius Quin
Reflections on the play from the case notes of former Superintendent Edgington, once of Scotland Yard.

Act Three

Perhaps a little imprudently, Inspector L'Estrange turns his focus to uncovering the identity of the man who is blackmailing Edward Buxton. I do not like the glib assumption in such works of fiction that, just because there is some other form of wrongdoing found to be occurring in the vicinity of a murder, the perpetrator of the two misdeeds must be the same person. Regardless of this, the inspector has no qualms about connecting the two crimes and even says that "Whoever is blackmailing Buxton must surely have killed poor Emilia." I scoffed rather loudly at that moment, and my neighbour in the theatre told me to hush.

Personally, I would argue that this makes no sense whatsoever, but then I am not a dramaturgist. I am merely a detective with a lifetime of experience solving crimes in one of the most complex and dangerous cities on earth. Had I adopted such a belief when patrolling the nefarious rookeries of London, like Frying Pan Alley and Sardinia Place, I would have had to arrest half the criminal population for every offence that occurred.

So, instead of focusing on the violent crime that had caused great panic in the peaceful southern holiday resort, L'Estrange interviews our suspects yet again to discover whether one of them is a blackmailer. My suspicions were then aroused by Edward Buxton's lover, Marjorie Whitstable. I couldn't help wondering whether she was more intelligent than she had first appeared. Perhaps her casual acceptance of the murder of Edward's first wife was not the naïve act of a mesmerised woman, but the clever ploy of a blackmailer. For one thing, we know that Edward told her of his crime, so perhaps she was using the information in order to extort money from him. Of course, this wouldn't explain why the man's second wife was murdered, or the significance of the play within the play, the protagonist of which bore a surprising similarity to Edward Buxton.

I must admit that I was mistaken on this count. The other characters spoke of Marjorie as if she was so saintly that I found myself suspecting her when the man whom L'Estrange finally identifies as the swindler is, in fact, Clive McCormack. Buxton's best friend, and the boyfriend of his daughter, had discovered Edward's dark secret and used it against him. The question is then raised – as it should have been half an hour earlier – of whether this automatically makes him the killer. However, instead of discovering the answer immediately, we are (for want of a better word) *treated* to a lengthy digression on the character of the detective himself.

In rather flowery prose, – in a scene that felt as though it had been added to the otherwise economical drama in order to give the lead actor another chance to amaze the audience with his theatrical prowess – L'Estrange explains his motivation and the reason he feels so compelled to find Emilia Buxton's killer.

We learn that his own father was betrayed by a colleague and disappeared when the detective was little more than a boy. In a lengthy monologue that was bordering on the banal, he describes his suffering and sense of abandonment. I don't remember a great deal of what was said, but the line "and that was when I knew that I wanted to do something for the downtrodden and unloved, the forgotten and the overlooked. I wanted to restore some justice to the world," sticks in the mind for some reason.

With this sad (and overly long) scene concluded, we return to the final stage of the investigation. L'Estrange raises the possibility that Marjorie Whitstable was only pretending to be in love with Edward in order to win his confidence and punish him for killing his first wife Carolina, who – it is then revealed – was Marjorie's close friend. By this stage, of course, I had gone off the idea. It was now too obvious a solution, and I felt that introducing such vital information late in the proceedings without any hint of foreshadowing was unfair to the audience. After all, any writer can bamboozle the amateur sleuths in the stalls if they simply don't tell the whole story.

The author of 'A Killer in the Wings', one Mr Marius Quin, won points with me for abandoning this idea at the last moment and placing the blame for Emilia's death on the blackmailer, Clive McCormack.

It was a clever trick to make the killer so unlikeable and so obviously criminal that I almost dismissed the possibility of his guilt. In fact, with this revelation, the play itself went up in my estimation.

We discover that McCormack had suspected Buxton of killing Carolina and ingratiated himself with both Edward's daughter and his second wife. He found out what he wanted to know from Emilia and set about blackmailing Edward, only for Emilia to realise what he was doing. That was why she was so nervous on the night she died, and why Clive McCormack met her in the woods and strangled her with her own golden necklace.

Denying his wicked crimes, the killer is led off the stage by the young constable, P.C. Dunts, and a frisson of excitement sweeps the theatre. The relieved faces of the other characters, as Marjorie embraces Edward and comforts his poor, beleaguered daughter, Miriam, made me smile. Well, that was until I realised that we'd reached the finale of the play and the scoundrel at its centre had not been punished for the crime that started the story right back in the opening scene.

There is an epilogue of sorts, in which we see the remaining actors who are still alive and unshackled preparing to perform the play within the play. The recreation of a theatre within the theatre is an effective technique for drawing the audience's attention to the artifice of all that we have observed. The real ushers bring a group of audience members up onto the stage to sit in a short row of seats on either side, whilst the character of Edward Buxton acts out an extract of this internal play.

In fact, he stands there with his mistress as they run through a scene that is remarkably similar to the opening of the play I'd spent two hours watching. They argue. Edward wrestles a knife from Marjorie's hand, and it seems as though both characters will survive the confrontation when a shot rings out from the side of the stage, and a red flower blossoms on the man's chest.

For a moment we wonder whether this is part of the story within the story, but that doesn't make sense as Edward would have been the main character in the play and couldn't possibly have died in the opening scene. This fact is confirmed when he falls to his knees and calls out his lover's name. Not the name of the character she's playing in the play within the play – yes, you have my apologies. It is all rather complicated – but, "Marjorie", the name of the character in the play we're watching.

The house fell to black then, and I can only imagine that, for some in the audience, this would have been a strange conclusion. However, I was up on my feet and clapping almost instantly at the impressive volte-face that Quin had executed.

You see, those last seconds before the curtains fall change everything. We know that Clive McCormack can't have shot Edward, as he is in prison for the murder of Emilia. We know that Marjorie isn't to blame, as she's standing on the other side of him. Assuming the waiter from the hotel hasn't followed all the characters back to London, this only leaves one person. Miriam Buxton has murdered her own father. She is the killer in the wings that the very title of the play told us we would encounter.

And as this concept sinks into the audience's whirring brains, another possibility announces itself. McCormack might be a blackmailer, but he is no killer after all. His supposed girlfriend, Miriam, has manipulated the whole thing. She killed her stepmother – who she blamed for destroying her family – before dangling the chance of a happy ending before her murderous father and, with the squeeze of a trigger, ripping it away on the opening night of his new production.

It was Miriam Buxton who sent the anonymous play to tempt the old friends to work together once more. She had assembled all the players in that hotel in order to enact her merciless though, let's be honest, understandable plan to avenge her real mother's murder.

And what I liked most about this, as the proverbial kitty is pulled from the bag, is the range of interpretations to which it lends itself. A lesser writer would have made the killer walk onto the stage to confirm her identity as the lights fade, but I appreciated Quin's use of ambiguity. It is not stated directly that Miriam is responsible for the killings, and my fellow audience members and I greatly enjoyed the feeling that we had been given the freedom to think for ourselves.

When the actors took their bow, I remained on my feet and clapped with all the power I could summon.

CHAPTER THIRTY

"Grandfather?" I asked when we were far from Gabriel Nelson's house on our way back towards the Underground station. "Did I get him? Is the evidence I produced enough to build a case?"

He sucked his cheeks in to consider the possibility. "I wouldn't go that far, my boy, but you did an excellent job. You hardly needed my input at all."

"And was what you said in there true? Was Brian Grimage really the target of the axe that killed poor Peter?"

He looked a little furtive just then. "Well... I can't say that for certain, as I haven't seen the whole play. As you noticed, the markings on the floor suggest that someone was meant to stand there, and it certainly made your argument more convincing."

"You little upstart!" I had to smile as he'd tricked us all. "But you are still convinced that Gabriel Nelson is the killer?"

He nodded ever so confidently. "It's the only thing that makes sense."

"And what about Lillian?" I asked. "Does the fact that they share a life together prove that they were both involved?"

He frowned pensively and so I continued.

"They may have originally hidden their courtship to spare Oliver's feelings, but they kept up the charade to grow their reputation as actors. This proves that they were willing to lie to protect their careers."

We walked a little more, and I thought a little more, but Grandfather said nothing.

"Yes, that must be it. The two of them were in on it together. If only we had a better explanation for why Peter Canning was killed... and we could say whether Nelson murdered his old partner Malcolm Delaney... and we had any idea what part Lillian played. If only we could learn these key facts – and a few more besides – I'm sure that we would be able to close the case."

I rambled on in such a manner all the way back to the Tube station, then southeast on the Bakerloo line to Trafalgar Square and along the Strand until we found ourselves at the Savoy.

It wasn't until we reached our suite that Grandfather spoke again.

"That's the spirit, Christopher. And, to help you in your task, I have devised a plan."

Delilah ran from her bedroom – yes, there was a spare one just for her – and Todd appeared from the far lounge to see us.

We all waited to hear what the old master would say.

"I'm leaving you here."

"I beg your pardon?"

"There'll be no more fancy restaurants for you until you can explain why Peter Canning and Brian Grimage were murdered."

My face (and stomach) fell. "That's not fair."

He marched off towards his bedroom, throwing a defence behind him as he went. "You're going to stay here in the suite whilst I meet Miss Alanson for a special dinner that the chef of the Savoy has designed just for me. Cook is down there giving him some tips as we speak."

I focused on the most important issue as he selected a black suit to wear from his wardrobe. "Have you not considered that I am incapable of solving a case on my own?"

His only response was a disbelieving laugh.

I suppressed a groan. "You've stood back from the action all day long to allow your underlings to do the work, and what have we achieved? Perhaps we need your brilliant brain to reach the truth."

He pulled a loose bowtie from a shelf so that it dangled from his hand like a fishing line. "You may think that, but there are two key factors you have not considered. For one thing, I have taught you well and, though you may not be able to tie a fishing fly without bleeding everywhere, I trust you to solve the mystery of Daly's Theatre."

"And the other reason?"

"Factor number two is the case itself. We are not dealing with a criminal mastermind here. The murders were haphazard, and the culprit could have been identified at the moment the crimes took place. In some of our investigations, we were almost outwitted, but this time too much was left to chance and the killer was always going to be caught."

"The killer who is definitely Gabriel Nelson?" I checked for the final time as he selected a shirt.

"Yes, Christopher. It's definitely him. Now that's all I'm going to tell you. I believe I've helped you enough."

I wanted to shout and moan, then lie on the floor and whinge for a good long while, but I knew it would do me no good. Either way, here are a few of the things I would have told him.

But you haven't helped me at all!

I'm beginning to think you have spent the whole day trying to confuse me just to make sure that you could dine with Miss Alanson alone.

Being told that I'm not allowed fancy food instantly makes me dream of caviar, which I don't even like!

Now, I don't know whether scientists have studied the possibility that dogs are so attuned to their masters that they can read our very thoughts, but dear, soft Delilah gave me the most sympathetic look just then. I could tell that she was saying, *Christopher, I feel your deep and resounding pain. I can only imagine what you must be enduring, especially in a luxurious hotel with so much fine food on offer. And, while we're on the topic, could you perhaps see your way to asking Todd to bring me my dinner? I feel rather peckish, and your grandfather didn't say anything about my diet.*

"Dear boy?" Grandfather murmured to pull me from my reverie.

"What's the matter?"

"You are. I need to change my clothes, and you're standing there staring at my dog."

I looked at him in the hope he might have changed his mind, but he just pointed to the door, and I mooned off feeling sorry for myself.

CHAPTER THIRTY-ONE

"Don't look so desolate," Grandfather finally relented as he prepared to leave. "You won't be having a lavish dinner tonight, but cook will be up before too long with sustenance. And if you untangle this particular mystery, I promise I will take you out to any restaurant in London. The choice is yours."

This brightened me up a little, though I still wasn't sure how I would solve the case.

"Chrissy, my dear boy," he said as Todd opened the door for him to depart, "I have no doubt that you will rise to the challenge."

Dressed to at least the eights – he didn't wear his diamond tie-pin, and his amethyst-topped silver cane had been noticeably absent all day – the old dandy left the apartment to dine with the most beautiful woman we'd met in months, while I stayed behind to do my homework.

Well, that's how it felt, at least. He'd even left a pile of books and papers for me to consider. There was a copy of the play script, a programme from the theatre and his surprisingly up-to-date notebook. I skimmed through them all and, far from finding the answers I needed, I just felt more confused (and hungry).

The play itself was a good read at least, and I certainly couldn't have predicted the dramatic ending, but unless Grandfather was saying that Tallulah Alanson – who played the real killer in the play – was to blame, I didn't see how it helped me. This made me believe for a moment that he had met her for dinner to make sure that she didn't kill again, but aside from the role she had in an entirely fictitious piece of theatre, there was sparse evidence to incriminate her.

What I found most puzzling was his conviction that Gabriel Nelson – the brilliant and beloved Gabriel Nelson – was to blame for two senseless murders. I was open to the idea, of course, but beyond the arguments I'd presented at his house that afternoon, I couldn't see any reason to single him out over all the other suspects.

I lay on my back on my room-sized bed with the books all around me and Delilah lying on my feet. If the truth be told, I thought that Dancing Denny or sweet, simple Oliver were just as likely to be the killers as anyone else. I played with the idea that Brian was behind the whole thing – perhaps he'd killed Peter and paid the price – but that didn't get me very far as Grandfather had sworn that we already knew the name of the killer and it was Gabriel Hercules Nelson. Fine, I didn't actually know that his middle name was Hercules, but my head was beginning to swim by this point, presumably from a severe lack of nutrition.

I had a long conversation about the case with Delilah and, for all the sympathetic looks she could offer, she did not land upon a realistic explanation for how the would-be star of 'A Killer in the Wings' could be responsible for the crimes. It was probably a good thing that, at around seven in the evening, there was a knock on the door to our suite. Todd soon opened it, and I was joined by a friend.

"Save me, Chrissy! They're after me again!" Marmaduke yelled as he ran inside, pursued by a bear… I mean, two large doormen from downstairs.

The first was as big as a house, and now as sweaty as a steam bath, and the second was somehow larger.

"We're very sorry to disturb you, Mr Prentiss," the well-mannered gorilla mumbled, before bending over to catch his breath.

"This young man says that he's here to see you, but he was behaving very strangely," the second continued when his colleague couldn't.

To be fair to them, Marmaduke was still behaving strangely. He had seized a pampas grass from a vase beside the door and was waving it in their direction like a sword. I stepped between them before he could use it.

"Don't listen to a word they say, Chrissy. They're thugs, and they've got it in for me."

One of them growled in response, and I felt that both sides had some valid points to make.

"I appreciate your diligence," I told them, "but you have no need to concern yourselves with my excessively spirited friend. He may seem odd, but it is merely his innate fear of authority that causes him to act in such a manner."

They shot doubtful looks at one another, then shrugged and, still panting, left the suite.

"Really, Marmaduke," I complained as he dumped himself down on the sofa and put his feet on the arm without taking off his shoes. "Why must you insist on causing such chaos wherever you go? They would have let you walk straight in each time if you hadn't acted like a loon."

He ignored me and looked indignant. "Never mind that. Where's my dinner?"

"I beg your pardon?"

"There was a note sent to my flat saying that if I helped you solve the case, I'd be rewarded with a fancy dinner. So where is it?"

I had to laugh at my grandfather's joke. He really was a wit. "I'm afraid that good old Lord Edgington has got you with that one. While it's true that there will be a reward for your assistance, it won't be coming tonight. Cook will bring us something to eat later, but there will be no grand prize until we can explain why the killer murdered the two victims."

"That snake!" He was up on his feet again, stalking the lounge like a furious gazelle. Wait... do gazelles stalk? "To think I came all the way here on the promise of some good, honest grub and now I'll have to work for it. The very idea appals me."

I imagine that he would have complained for a while longer if someone hadn't knocked at the door just then. Ever discreet, Todd arrived to open it, and Marius Quin entered the room with a bottle of wine in his hand.

"I'm not too late, am I? I would have got here sooner, but my aunt and uncle were busy dancing around the living room and my mother insisted that I accompany them on the piano. If I've got one piece of advice for you boys, it's to think very carefully before inviting your relatives to live with you. I've met quieter monkeys at the zoo."

"Did you come here for dinner, too?" Marmaduke asked, and our writer friend looked bemused.

"No, I came here to help Chrissy with the case. I heard that you were doing the same."

Todd knew his orders well and, as he helped Marius out of his officer's coat, he explained the situation. "That's correct. Lord Edgington believes that the three of you working together should be up to the task."

"Us?" Marmaduke replied with a hint of shock in his voice. "An author and an actor are hardly the sort of people you would think of calling if you wish to keep the streets free from crime. He can describe the problem and I can dramatise it, but I wouldn't expect much more from us than that."

Rather than complain loudly as my friend usually did, Marius was a little subtler in his approach and took our factotum aside for a quiet word. "I must warn you that I've been telling Lord Edgington that I'm no detective since the first moment we met. I'm as much use as that dog over there when it comes to identifying murderers or working out motives."

"I'm sorry, Mr Quin," Todd replied. "I don't know why he chose the three of you, but I trust my employer's instincts, and I'm certain he had his reasons for doing what he did."

Marius just smiled in that co-operative manner of his. "Very well. I'm game if you lot are, and it beats dancing about the flat with my family."

"I'd do anything for a slap-up meal," Marmaduke informed us – he had already found a box of raisins from somewhere, which he was emptying into his mouth. "Let's just say that Lillian is to blame, and then we can head down to the restaurant."

I went to stand before the fireplace between two large palms. I don't know why, but a mantelpiece is a wonderful thing to hold whenever one's in need of inspiration. "I'm afraid it's not so simple. Grandfather has already picked the killer; he says that it's Gabriel Nelson. What we have to do is prove it."

"Gabriel Nelson?" Marius sped over, already energised by our task, despite his claim that he would not be any help. "Well, I never. I wouldn't have picked him in a century or longer. The man's a living legend – a true great of comedy and tragedy alike. I would have put Dancing Denny ahead of him in the probability stakes."

"It's easy." His snack consumed, Marmaduke was back on the sofa with his feet in the air. "Nelson did it because he was in love with Tallulah Alanson and didn't want any of the other gents taking her away from him."

I had to disappoint him once more. "Not even close. Nelson is walking out (and staying at home for that matter) with Lillian Bradshaw. They've been sweethearts for decades."

He threw the paper box towards the wastepaper bin and brushed off his hands. "Oh, let's get on with it then. You obviously know more than we do. You had better tell us everything you've learnt if there's to be any hope of our leaving here before dawn."

CHAPTER THIRTY-TWO

The time passed swiftly and, once I'd explained all I knew, the moment came to put forward our theories.

"So what have you got?" I asked, quietly expectant that they would amaze me with some clever perspective that I hadn't considered before.

Marius looked at Marmaduke, and Marmaduke would have returned his gaze, but he appeared to be dozing.

"Adelaide!" I yelled, knowing that, shouted loud enough, his surname would transport him back to our school days.

"I'm not asleep, sir, and if I was, I was almost certainly dreaming of schoolwork."

I gave him a thump on the arm to wake him and turned to my other helper. "Very well, Marius, have you come to any conclusions?"

"I have indeed." He started brightly enough. "I've come to the conclusion that Lord Edgington lied, and this is not an easy case by any measure. Is he certain that Nelson is the killer?"

"He is," I replied.

"Of Peter Canning and Brian Grimage? Not flies and spiders around his house?"

"My brain may not be the finest around, but my ears work just fine."

He shook his head despondently. "I don't see it. I really don't." He had an odd habit of standing completely still when he needed to consider a point and then jolting back to life a moment later. "It doesn't seem possible that Nelson would risk his reputation as an actor in the way that he has. By murdering two members of the cast and setting all those traps, he must have known that we wouldn't be able to continue. If it was a real stinker of a play, I could understand him sabotaging it, but the general feeling was that it was rather good."

"If you do say so yourself," Marmaduke put in, which confirmed my suspicion that he was only feigning sleep to get out of having to do any work.

"I agree that it would certainly take something dramatic to push Gabriel Nelson to those extremes," I told them. "But why would my grandfather insist that he was the culprit if it wasn't true?"

This drew some blank looks from my friends, but luckily Todd had stayed behind to help. "If I may offer some advice, Master Christopher. Might it not be a good idea to set aside the biggest questions of the killer's identity and the reasons the two men were killed and focus instead on the minutiae of the case?"

"The minutiae of the case?" I was certain that Lord Edgington himself had put this phrase in his servant's mouth and wondered what other instructions the man had been given. "Yes, that's just what we should do. And would you happen to know the exact sort of minutiae which we should be considering?"

He stood between two windows that gave onto the Thames. "I was thinking of the list of small questions you will have accumulated since we first arrived here."

Marmaduke opened one eye. "Isn't that the same thing?"

"No, Mr Adelaide, it's actually a little different." Todd was such a calm, efficient person that the three of us, and even my irrepressible hound, had fallen quiet to listen to his advice. "Think about all the different interviews you conducted with your suspects. Think about the inexplicable moments you witnessed at the theatre. In each of them, you came away with doubts – minor, potentially vital points that puzzled you. It's my understanding, from having spent no short length of time with Lord Edgington as he investigates such cases, that by finding the answers to all of those small questions, you might just arrive at the big ones."

Marmaduke marched across the room then to shake his hand. "Todd! You're a genius. Take the rest of the night off!" He was clearly hoping that our supervisor would accept the offer – leaving us free to order food from one of the hotel restaurants – but Todd was too smart for that.

"That is terribly kind of you, sir, but I couldn't possibly deprive you of my assistance this evening."

I could only imagine that Grandfather paid him a handsome salary. I'd rarely met such a loyal employee.

"I've read of this very idea any number of times in my research," Marius stated with great enthusiasm. "A mystery is made up of a thousand tiny uncertainties. That is why a methodical approach is so important."

He was invigorated by the possibilities now open to us and ran to the neighbouring toilet. Wait a moment, I don't mean he was so excited that he... I mean to say... Well, he returned a moment later with a bar of lavender soap and used it to write on the mirror above the fireplace.

"First things first," he began, and even Marmaduke sat up to take notice, "the photograph of Peter Canning that was found on Brian's body is a perfect example of a mystery within a mystery."

He set to work writing out the question, *Why was Brian carrying a photo of Peter?*

I thought of another before he'd finished. "The next could be, *What did the killer gain by laying so many traps in the theatre?* I don't just mean the one that killed Peter, but the light that nearly squashed Oliver and cut Denny's leg, the scenery that fell on Gabriel, and whatever it was that sent Marmaduke down the stairs on his bottom."

"Slow down," my old school chum said, laughing a little as he relived his slippery experience. "If Gabriel is the killer, why did the scenery collapse on top of him?"

I thought Marius might provide an answer, but it was down to me. "That's simple enough. If the killer had been the only one left unharmed by the accidents, it would have been rather obvious who had been causing them."

"In which case, we already have an answer to your last question!" the man with the Yardley soap suggested. "The minor accidents were designed to suggest that, when the time came to kill someone, the killer himself couldn't be to blame."

"You're right." Marmaduke clicked his fingers. "And what we've all forgotten is that there's one person who was never hurt."

"How do you mean?" I asked, as it was all getting a little complex for my liking.

"I fell down the stairs. Oliver was nearly killed by the falling light. Denny's leg was cut. Gabriel got flattened, and Tallulah was both trapped beneath the stage and nearly broke her neck on those metal balls."

"Which only leaves Lillian from the main group of actors." This seemed as though it would be hugely significant, but I couldn't quite tell how. "Wait, does that mean that she's not too smart, but she's also the killer? Or could it suggest that the real killer wished to suggest that she was to blame?"

"Or it could mean that he didn't want to put her life at risk in the same way that he had the others."

"Gabriel Nelson!" we said as one.

There was one exception, of course. Todd had been listening to every word we spoke and chimed in with a point of order. "I'm afraid that's not enough to prove he's guilty, though. It's quite possible that the hypothetical killer would have known about Gabriel and Lillian's relationship and avoided hurting her to implicate him. You'll have to keep going."

"What else should we put?" Marius asked as we reversed out of that particular cul-de-sac.

"Oliver and Gabriel's dead partner from their days in the music hall," I eventually responded. "His name was Malcolm Delaney, and his safety net was sabotaged on the night of their big opportunity at the Alhambra."

"That is an interesting point," Marmaduke murmured, and I assumed he would make another flippant comment, but he actually said something rather smart. "You found out about this Delaney fellow's accident but, when you arrived at Gabriel's house, your grandfather sat back and let you do the talking. It was almost as if he didn't want to address the great big secret you'd discovered."

I'd been walking around the coffee table in the centre of the open salon and stopped as I was making myself dizzy. "You're right. That could be the key element, and I completely forgot to discuss it with our main suspect. Grandfather is nothing if not a hard taskmaster; he refuses to do any work for me and didn't raise the issue when I failed to do so."

Marius wrote the question on the mirror, then set down the soap to engage with the discussion. "Let's imagine that Gabriel was responsible for disconnecting the safety net in the orchestra pit that day. We still have to work out how that could relate to the other crimes."

"Perhaps we've been distracted by so many of the big parts of the story that we've overlooked the mew-nish-ear." Marmaduke was so earnest as he said this that I didn't have the heart to tell him that the word minutiae is pronounced *my-new-she-eye*. "Take the blackmail,

226

for example. We assume that was the reason why Brian was killed, but what if there was something else? What if he'd offended Gabriel by flirting with Lillian? There's no evidence it happened, but we can't rule out the possibility."

I let out an exasperated sigh. "If we extended your point to its logical conclusion, we would have to question everything we know."

"I've thought of another gap in our knowledge," Marius said more cheerfully and got busy with the soap again.

We were running out of space, and he would soon need a chair to reach the top half of the mirror. I must say that he was a very neat writer. I struggled to read my own handwriting even with a pen, but his soap letters were perfectly formed.

"Why did Tallulah come to the hotel last night to speak to your grandfather?" he slowly read as he wrote the words.

"We wondered the very same thing," I replied and went to look at the growing list. "She seemed terribly flustered but didn't have anything to tell us except that she thought Peter Canning was a nice man. It was all very strange."

Before long, there wasn't an inch of mirror free. Additional questions, and their possible answers, were squeezed into corners and between longer sentences in the tiniest of writing.

Marmaduke could take it no more and finally surrendered. "It's hopeless." To give credit where it's due, he'd lasted longer than I'd expected. "We have more holes in our knowledge than actual knowledge. We have more questions than evidence – more queries than certainties. We're never going to solve this case, and I will never win the extravagant dinner I so richly deserve!"

I would have said that he was being overdramatic but, as he was an actor, the correct term is *completely normal.*

"There's no need for negativity," Marius suggested, but when he took stock of the sheer number of doubts we'd listed, he seemed to change his mind. "Oh, my…"

He and Marmaduke sat on the floor looking quite confuddled. Delilah couldn't make her mind up which of them to comfort and so she licked Marius's hand and flicked Marmaduke with her tail.

You know times are bad when I'm the one who has to be optimistic. "We can't give up," I tried in a confident voice. "There are so many things we don't know. So many questions still to answer. So many—"

"Christopher…" Marius put one hand to his head. "…you're not helping."

I would probably have accepted defeat like them, but something happened to lighten the mood. The chimes on the grandfather clock struck the hour just as our cook, Henrietta, arrived at the suite. She had her own key and pushed through the door with a trolley laden with silver cloches and condiments. "Good evening, Master Christopher." She looked as though she wished to say the same to my two friends but didn't know their names. Instead, she curtsied and offered a quiet, "Good evening, gentlemen." With a smile on her face, she hurried over to the dining table, her skirts swishing loudly as she went.

"Thank goodness you've come," I told her. "It feels as though I haven't eaten in days."

"I believe that you had a sizeable lunch, sir," Todd replied with a more accurate description of how the day had progressed.

"Oh, yes. I'd forgotten that."

"Have you solved the case yet?" Cook asked brightly as she and Todd prepared our plates, and the three of us shot forward to see what delights she had brought.

The staff were gradually assembling an English breakfast with everything we could desire on the table in front of us.

I had to laugh as I realised the old lord's trick. "He said I wouldn't have a lavish dinner until we'd solved the case, but he didn't say anything about breakfast."

"I love you, Cook," Marmaduke declared, suddenly finding the positivity he'd been lacking. "If you're not already married, then I will happily make an honest woman of you."

Henrietta had received such proposals many times in her life and knew to ignore the impish giant as we settled down to a feast.

There comes a point in any such meal at which you realise that your stomach is resisting the constraints of your trousers, your head feels a little noddy, and you never want to see a rasher of bacon for as long as you live. We reached that stage within half an hour of rowdy noshing and, as one, we turned back to the mirror feeling just as uninspired as before. I had to wonder whether Grandfather should have held our food back a little longer.

"It's hopeless," I murmured, and there was no one to tell us otherwise.

Even Todd couldn't find a ray of hope. He opened his mouth to encourage us before his cheerful expression went into hiding and he said, "I'll clear the plates while you consider the evidence."

Delilah produced a mournful note, and Marmaduke made his excuses. "Sorry, Chrissy. I think it's best if I go home. I didn't just come here for the food. I would love to have helped, but I think this is one case that is beyond me."

He rose to leave, and Marius joined him. "I'll go, too, but you can telephone Mayfair 7001 if you need me. Just don't be surprised if my uncle answers the phone and starts singing." He couldn't hide a smile at the thought. "He's something of an eccentric."

Marmaduke gave me a punch on the arm for old times' sake and left with a sorry expression on his face. Todd squeezed my shoulder and went to help Cook with the trolley, so then only Delilah and I remained.

I sat on the thick rug before the unlit fireplace with that living blanket on my lap and stared at the list of mysteries we were yet to solve. I felt certain that, if I could just think hard enough, everything would make sense. I cast my mind back to the point at which Grandfather had become certain of the killer's identity, and I wondered what had changed at that moment to make him so sure. Chief Inspector Darrington had been interviewing Gabriel Nelson, which hadn't got us very far, and then Nelson behaved as though he'd outwitted us.

I kept looking at the mirror. I practically drilled holes through the glass, but the words soon became blurry and lost all meaning. In fact, they started dancing about in my head. It was quite pretty as floods of colour washed over them and the letters pirouetted and pranced like ballerinas at the Royal Opera House. I must have noticed at some point that this was all a dream, but I was swept right along with it. When I woke up the next morning – with the rising sun reflecting into the room off the river below – all those bothersome words had found their right places again.

I looked up at the jumble of questions on the mirror and could finally see my way to answering some of them. One in particular stood out for me. In his neat, soapy script, Marius had written, *Was Brian the only one who was influenced by the play, or did the killer take inspiration from it too?*

I don't know if this is how the great detectives go about solving their cases, but it turned out that all I needed was a good night's sleep.

CHAPTER THIRTY-THREE

The only downside to my lengthy repose was that, at some point in the night, Delilah had fallen asleep on my chest. I woke with a mouthful of dog hair and had to run to the sink for a glass of water.

Todd was already dressed and ready with some orange juice. I've yet to see any evidence that the man sleeps and, if he does, he almost certainly does so standing up.

"Have you solved your grandfather's puzzle, Master Christopher?" he asked as he produced a wicker basket of fresh French pastries and sat me at the dining table.

"I think so, Todd. I am not blessed with my grandfather's sense of self-confidence, but I really believe I've cracked it."

"Good morning, Christopher!" the man himself sang as he appeared from his wing. "You seem oddly..." He searched for the right word. "...sunny."

Todd explained this unusual sight. "Your grandson has just told me of his success in solving the murders, M'lord."

Grandfather showed no surprise at this but picked up a newspaper from the table. "I should think so, too. I've asked everyone to meet us at eleven at the theatre for you to explain what happened. Which reminds me, Todd, you must call Miss Craddock at The Chronicle. Tell her to bring as many of her fellow journalists as she can to witness Christopher's first solo endeavour."

"Solo?" My throat suddenly felt very tight as he flicked through the pages of *The Times*. "Wouldn't you prefer to share the stage with me?"

"No, no. Consider this the next step of your apprenticeship. It's high time that you rise to the challenge before you."

I was beginning to panic. "Fine, but couldn't I do it somewhere a little less intimidating than a theatre? What about a nice, quiet library? Or in a tearoom over sandwiches and scones?"

He seemed to think I'd said something whimsical. "Oh, Christopher, you are funny."

"But what if I've made a mistake? What if the whole thing is a big mess and half the scribblers in London are there to witness my inability to solve what, in your own words, is one of our less-taxing cases?"

"Nonsense, my boy. I've taught you everything you know." This did not mean I had the brainpower to solve the case but, before I could say anything, he held up the immense broadsheet and pointed at an article. "The papers are already reporting the closure of the play, and Brian Grimage's murder made it onto the front page." He put his hand on my shoulder to comfort and scare me at the same time. "This is your big day, Christopher. The debut performance of your first major role."

I carefully considered the best response before settling on, "Oh, dear."

We had a long, delicious breakfast. It was my second in the last twelve hours, but I don't think that was the reason I had so little appetite. I barely finished the cheese muffins that Cook had made and, as for the sausages, I gave half of them to Delilah.

We left the hotel to wander through Theatreland, and, by the time we reached Leicester Square, twenty or so reporters had already assembled. They stood in a huddle, just as the star performers' excited admirers would have on opening night. It was my grandfather they were most interested in seeing, and I only caught the attention of a curly-haired journalist we'd met on a previous case.

"Lord Edgington." A tall, slimy-looking man stepped into our path to get his attention. "Thomas Overton from the *Daily Mail*. Is it true that the two victims were known drug fiends?"

Grandfather looked appalled and would not answer his question. "I have nothing to say on the matter. Everything you need to know will be explained by my brilliant grandson up on that stage."

"Gareth Walker, *The Times*," another came forward to say. "We've heard rumours that the killings could be the work of the infamous Fenwick brothers. What do you think of the idea that they've come back for revenge after you put them in prison all those years ago?"

"I think it's nonsense. The last I heard, Roger Fenwick ran a garage in Potters Bar and his brother sends me a Christmas card each year from his home in Devon. Now please let me through before I have to clear a path with my cane." He brandished the amethyst-topped stick, and the crowd neatly parted.

I nodded to a few of the more polite members of the pack, and we entered the building. Inside the auditorium, there was already a bustle and buzz to the place. Though the stalls were lightly populated, the cast and stage crew were sitting together at the front. I noticed Marius at the side of the stage talking to an elegantly dressed man whom I took to be the owner. He was pale-faced and looked uncomfortable as the press swarmed inside behind us.

Grandfather had allowed Delilah to come as, though he insisted the theatre was no place for an animal, he decided that he could not deprive her of seeing my big moment. Such talk did little to reduce the pressure on me, and I was relieved that he hadn't invited my family.

"Christopher!" my mother called as I shook hands with Marius and his associate. She rushed down the side aisle to see me, followed closely by my father, brother, grandmother, and several cousins.

"The only thing that surprises me," I told my grandfather when they'd all taken their seats, "is that you didn't invite the staff from Cranley—"

Before I could finish the sentence, Todd directed a gang of maids, gardeners and footmen to their seats. I didn't dare make any other such jokes; the England Cricket Team had yet to show their faces, for example, but I would not be mentioning them.

Once Chief Inspector Darrington and twelve or so of his subordinates had filled the aisles, there was no turning back. I had to conclude that my grandfather had designed this whole event to be as daunting as possible, but he seemed to relent a little and spoke to me in a hesitant tone.

"I have no doubt that you will rise to *the challenge*..." He placed added emphasis on these last two words, and I didn't know what to make of it.

"Sorry, Grandfather. That's the third time you've used that expression in the last day, but what exactly do you mean?"

"Trust the evidence, Chrissy. Ignore any distractions." From his tone, I could only assume he was worried I might make a fool of myself. "Of course, if you prefer not to go through with it, I'll fully understand."

Something in what he'd said gave me the burst of optimism I required. "Do you know what, Grandfather? It's absolutely fine. I'm going to go onto that stage and solve some murders."

"That's the spirit, my boy." Perhaps inspired by Dancing Denny, he looked as though he might break into a jig. The lights in the auditorium fell just then, and he pointed at the brightly lit stage. "It's time to begin."

He and Delilah took their seats in the middle of the theatre, and I veered between extreme confidence and self-doubt. Just lifting my legs to climb the stairs was difficult enough, and I had to wonder whether all the breakfast food I'd consumed had sunk to my feet. I didn't dare count how many pairs of eyes were on me as I walked to the centre of the stage. I was afraid of a wave of nervousness washing over me and leaving me speechless and so, instead of giving in to my fear, I launched straight into my tale.

"My name is Christopher Prentiss, but if any of you know me, it's most likely as the grandson of Lord Edgington." I could hear the scribbling of pencils at certain moments but, every time I stopped speaking, the sound would cease as though the reporters didn't want me to know what they were doing.

"Over the last few years, I've helped my grandfather to investigate a number of murders, though *help* is probably too strong a word. Until fairly recently, I was more likely to get in the way and suggest nonsensical solutions than actually offer much insight into the crimes."

There was some polite laughter at this moment, and I would be happy with any positive response I could get.

"Solving a murder is not like acting in a play. There's no script to follow and, sadly for me, you cannot skip to the end to find out the name of the killer." I realised then that I didn't know what to do with my hands. It may sound odd, but they felt like ton weights that were swinging clumsily from my wrists. I hid them behind my back in case anyone else had noticed and got on with my task. "My grandfather is normally seven to seven hundred steps ahead of me and, try as I might to convince him, he never tells me who he thinks the culprit is or even which of my theories are closest to the truth."

I peered around the audience in search of friendly faces. Mother and father both looked interested, and my grandmother had yet to boo or throw anything, which was fairly promising behaviour by her standards. In the row just in front of them, Delilah was sitting on her seat, her mouth open and tongue lolling. Though her master was just next to her, it was our dear canine's cheerful face that most reassured me.

"The point is that, when he told me who had killed Peter Canning and Brian Grimage, I couldn't believe my luck. We were only halfway through the investigation, and he had finally trusted me with the information I wanted without a single condition. Sadly, it wasn't quite that simple. You see this time, instead of hiding the name of the killer from me, he decided not to reveal the motive instead."

I'd been standing in the same spot for some time and decided to perch on the rim of the fake fountain that was still on the stage. It was quite comfortable, and I really felt we should do all our detective work sitting down.

"And so it occurred that I was given the task of figuring out a case that Lord Edgington had already solved. I would come to question every last piece of evidence and reexamine all the interviews we had conducted, but the one thing I knew for certain, the only fact that my famed companion had seen fit to impart, was that Gabriel Nelson killed his two colleagues."

CHAPTER THIRTY-FOUR

For the spectators in that auditorium, this revelation was hugely arresting. Sitting a couple of rows behind her secret lover, Lillian Bradshaw was the only person who would not betray her feelings. A look of stony concentration remained on her face as my words reached her and the others chattered in amazement. Even the Fleet Street hacks seemed stunned by the news.

"The men were murdered less than a hundred feet from this very spot. The first, Peter Canning, was a victim of circumstance, whereas Brian Grimage was dispatched in order to hide the killer's dark secrets. Canning died as he performed his part in the play, and Grimage was discovered in a room behind this stage yesterday morning. On his person when the body was found were letters blackmailing two of his fellow actors and a photograph of the first dead man."

With the details of the killings established, I returned to the assassin. "Nelson himself started his career in a comedy act known as the Beaconsfield Three. They became popular in the theatres and music halls of London and might have gone on to bigger things had one of them not suffered a terrible accident on their first night performing at the legendary Alhambra Theatre just across the square from here. This was not a problem for Mr Nelson, of course. He continued to appear with his remaining sidekick, Oliver Hartley, and went on to become one of the most beloved actors in Britain."

This tribute might have meant more to the flamboyantly dressed man in the third row if I hadn't just accused him of murder. Instead of accepting the compliment, he looked blankly up at me, perhaps trying not to think about the uniformed officers who were blocking every exit.

"As the lead detective in 'A Killer in the Wings', Mr Nelson found the perfect role to prove how capable an actor he still was. From what I've seen of the play, it is a great piece of theatre, written by a hugely promising author." I didn't want to make a big deal of it, but Marius Quin happened to be a friend of mine. "Nelson heard about the production after his comedy partner had been cast in a leading role, and the producers were over the moon to have him take on the part of Inspector L'Estrange in their serpentine play.

"When I first considered the possibility that he was to blame for the killings, it didn't make sense to me. Gabriel wouldn't have wanted to put the play at risk when he was its biggest star. But that was only true if the role burnished his reputation and, judging by the way he reacted when he discovered that his best friend had put his enemy forward for a part in the play, that wasn't the case. The problem Nelson faced was that he was appearing opposite a hugely talented actress who made his overly expressive style of acting seem old-fashioned."

If nothing I'd said up until now had bothered the man, this certainly did. It turned out that there was something worse than accusing a thespian of being a killer: telling him he couldn't act his way out of an imaginary paper bag.

"He must have known that he wasn't the best on that stage, and I believe that it cut him to the quick. The fact is that he was no match for Miss Lillian Bradshaw, but after the long, antagonistic history the pair had shared, he would not want his adoring public to know that."

The trouble with me perching on the fountain was that the people in the front row couldn't see me and had to sit up higher in their seats. Feeling a touch guilty, I stood up instead and walked towards the glare of the footlights.

"What greater motivation is there for an actor than to be the best in his field?" I paused then as I thought this bore some consideration. "Gabriel Nelson wasn't the best actor in the play. He wasn't even the most admired. Peter Canning was a quiet, reasonable sort of person, but he was appreciated by every other member of the cast to the extent that no one could fathom why he had been killed." I had come to a stop right in front of Tallulah, and so I asked her a question. "You were good friends with him, weren't you, Miss Alanson?"

She gripped her seat more tightly and replied with a sad nod.

"You admired Peter Canning, not for his talent or fame, but because he was a very nice man."

"That's right." The melancholy that was usually present in her voice was even more pronounced. "Peter was special because, in the artificial world in which we actors exist, he was real."

"And that's why you planted his photograph on Brian's body, isn't it?"

"I…" She held her breath for a moment, and I thought she

238

might not have the strength to respond. "Peter was a good man, and I wanted his death to get its due consideration. I thought that, if it was connected to the other murder, the police would have to take notice." Her voice fell quiet for a moment, but then it rose back up far stronger than before. "I came in early yesterday morning and found Brian's body hanging in the prop room. I had the photograph of Peter in my dressing room and thought, why not? He didn't deserve to be forgotten, and I hoped that Lord Edgington would see that his death hadn't simply been an accident."

"But you weren't to blame for the killing?" I thought I should check... just to be on the safe side.

"No, he was already dead. The blood still looked wet on his clothes, so I assumed he'd been killed a short while earlier. "

"Thank you, Miss Alanson." I offered her a sympathetic look. "Both by interfering in the crime scene and coming to the Savoy Hotel two nights ago to petition my grandfather, I believe you were influenced by the character you played. Though it may not seem it at first, Miriam Buxton is integral to the action in 'A Killer in the Wings'. She pulls the other players' strings just as the gods motivated the heroes of ancient Greek dramas. But you were not the only person involved in this play who was affected by the role he inhabited."

As I moved from one victim to the next, I turned from one side of the audience to the other. "Brian Grimage was not a popular man. He was a petty criminal and an out-of-luck gambler. His character in the play becomes a blackmailer and, with various nasty figures leaning on Brian to repay his debts, it must have given him an idea. As we discovered when we found his body, he wrote letters to various members of the cast demanding money in exchange for his silence."

The senior police officer was standing on the left of the auditorium, listening to every word I said, and so I looked to fill in another gap in the tale. "Chief Inspector Darrington, did your men find anything around the bench where Grimage had demanded that his victims leave money?"

He nodded resolutely. "They did. They found a note saying, 'You'll get what you deserve, and nothing more.'"

I think it's fair to say that this was where the audience got the first hint that my theory was not quite as solid as it needed to be.

I swallowed hard as I considered this unexpected fact. "I see. How interesting." I peered down at Gabriel Nelson, who looked increasingly alone in the middle of his row. "Right, yes… so it's safe to assume that Grimage had already blackmailed someone, and the two unsent letters we found in his pocket were not the cause of his death."

"That does seem to be the case," Darrington confirmed.

I finally thought of a way to explain this. "Or perhaps that was what the killer wanted us to think. You see, the letters were addressed to Gabriel Nelson and Lillian Bradshaw who, as it happens, lived mere yards away from one another. It came to our attention that, despite the public feud between them, the pair were concealing a long-standing love affair."

This drew some gasps and any amount of scribbling. Oliver's jaw dropped as he made sense of the news, but I had bigger matters to address.

"The evidence at the scene of the crime suggested that Grimage had discovered this secret liaison and was about to blackmail the clandestine couple when another of his victims killed him first. This would seem to clear our friend Gabriel once and for all, but what if the letters were placed on the corpse for that very purpose?"

"This is becoming ridiculous." He raised his voice a little louder. "All you've got is theories and hearsay." Despite this complaint, he stayed where he sat to listen. I watched him for a moment, and something wasn't quite right about his reaction. It was too calm, too casual, which only made me more certain that I was on the right track.

"Miss Alanson, I believe you constructed a theory to explain how the axe fell on the top of Peter Canning's head. What was it?"

She glanced at Nelson before speaking, as though afraid of what he might do. "I wondered whether someone he admired had directed him to that spot. One of the other actors might have suggested that the scene would be more dramatic if he said his final speech beside the suit of armour."

"And so it would fit if your highly esteemed colleague Gabriel Nelson was that actor." I moved to the very place where Canning had died. "He set the trap, told Peter to stand here and, when the sound of the orchestra reverberated around the stage, the axe fell, and the poor man was killed."

Grandfather's favoured suspect glanced at the line of officers to his right, and yet he showed no fear. Instead of confessing to the crime, he leaned forward in his chair with a sympathetic expression on his face. "Now, listen here, Christopher. It's a colourful story that you're telling, but it's not true. I'm not a killer. I liked Peter, and I didn't know anything about Brian's attempt to blackmail me until the police told me about it."

"But… but it's the only thing that fits with my grandfather's theory." I attempted to match his confident tone, but it was no good. The case was unravelling before me.

"I'm sorry to tell you, but I'm not the man you're after." Nelson was far too relaxed, as though he was certain that none of this would affect him. "I've never killed anyone in my life. Although I did once murder the part of Mercutio in Romeo and Juliet."

This provoked a few chuckles from certain members of the audience. Others wore sympathetic grimaces as they witnessed the idiot boy-detective floundering. My dear mother looked as though she wanted to rush up to the stage to put things right, whereas my brother Albert hid behind his hand to avoid having to see the sorry spectacle. Even the staff from Cranley Hall winced painfully, as if they were watching an inferior actor fluff his lines.

Well, they were right. I was no great actor, but they'd still believed every word I'd said up to now, and I'd been lying the whole time.

"I must make an apology, ladies and gentlemen. I spent all last night trying to prove my grandfather's theory, and I failed." My voice was sad, my hands unsteady, before a smile lit up my face like a spotlight. "I woke up this morning with one thing clear in my mind; Gabriel Nelson is not the culprit. My grandfather played a trick on me, and I fell for it."

CHAPTER THIRTY-FIVE

Even the journalists' pencils had fallen still, and I luxuriated for a few moments in the quiet of the theatre. Lord Edgington patted our dog, and the pair of them looked very pleased with themselves. I had a feeling that he was a little pleased with his grandson, too.

"Gabriel Nelson is innocent." I looked down at him, not as a menacing detective but as the apologetic and entirely human nineteen-year-old boy that I was. "I am very sorry that I put you through that experience, Mr Nelson, but I needed everyone to understand the conundrum I faced." I realised that there were a number of things I should apologise for and kept going. "I'm also sorry that I told everyone about you and Miss Bradshaw, but I can only assume that my grandfather let you into a few of his secrets."

He laughed a little to dismiss my fears. "Don't worry, boy. Lillian and I had been hiding for far too long. And, as you guessed, your grandfather warned us what might happen here this morning." This rather explained why he had barely reacted to my accusations. "I know I'm not the killer, so I'm not afraid of what you might have to say about me."

His generosity made me want to explain what had really happened as swiftly as possible, and so I addressed the audience. "You see, this is my first time trying to tie up one of our cases on my own. My mentor doesn't like things to be too easy, so he complicated matters. Right from the beginning, he acted strangely. He clung to the idea that there could only be six suspects, and that we could eliminate certain other people simply because he had a positive feeling about them. I should have seen then that he was confusing the evidence in order to test me."

Even if I knew the solution, it was still hard to put everything in order, and I took a deep breath before continuing. Oh, and those electric lights were still very hot. I had already decided that I was not built for the stage.

"Normally, it is my job to profess improbable presentiments and imagine one unfeasible theory after another. On this investigation, Grandfather took up that mantle, leaving me to do most of the detective work. He barely said a word in our interviews, perhaps afraid that he would give away too much of the solution and lighten my load. When he did speak, it was to tell me of his unsubstantiated opinions on the case. That's right. He was Christophering me!

"My demanding forebear didn't just want me to solve a mystery. He wanted me to do so in the most difficult of circumstances so that I would learn even more. Soon after we came to investigate Peter Canning's death, it was evident that Lord Edgington was keeping things from me. A light fell onto the stage, almost killing Oliver Hartley, and he bent down to retrieve a piece of evidence but never revealed what it was.

"Furthermore, in the hours following Brian Grimage's murder, Grandfather told me that Gabriel Nelson was to blame. To my knowledge, little had changed in our understanding of the crimes, but he insisted that, through a combination of observation and instinct, he had picked the killer, and I would have to work out the rest.

"I knew at the time that his claim went against much of what he had taught me, but my grandfather can be a forceful character, and I didn't contradict him. It wasn't until this morning that I was willing to accept he was wrong about Nelson. First, I thought he'd made a mistake. Then I assumed old age had suddenly caught up with him and, finally, I realised that he knew just what he was doing. Before I walked on this stage, he told me he was confident I would 'rise to *the challenge*' if I trusted the evidence at my disposal. He set me that challenge and I very much hope that I am about to complete it."

The old devil mimed a brief round of applause from his seat, his smile only growing as I descended the stairs at the side of the stage. I had no desire to be a showman, talking down to them from my pedestal, and so I walked into the audience to present the next part of the story. Chief Inspector Darrington nodded as I passed, and I had no doubt that, as Lord Edgington's former pupil, he could sympathise with everything I'd been through that weekend.

I stood at the front of the stalls and looked at the remaining suspects. The air crackled with suspense as the audience waited for me to speak again, and, although I felt confident that I'd picked the right culprit, I was still on edge. The seconds ticked by, and I realised how difficult it was to say what I had come there to say.

"Do get on with it, Christopher," my tetchy grandmother shouted when I'd been standing in silence for too long. "We don't have all day."

A crisp muttering broke out among the pack of journalists as they concluded that there would be no story to report beyond Lord Edgington's hapless grandson making a fool of himself. *Apple Falls Far from Great Detective's Tree,* the headlines would say, and I would be a national joke. I don't actually know whether that's what they were thinking but, nevertheless, it motivated me to prove them wrong.

"We started this case with six main suspects." I said in my clearest voice so that every last person in the theatre could hear. "One of them is now dead, and one of them is a dancing stagehand."

I considered pointing out how meagre a connection he had to the rest of the case, but I decided this was enough of a rebuttal. Denny, meanwhile, looked as though he'd been holding his breath for the last ten minutes and could finally breathe.

"That left us with four suspects, three of whom have known one another for the last four decades. The fourth is a relatively new actress who has only made a name for herself in the last few years. Certain evidence pointed towards Tallulah Alanson's involvement in the crime." I paused then, as I didn't think it was fair to incriminate her when she hadn't done anything wrong. "None of that is important anymore, though, as Miss Alanson is innocent."

Tallulah offered a grateful smile, and I continued along the front row past the central aisle. Marmaduke doffed an imaginary cap and whispered words of encouragement. I ignored my grandfather, as the whole thing was his fault for making everything so difficult, and I gave Delilah a quick stroke before coming to a stop on the right-hand side of the theatre.

Gabriel Nelson, Oliver Hartley and Lillian Bradshaw. I looked at the triumvirate of stars and realised that it was always going to come down to them. I'd dismissed Nelson as a suspect once but hadn't yet ruled out the possibility that Grandfather had wanted me to think he was lying when he was actually telling the truth so that I would think he was lying… or something along those lines.

"I said from the beginning that Peter Canning was unlucky, and Brian Grimage had to die, and that still holds true. One of the three people in front of me caused their deaths. The killer put personal pride and reputation before everything else and snuffed out two lives. When I discovered that, before he was famous, Gabriel Nelson argued with his former partner just moments before a terrible accident, it seemed there was only one explanation. This idea was only strengthened when my grandfather made no further reference to this important discovery. It seemed inevitable this was an essential piece of evidence that Lord Edgington was playing down in order to throw me off the trail of the killer.

"However, I can see now that Mr Nelson had no reason to endanger the production which offered so much to him. He has a happy life, has achieved all that he could hope to in his career and would only benefit from the success of the play. He was doing what he loved at Daly's Theatre, and none of the motives we discovered were enough to explain why he would have murdered two people and put everything he had here at risk."

Pencils were laid to rest now. Eyes narrowed to study my ambiguous expression, and every last person in the audience was eager to hear what I had to say.

"The missing piece of the puzzle simply had to exist, and so I considered what part Gabriel's friends had played in the crimes." I took a moment to glance from Lillian and Oliver and back again, before settling on the latter. "You were the one who told us about Malcolm Delaney's accident, weren't you, Oliver?"

He was his usual nervous self. "I didn't want to. You know I didn't, but there was no other choice. I truly believed that Brian had discovered Gabriel's part in Malcolm's accident and was blackmailing him. Gabriel and I have been friends since we were boys, and it was the only thing that made sense."

I was also my usual nervous self, but I tried not to let it show. "Perhaps. But you can understand why it might seem strange. After all, you were providing evidence of a potential crime that could neatly sew together the case and lead your supposed friend to the gallows."

He put his hand to his throat in that hesitant manner of his, but he didn't reply.

"The very fact that you are still friends with Gabriel after you've spent so long in his shadow is significant. He took a part in your play and stole the limelight, not to mention the girl who you'd been in love with all that time."

He at least thought up a good defence. "But I didn't know about Gabriel and Lillian until you mentioned their involvement just now. I was as shocked as anyone else."

"You never went to their houses and realised how close they live to one another? A fact that is even more suspicious when you consider that Lillian could have moved her boat away with great ease."

He looked at her then, and I believe he was questioning how she had kept the truth from him for so long. "I'd been to her barge once or twice, but Gabriel never entertained at home. He said he was too private for that, and I accepted what he told me." He seemed a little calmer and presented the last proof of his innocence with a gentle smile. "And besides, I was never in love with Lillian. I thought that she and the other girl in her act were both very pretty, but they weren't the only women around. Gabriel and I both did fine, didn't we, Gabe?"

He sent a soft laugh in his old friend's direction, but I don't think anyone was listening anymore. Every head was pointed in the direction of the great actress.

"Lillian Bradshaw," I began, drawing the words out just as Inspector Rupert L'Estrange would have so that everyone there knew I had reached the pivotal moment, "did you kill Peter Canning?"

There wasn't even a flicker of panic in her eyes, and I realised that she was the only suspect who hadn't said a word since I'd arrived at the theatre.

"No." Her response was as clear as if she'd spoken it on the stage. "No, I didn't."

"Then what about Brian Grimage?"

"I'm not a killer."

As she replied, I caught the faintest glimpse of a smile from another of the suspects.

"Of course you're not, but Oliver Hartley is."

CHAPTER THIRTY-SIX

This isn't one of those false endings where it turns out later that the person who seemed to be the killer is innocent and someone else is to blame. Oliver Hartley was a murderer, and my greatest achievement that week came when I wiped that disgusting grin off his face.

"You've just been through all the evidence," he said with a flutter in his throat. "You accepted that I wasn't to blame."

"No, I didn't. I discussed a few minor concerns which I knew you could explain. There were only two suspects left and, if I'd talked to Lillian first, everyone would have guessed that it was you."

He looked at me then as though I was the strange one. That's right; the double murderer thought *I* was odd! The cheek of the man!

"The key factor that we kept returning to throughout this investigation was that whoever killed Peter and Brian was clearly willing to sabotage the play. Well, you were the only person here who actively tried to do that. You were angry at Gabriel for trying to steal your thunder in a production that was supposed to win you the respect of the public. You knew his presence would eclipse yours, just as it had throughout your career. To get even, you recommended Lillian for a part, hoping that the confrontation between them would be too much and he would leave."

I walked closer so that I could see the panic in his eyes. "When that failed, you took more drastic action to get 'A Killer in the Wings' shut down. You no longer cared about the play that he'd spoilt, and so you set out to destroy it. You planned a series of accidents to make your fellow players think that the theatre was cursed. That still didn't work, though, and you conceived of something more dramatic. Sadly for you, the falling axe you'd set to terrify your superstitious colleagues killed Peter Canning, and then your troubles really began."

Hartley was stuck to his chair – just as all members of the audience should be at the finale of a mystery play – and I felt I understood why Grandfather had devoted so much of his life to detective work. The duplicitous actor had committed a crime, and we'd made certain that he would face the reckoning he deserved.

"You were the killer in the wings, just like in the play," I told him to dive my message home as the others around him looked on in disbelief.

"You set the axe to fall on a specific point on the stage where no one was supposed to be standing. It wasn't your fault that Peter strayed from his usual position. Perhaps the pressure of the rehearsal got to him, and he lost concentration at his big, dramatic moment. It was just bad luck, and I might feel sympathy for you if you hadn't killed again."

"He saw me!" Oliver rose from his seat then and I thought he might deny it, but he almost seemed relieved that he'd been found out. "Grimage saw me pull the thread that was attached to the axe as we stood in the wings. It was dark, and I had my back to the stage so that no one would think I was doing anything wrong. I never meant to hurt poor Peter. It was just supposed to scare people and get the play shut down. I thought I'd got away with it, but then I found a letter in my dressing room the following day, and I knew it must have been from Grimage. He was the only one who could have seen me. He wanted me to pay for his silence, but I had a better idea."

Hartley didn't look at me as he spoke. He walked to the front row and turned to his audience one last time. "I wanted to do it somewhere that the police would never find the body." Not for the first time, his words echoed those of the character he had played. "He was a stubborn sort and would only see me at the theatre. We arranged to meet an hour before our rehearsal, and I killed him with a prop from the play. There's a torch which several characters touch, and so I thought that would be enough to disguise any fingerprints or what have you." He paused to study the faces who sat judging him. "None of this was my doing. I'd never have become such a bitter person if my *friend* over there had shown me the slightest respect."

Nelson actually sounded a little hurt by this. "Come now, Oliver. You can't say I wasn't fair to you. I've always given you roles in my productions. I always found you work."

"Oh, you gave me work, all right: as the butt of every joke. For nigh on forty years, you've humiliated me. I thought this play would change everything. I thought I could escape the past, but you wouldn't allow it."

Another key element of the story came into focus, and I cut through his self-pity. "You told us yesterday that you identified with your character, but he becomes a killer in the very first scene. You saw yourself in him because you tampered with the net that injured

250

Malcolm Delaney. You've lived with the knowledge of your crime for years, just like Edward Buxton in the play."

His eyes glistened beneath the lights as he turned to look at me. "The only one worse than Gabriel was that thug, Malcolm. It wasn't just that he liked smashing planks of wood over the back of my head and tripping me up. He took pleasure in the pain he could cause. He deserved what he got, and I was never haunted by my actions, if that's what you were thinking."

"You're a killer, Ollie," Gabriel said, as though he couldn't bring himself to believe it.

Her face bloodless, Lillian studied her former friend before adding a comment of her own. "We did all we could to make you happy, Oliver, but you never appreciated it. We sacrificed ourselves so that you wouldn't suffer."

"Don't you dare say another word." Hartley's face was raw with anger as two officers approached him. There was nowhere left to go, but he looked at the stage in desperation. I had to wonder whether he was searching for an escape route or picturing himself up there, playing to a packed house. "You odious traitors. At least I won't have to hear your voices ever again."

He held his wrists out to be handcuffed, but he wouldn't look directly at the constable who arrested him. He never took his eyes off the stage, even as they led him away.

CHAPTER THIRTY-SEVEN

"That was quite difficult," I confessed as I sat with my grandfather and our dog in the front row of the now quiet auditorium. Most of the officers had left, and my family were having a tour of the theatre with the owner while the cast packed up their possessions.

"Then you have my apologies, Christopher. I wasn't trying to traumatise or terrify you by putting you on that stage before you were ready. And I think it took great courage to go up there alone."

I bit my lip as I considered the events of that morning. "On the way over here, I did wonder whether you wanted me to fail so that I would learn from my mistakes."

He shook his head and looked quite sincere. "No, of course not. If I'd been worried that was the case for even one moment, I would have come to your assistance and helped you to the right solution. I never really felt that you required my help… Well, perhaps for a moment or two, but only because you tricked me." He sat straighter in his chair and placed one finger on his cheek. "Seeing as our roles have reversed, I have a question for you this time."

"And if you're lucky, I'll answer it."

We both smiled as he continued in a hushed tone. "How did you go from realising that Nelson wasn't to blame to identifying the correct killer and motive for the crimes?"

I stroked Delilah's velvety coat at the back of her neck and considered my response. "As soon as I knew that I didn't have to mangle the facts to find the answers, the evidence became clear to me. Before then, I'd had to invent explanations to fill in the gaps. Nelson was rather melodramatic compared to the rest of the cast, so I wondered whether he could be considered an inferior actor. That would have provided a motive but, as he is one of the most famous men on the London stage, people must like what he does.

"When I was certain that you'd lied to me and that he wasn't the killer, I was suddenly free to join the dots in the right order. I thought back to Oliver Hartley's story about their dead partner from the Beaconsfield Three, and I realised that, as much as the account incriminated Nelson, it also distracted us from the possibility that

Hartley could be the culprit. After that, everything fell into place."

He nodded as he considered this, then raised another point. "I must admit that I had considered Tallulah Alanson a likely culprit until Brian Grimage was killed. You said that there was evidence to link her to the crime, but you didn't say what it was."

Going back over the case now that it was concluded was like reading through old files, and I would need a moment to gather my thoughts. "Well, we knew that she and Peter were close."

"Yes, she was in love with him. She confessed as much at dinner last night."

"Indeed, and if Brian had killed Peter for some reason, Tallulah might have sought revenge. She turned up late to the rehearsal after he was killed and was the only actor to come through the front door, so I wondered whether she was trying to hide the fact she had already been there that morning."

Grandfather couldn't resist filling in a few gaps himself. "That's just what happened. She was the first to find Brian and, as you revealed on the stage, she placed her photograph of Peter on the body."

"Exactly, but she wasn't involved in the killing. She just put the photo there so that we would believe the killings were both murders. Of course, she gave that away when Denny found Brian hanging in the storage room. She broke off her rehearsal and ran to see why he'd screamed because she already knew what she would find there."

The longer I spoke, the happier he became. His cheeks were positively rosy, and his moustaches wouldn't stay still.

I thought I'd keep up the good work. "If Tallulah really was the killer, it would have been sheer madness to plant Peter's photograph on Brian's body, as we could trace it back to her. And why would Brian have killed Peter in the first place? As promising as this theory had initially looked, it was half-baked, like all the others."

"Ooh, what others did you have?" He leaned forward to concentrate and, had there been a girl there selling refreshments, I'm sure he would have bought a packet of chocolates.

"Take Denny, for example. The story he told us about how he got his first job in the theatre through Gabriel Nelson could have suggested a closer connection between them than he was willing to admit. I wondered whether Nelson and Lillian were really his parents, and he had procured—"

"You're right," he interrupted. "That is a truly half-baked theory."

"Thank you, Grandfather." I laughed at the idea myself then, as it was rather farfetched. "As for Lillian, everything that I said about Gabriel could also have incriminated her. At the same time, though, everything that told me he couldn't be the killer applied to her, too. I'd like to believe that I would have picked Oliver sooner if you hadn't sent my head spinning. I was so busy trying to fashion a motive to explain Gabriel's involvement that I failed to consider the possibility that Brian had seen the first murder and was killed as a result."

"You did a fine job." He kept his eyes on me as he replied. "I am genuinely impressed."

"That's good, because I still have a question or two of my own."

He sat back and waited to hear what I would say.

"You removed something from the light that fell on Oliver, didn't you?"

"I did."

"I believe it was a piece of strong thread. I found a similar item near the suit of armour and didn't think anything of it at the time, but that was how Oliver set off his traps. You were right that a killer couldn't have relied on the vibrations of the orchestra to tip the falling axe."

"I do like to get things right from time to time," he joked, before letting me continue.

"There was a moment in the first scene we saw them practising when I assumed that Oliver was overacting. He reached his hands up to the sky, as though cursing the gods, and I thought it was excessive, especially as he was a perfectly capable actor when he tried. It was only after I knew he was the killer that I realised what he'd done. The thread must have been dangling a little above head height so that no one noticed it. He pulled it a little lower, and then, after another sharp tug, the stage light came down on top of him. He must have loosened the fixings when no one was around. It was worth it to suggest that he wasn't to blame for the run of accidents."

"That's a wonderful effort, Christopher," he said, and from his phrasing, I wondered if I'd got it all wrong. "I mean it. You've reconstructed the case just beautifully."

My next question was harder to put to him. "Was I right that you were giving me a dose of my own medicine? Was that the challenge to which you referred this morning?"

I loved my grandfather's smile. It curled the ends of his moustache and transformed his face so that, for a moment, he looked terribly mischievous.

"If you are to become one of the great detectives – as I hope you will – you must learn to overcome all distractions. I can honestly say that, when you first became my assistant, your wild speculation, refusal to accept anything but the most obvious solutions and constant assumptions without proper evidence made my job far trickier. I thought that my behaviour on this case would stand you in good stead when you one day have an assistant of your own."

The idea of investigating a crime with anyone other than him made me a little sad, but I preferred not to think about that just yet.

"Marius was right," I said instead. "As soon as we pick a killer, it's relatively easy to divine an explanation for his behaviour. I just about managed it with Gabriel and, now that I know Hartley really was a monster, I understand much more about his motives and the group as a whole."

He leaned away from me as though to get a better view. "In what respect?"

"Several of the actors were influenced by the play. Brian got the idea of blackmailing his colleagues. Tallulah became more calculating in trying to spark the investigation into Peter's death, and even Gabriel copied Inspector L'Estrange a little and developed strategies to hide his secrets from us. But it was Oliver who really transformed into his character. He found a way to justify his violence, just as Edward Buxton did in the play."

"That is very insightful, Christopher." He paused then, as though to give his words greater importance. "I hope you can see that, having overcome my test, you have every reason to regard yourself as a detective in your own right."

He was so serious then that I had to tease him. "Either that or I could become a theatre critic for a newspaper."

"You have many options still open to you."

I realised there was one part of the mystery that I still hadn't solved. "Wait just a moment, why did you take Miss Alanson to dinner at the

Savoy last night? Please tell me you're not about to marry a woman who's less than half your age." She was actually less than a third his age, but it would have felt mean to point it out.

"I'll stop you there, Christopher." He held his hand up to silence me. "I met Miss Alanson last night because I was worried about her. She seemed so desolate about the loss of Peter Canning, not to mention the closure of the play, and so I've offered to become her patron. I will help her financially whenever she needs it, and she can choose her roles more carefully on her way to becoming the exceptional actress that I know she is meant to be."

"That's incredibly kind." I was impressed by his generosity. Most other lords I'd met were real skinflints. "I hope you know that you really are a very nice man."

"You have mentioned it on occasion, but thank you, Christopher. I'm most fond of you, too."

Marmaduke arrived then to interrupt this tender moment. "Why don't you buy everyone lunch again, Lord Edgington? We had such a good time at the Café Royal that I thought you might like to take us somewhere equally grand that I haven't tried yet."

"Oh, you did, did you?" my grandfather began but, before the discussion could go any further, Marius appeared on the stage and began to issue orders.

"I would like all the actors to come up here, please."

It appeared that Marmaduke was the only one missing and, in his usual lazy fashion, he sauntered over to see what was happening.

"Jolly good, and now, if everyone else would like to take your places in the stalls, the first, last and only performance of a 'A Killer in the Wings' will be starting very soon."

"But we don't have enough actors," Denny replied.

"Yes, we do. I'll take Oliver's part. I wrote it, so I should know most of it. And then…" Marius had a script in his hand and was peering around the auditorium in search of an understudy. I was fairly certain he would choose the stentorian detective beside me. "…Chrissy! That's right, Mr Prentiss, come up here. Take this script and you can play the character that Brian—"

"No, no," Marmaduke interrupted. "Christopher would be awful as Clive McCormack. He's far too innocent. He can play P.C. Dents, and I'll take over from poor, dead, criminous Brian. I know that role off by heart anyway."

There was a quiet buzz of excitement just then as the actors realised they were about to get their chance to perform after all. Even Gabriel and Lillian looked energised by the news, though they'd been deathly quiet since their friend was arrested. My family and the staff from Cranley Hall returned to their places, and several of the reporters who were still lingering came to claim the best seats.

Surprised by what we were seeing, I looked at my grandfather, and he did his best to make sense of things.

"It was your beloved Dickens who said that 'It is a hopeless endeavour to attract people to a theatre unless they can be first brought to believe that they will never get in.' Evidently those here today will feel ever so lucky to see whatever is about to take place. The fame of Mr Quin's aborted play will spread and, whenever he finally recovers from his slump and writes another book, it will be more popular than chocolate dipped in liquid gold. Now, run along, boy, and try to enunciate up there. There really is nothing I like less than actors who mumble."

Rather than point out that he'd said the same thing about dawdling, green tea and blue cheese, I ran to the end of the row and up the steps to the stage. The author turned playwright turned director turned temporary detective's assistant handed me my script just as the curtains were going down and everyone found their seats.

I read out the parts marked for P.C. Dunts (along with the odd line belonging to the characters who spoke after me) and I believe that what I said largely made sense. Marmaduke was exceptionally believable as slimy Clive McCormack, and Marius made a good Edward, but it was Tallulah, Lillian and Gabriel who carried the rest of us. They were consummate performers and couldn't have done a better job.

We made it to the play's epilogue and, with no one else eager to do the job, I fired the shot from the side of the stage that brought the play to its grim conclusion. Thanks to the curse ascribed to 'A Killer in the Wings', I greatly doubted that it would ever be performed again, but for two hours it was the greatest play in London. I just had to hope that everyone involved would go on to find the success they deserved.

One thing that seemed certain was that, as Grandfather had predicted, the author of the play would soon have his time in the spotlight. When we said goodbye that day, and the doors of Daly's Theatre closed behind us, I had the definite feeling that we hadn't seen the last of Marius Quin.

The End (For Now...)

"LORD EDGINGTON INVESTIGATES..."

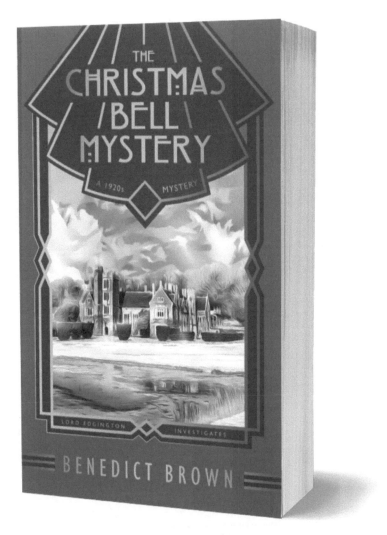

The twelfth full-length mystery will be available in **November 2023** at amazon.

Sign up on my website to the readers' club to know when it goes on sale.

ABOUT THIS BOOK

I don't think I've written any other book that was so much fun to write and such an ordeal to edit. I knew from early in the series that I wanted to set a book in the theatre. Not only is it a classic mystery setting, I spent a lot of time in such places as a child. From the age of about eight, my brother and I went to a drama group in our town and performed in competitions and plays each year. We spent far too much time hanging around in theatres, and my brother Daniel even went on to study drama at university.

I should point out that, although several of my books have jokes at actors' expense, I really have nothing against them – I think the phrase 'low-hanging fruit' may apply here. I have become good friends with a very talented actor over the last year or so and I have to say thank you (and sorry!) to my audiobook narrator George Blagden for helping with some of the details of how the backstage world of a theatre works. George's wife Laura Pitt-Pulford was the lead in a West End musical when I started writing this book, so it was handy having him on WhatsApp to fire off questions when they arose. I had a particularly interesting response from him on exactly how dressing rooms are distributed to the star actors in a production.

Growing up in south London, my parents often used to take us to the West End to see plays and musicals, and it really was the most exciting place in the world for me. In a city that changes so much every year, the beautiful old Victorian and Edwardian theatres that have survived are to be treasured, and I loved finding out about their history when writing this book.

I spent a good while choosing a lost theatre as the setting, and Daly's fits the bill perfectly. It was built in 1893 by an American called Augustin Daly who owned a similarly named sister theatre in New York. He had been the first person to bring a whole company over from the States, but when he splashed out on a theatre of his own there, he never made much money. A couple of years later, Daly's heyday began when a hugely influential British producer named George Edwardes took over running it. For thirty years, it was known and loved for musicals and operettas and had a massive hit with a show called 'The Maid of the Mountains', which ran for over a thousand performances.

By 1927, though, the theatre was struggling and would have a run of flops, including the hit writer of the day Noël Coward's disastrous "Sirocco". The play starred the popular actor and composer Ivor Novello, but the audience's reaction to its scandalous themes meant that the cast were booed off the stage on opening night, fistfights broke out in the auditorium, and Coward was confronted at the stage door and spat at by his previously adoring fans. Suffice it to say that the play soon closed, costing the theatre a fortune.

It was owned at the time by an interesting character called James White. White made his fortune as a boxing promoter before moving into racehorses, property development and the theatre. His time in charge was not a success, and he ended up running up immense debts across his businesses and killing himself that same year. He was a hugely popular figure in Britain and five-thousand people turned up at his funeral. He left his family penniless and bankrupted many investors, but even at the moment of death he had a sense of humour and wrote to the coroner in his suicide note, "Go easy with me, old man. I am dead from prussic acid. No need to cut any deeper. – Jimmy."

While a lot of my books are set in one main location, this book takes in a theatre, a whole city and, of course, the Savoy Hotel. The sumptuous establishment fits well with the theme of the book, as the Savoy not only has a theatre of its own attached to it, the original owner, Richard D'Oyly Carte, had made his fortune through his incredibly successful English opera company. Carte staged the light operettas of W. S. Gilbert and Arthur Sullivan and built two important London theatres as well as the hotel. His businesses were passed down through his family and the hotel remained with them until the 1980s, just shy of a hundred years. The Savoy is undoubtedly one of the most luxurious hotels in London and the only one with its own archivist. I was grateful to be able to meet her when I was home in the summer, and she talked to me about the hotel in the twenties, the famous band The Savoy Orpheans, and some of its incredible features (including directing me to the toilet once used by Winston

264

Churchill). You'll find out a lot of incredible facts about the hotel in the research chapter of this book.

This also might be the first time I've been in the place one of my books is set while writing it. I was home in the summer at my family home, which is twelve miles (or approximately ninety minutes in slow traffic) from the centre of the city. My daughter had been studying famous landmarks in school and had a list of places she wanted to see, and it really inspired me to walk through the streets where Chrissy and his grandfather roved and visit the theatre there before racing home to write about it. I've talked at length in previous books about what my home city means to me. This is my third set in London, and I very much doubt it will be the last.

If you loved the story and have the time, please write a review at Amazon. Most books get one review per thousand readers so I would be infinitely appreciative if you could help me out.

THE MOST INTERESTING THINGS I DISCOVERED WHEN RESEARCHING THIS BOOK...

Oh, where to start! The research for this book was a fairly large undertaking and even involved me leaving my house for once, so let's see where we end up today...

Let's begin with my favourite coincidence this time around. Readers of '**What the Vicar Saw**', the previous-but-one book in this series, will know that I love the works of John Masefield and borrowed names and settings from his children's book 'The Box of Delights'. Six months later, when writing this one, I was looking for a spot in London where a houseboat would be handily located near some nice residential buildings and thought of Little Venice in the north-west of the city. The first thing I discovered was that, though the quaint name for the area where the Grand Union and Regent's Canal meet is attributed to both Robert Browning and even Lord Byron, it was not in common use until the mid-twentieth century.

Either way, I found a nice quiet stretch of the canal near Maida Vale, picked a spot in front of some grand white villas to moor Lillian's boat and was scrolling through Google Maps to find the prettiest house on the road. When I chose the one I liked, I zoomed in on a small blue plaque above the front door at 30 Maida Avenue and what should I see there? Boom! John Masefield's name! Mind blown, I looked it up online and found a clearer image of the plaque which states, "John Masefield... Poet Laureate lived here 1907-1912". It seems he lived there with his wife and two young children.

Meanwhile, (in a completely unrelated discovery) his wife's brother, Andrew Claude de la Cherois Crommelin, not only had a brilliant name but was an astronomer and, in 1910, won various prizes for his study of Halley's Comet. Crommelin was an expert on comets and calculated the orbit of a significant one that now bears his name. He also investigated the impact of the sun's gravitational field on light deflection, and the data he collected would be used to confirm Albert Einstein's General Theory of Relativity. What an impressive chap!

Maida Vale itself is one of several areas in London (including Swiss Cottage, Royal Oak and Elephant and Castle) that were named after pubs. The Hero of Maida pub took its name from a general who became famous for his valour in a Napoleonic battle in Italy. As I would rank the British pub as being one of the finest institutions in the land (alongside the NHS and BBC), I heartily approve of this naming custom.

There was previously a long description of Maida Vale Tube Station in this novel, but I cut it out for the sake of brevity. Opened in 1915, it is a very neat little station, with oxblood tiles, art nouveau touches and two incredible mosaic Underground signs. It is perhaps most remarkable for being the first station to be staffed entirely by women who were (even more surprisingly) on equal pay with their male counterparts. Of course, once the war was over, they were all fired so that the men could have their jobs back, but it was nice while it lasted. Maida Vale was also one of the first stations with escalators, which Chrissy clearly enjoyed immensely.

Playing about on Google maps around the old site of Daly's Theatre in Leicester Square, I noticed a large circular building stuck rather uncomfortably between two cinemas. The church of Notre Dame de France also stood out to me for its name, and it turned out to be a French Catholic church in the absolute centre of tourist London that was set up to serve the immigrant community in the mid-nineteenth century. The church is also interesting as it has a mural by the surrealist artist Jean Cocteau, which depicts three key parts of Jesus's story. Most surprisingly, though, the perfectly round building which houses it was originally built at the beginning of the 1800s to hold panoramas.

Wait a minute! What are panoramas? I asked myself and then spent half an hour reading about them. It turns out that panoramas were humongously vast paintings of cities or landscapes that were so intricate that people couldn't tell the difference between them and reality. They were a hugely popular form of entertainment at the time and "Burford's Panorama" was one of London's top attractions. The building offered a three-hundred-and-sixty-degree view of the city via a platform in the middle of a two hundred and fifty metre square painting on two levels. The paintings employed clever use of perspective and the artists intended for the viewers to lose their sense of place and time when looking at them. They didn't only depict places but also battles and famous moments in history, and it is believed that over a hundred of them were displayed in the seventy years that the Leicester Square panorama was in use. Some such paintings still exist today, and I really recommend looking online to see examples.

From London to Germany now, and I had not realised before writing this book that the story of the Pied Piper of Hamelin is believed to have been inspired by real events. The first known depiction of the incident was a stained-glass window from 1300 depicting the piper with his young followers. Most frighteningly, the very earliest records from the town simply state, "It is 100 years since our children left." The details of what actually happened evidently have no contemporary sources, and the mention of rats was only added in the sixteenth century, but it does seem that a lot of children really did vanish from the town.

The first written document attesting to the story comes from the mid-fifteenth century and describes a handsome, well-dressed man with a silver pipe, playing so sweetly that one hundred and thirty children followed him from the town, never to be seen again. A similar account is found inscribed on a building known as the Ratcatcher's House, which gives the date of the disappearance as 26th of June 1284.

Historians have found a number of potential explanations for the disappearance, including emigration, a natural disaster, mass hysteria and, noting its occurrence on midsummer's eve, a clash between pagans and Christians. I had always assumed that it was just a fairytale, but another thing I really like about this story is that it occurred in the diocese of Minden where, aged eleven, I went on a theatre trip with my brother to put on a play of Dicken's first novel "The Pickwick Papers". It was only on reading about the Ratcatcher's House that I remembered that I'd actually stood in front of it on a day trip. Mind blown again! Coincidences are the best.

Before I looked into specific theatres, I was interested to find out what had been happening in the West End in general around the time of this book. British theatrical history is fascinating and was heavily influenced not just by contemporary tastes but the demands of the monarch and government of the time. Since 1737, it had been the job of the most senior officer in the Royal Household, the Lord Chamberlain, to review and issue licenses to all publicly performed plays. This meant that there was a huge amount of censorship for over two hundred years, and playwrights had to be cunning to get around it. The clash between artistic and political expression and the expectations of the state was starting to heat up in the 1920s, but for many years before, productions had shied away from controversy in order to ensure their success.

Classic works had fallen out of fashion by then. As Lillian Bradshaw attests, Shakespeare was not drawing the crowds and only had a resurgence with the emergence of actors like John Gielgud in the 1930s. Instead, in the nineteenth century, along with lighter forms of entertainment such as music hall, melodrama and burlesque, there was a trend for spectacle. Theatres tried to outdo one another to produce the most sensational visual effects possible. This gave rise to productions depicting chariot races and train crashes on stage, using sophisticated combinations of engineering and art to whisk the audience away to another place or time.

By the dawn of the new century, more serious works began to be produced, influenced by dramatists like Ibsen and Chekhov. But even George Bernard Shaw, who is often considered the eminent playwright of the era, regularly clashed with the censors and, because of his social messages and risqué themes, he had several of his plays banned. Companies tried to get around the law by forming private clubs to put on plays so that they could discuss issues such as suffrage and poverty without the police raiding the theatre. It wasn't until 1968 that this system of censorship was finally abolished.

So things were starting to change by the twenties but, for the large part, big West End theatres made their money with comedies, operettas and musicals. Daly's Theatre in Leicester Square was particularly well known for comedy musicals (or musicals, as we'd now call them). I've tried to stick to the facts as much as possible, and you can find out all about the theatre and countless other lost ones on the brilliant website ArthurLloyd.co.uk. Chrissy's description of its impressive
270

décor is hopefully accurate and the entrance to the theatre had the unusual look of a comfortable living room which you had to pass through before getting to the grand Italian style foyer built on two levels with an upper gallery. As for the theatre itself, to quote *The Daily Graphic* from 1893...

"On entering the auditorium, the first thing to impress the spectator is the bold originality of its outline and decoration. The general scheme of colour is a blending of red, gold, silver and bronze. The circle fronts and boxes have been modelled in such a way as to represent boatloads of sea nymphs and Cupids in the act of blowing bubbles, which bubbles have been ingeniously converted into electric lights of many tints."

Which sounds pretty dang fancy if you ask me. The article goes on to describe the vibrant decoration, which apparently went against the fashion of the time, and says it was "one of the boldest experiments in theatrical architecture that we have for some time seen." As I wrote the scenes there, I enjoyed imagining myself walking around the building, as if it hadn't been lost forever.

What I also found impressive throughout this period was the sheer number of theatres, even in provincial towns. Sadly, the vast majority of them have been lost, but my famously cultureless town of Croydon had several, including The Croydon Grand Theatre and Opera House. When first built, the French Renaissance style venue could house two thousand people and played host to all the great actors of the late Victorian era like Henry Irving, Sarah Bernhardt and Ellen Terry. It managed to survive the intensive bombing to the area in the Blitz but was sacrificed to make way for offices in 1959 – despite a campaign to save it and a petition signed by 100,000 people. That sort of thing breaks my heart, and I can't believe that, to this day, governments don't do more to preserve historic buildings.

Speaking of The Croydon Grand, like Daly's, it was also owned for some time by George 'The Guv'nor' Edwardes, who helps tie together several of the different elements in this chapter. Not only was he linked to these two theatres, Edwardes managed theatres for Richard D'Oyly Carte, who owned the Savoy. In fact, the producer-manager had a massive impact on this period of history and helped shift trends away from the burlesque towards a form of light musical comedy that would dominate the early twentieth century.

He was already managing theatres at twenty-years-old and would go on to run several of the most important venues in London and send the musicals he produced around the country, too. The most curious part of his massive success, though, was a group of women who became known as the Gaiety Girls. Many of his productions featured this troop of elegant and respectable young ladies, who dressed in the most up to date fashions. In an early example of product placement, famous designers would provide clothes especially for the shows, and the Gaiety Girls came to epitomise the perfect woman of the day. They were so admired, in fact, that many of the actresses went on to marry peers and wealthy men. It became so problematic for the continued running of the shows that Edwardes wrote in a 'nuptial clause' to prevent his actresses from running off to marry the dukes, earls and marquesses who hung around the theatre each night looking for a wife.

As for murder mystery plays, like Marius's 'A Killer in the Wings', they weren't identified as such for some time, but there had been certain works that could fall into that category. The famous actor who has appeared in a number of these chapters, Henry Irving, had made his name in the drama "The Bells". First performed in 1871, it focuses on the guilt the main character feels after robbing and murdering a wealthy merchant. The opening-night audience was so affected by what they saw that one woman fainted and the end was greeted with stunned silence. Irving became synonymous with the play and appeared in over thirty productions of it, with the last occurring the night before he died.

Similarly suspenseful plays included, in 1923, "The Ghost Train" by Arnold Ridley (who played the loveable Private Godfrey in the sitcom Dad's Army). But it wasn't until 1928 that Agatha Christie's "The Murder of Roger Ackroyd" was adapted as "Alibi". She didn't think much of it – and largely adapted her own novels and wrote her own plays from that point forward – though Ridley himself adapted "Peril at End House" in 1945. As it happens, the Savoy is mentioned in at least nine of Christie's books and she celebrated the tenth anniversary of her biggest play, "The Mousetrap", there at a grand party in 1962. Ngaio Marsh was also in attendance and there was a cake shaped like a mousetrap that was approximately the size of my desk. The play is still running, is about to celebrate its seventieth anniversary, and has the Guiness Word Record for the longest-running play at over 29,000 performances since 1952.

Right, that's enough of the outright theatrical for the moment. Let's take a trip to the Savoy. Whole books could be written of the hotel's claims to fame, which, in fact, they already have. It was one of the first in Britain to have electric lights throughout the building and was always at the forefront of modern technology, with lifts and speaking tubes for guests to communicate with hotel staff. The road in front of the hotel has the curious honour of being the only street in Britain where you have to drive on the right-hand side. This was supposed to accommodate horse-drawn carriages, as it meant that drivers could open the doors for their passengers without getting out of the cabs. Of course, that doesn't explain why it hasn't changed since. STOP THE PRESS. The night before I was due to publish the book, I got the scoop on the real reason that cars drive on the right in Savoy Court. The Savoy archivist informs me that this came about in the late 1920s and was a measure to separate the nightly influx of theatre traffic from hotel traffic. It had nothing to do with carriages; the internet has let me down!

From early on in its existence, the Savoy's staff would go the extra mile for their guests and, as Christopher guesses in the book, they kept files on regular visitors. Information such as age, the names of their companions, and a Who's Who-style list of their achievements were stored on index cards. These became so extensive that they eventually required a room of their own to house them. Two interesting examples of information noted are Noël Coward's very specific way of organising his toiletries – a trait he shared with my father-in-law – and Marlene Dietrich's expectation of twelve pink roses in her room each time she stayed. Apparently, her suite is still adorned with such flowers to this day.

Okay, this is getting long. Let's switch to bullet points!

- The hotel was named after the Savoy Palace, which had stood on the spot between the Strand and the River Thames six hundred years before the hotel was built.

- Monet painted several scenes of the Thames from his room on the fifth floor. When he stayed there, he would start each morning with two whole English breakfasts – which makes Christopher look quite reasonable.

- I would take this next claim with a pinch of salt, but apparently, one night during dinner at the hotel, the Duchesse de Clermont-Tonnerre became the first woman ever to smoke in public. Ummm… the hotel opened in 1889. Surely a woman somewhere in the world smoked in public before then? I've found it mentioned on some fairly reliable websites, but this is why I don't trust the internet.

- To do their bit for the war effort, the hotel started its own poultry farm to ensure they had enough eggs. Apparently, it was the first hotel to do so. I wonder if it was also the last.

- A famous icon of the hotel is the seventy-five-centimetre Art Deco sculpture, Kaspar the cat. It was introduced after a party of fourteen was one guest short and one of the diners predicted that whoever next left the table would be the first to die. The diamond tycoon who had organised the dinner did just that and was shot dead a few weeks later. As a result, the hotel would add a member of staff to any groups of thirteen and eventually, in the mid-twenties, commissioned Kaspar the cat to fulfil this role.

- Among other notorious celebrity moments that have taken place there, the time that Oscar Wilde spent in room 361 with his lover, the poet Lord Alfred Douglas, received a lot of attention at his trial for gross indecency. Stories of them entertaining dubious company, quaffing champagne and scoffing ortolans enlivened the already outrageous trial.

- And, last but not least, as we learn in the book, the actress Sarah Bernhardt stayed in the hotel with her red setter, Tosco. This is not exactly a fascinating fact, but I was glad to discover it, as it meant that I could include Delilah in Lord Edgington's visit. Perhaps more surprising was the night in the 1950s when the hotelier Billy Butlin turned up to a party with his pet leopard, Chiefy, who had starred in a film adaptation of Tarzan. Poor Chiefy was not admitted to the party and spent the evening tied to a no parking sign in front of the hotel.

Another incredible chapter in the hotel's history is the murder described by Lord Edgington when they head to the Savoy Restaurant. Marguerite Alibert was a prostitute who the future British king Edward VII met and fell in love with in France. A few years later, she married an Egyptian prince called Ali Fahmy Bey. Whilst staying at the Savoy, they went to the theatre one night and, on returning to the hotel, they had a blazing argument, and Marguerite shot her husband in the back.

The interesting part of the case comes in the trial, when the killer was represented by a slick barrister and her past as a courtesan was deemed inadmissible. The prince was depicted as a violent and sadistic foreigner who had terrorised his innocent European wife. She was cleared of the crime, but a recent book claims that the trial was a sham and Marguerite made a deal with the crown to return intimate letters that Prince Edward had sent her in exchange for her freedom – scandalous (possibly true) stuff! Oh, and which theatre did they attend on the fateful night? None other than Daly's itself! The murder at the Café Royal, meanwhile, really did happen, and the victim really was called Marius. Poor chap.

Returning to prostitution, the area around Covent Garden was well known for its brothels. In fact, they were an accepted part of some high society gentlemen's existence, and "Princes, Peers and men of high rank" (including King George II's youngest son, William) were often seen there. Some of the courtesans were immortalised in art and literature, and there was even an annual guide published to the ladies and their keepers. The brothels were perhaps less fashionable by the 1920s, but they still existed, especially in the area around Seven Dials.

Oh, and the password that Lord Edgington provides in order to have access to the delicious sandwiches on offer? Well, I don't really know why I came up with such nonsense, but Saint Vitalis of Gaza was a holy man in Palestine in the seventh century who would work all day as a labourer and, with the permission of his bosses in the church, use his wage to pay prostitutes for the night to keep them away from sin. He would spend that time praying, and many of the women abandoned their work to take up a more wholesome existence. As a result, Vitalis became the patron saint of day labourers and prostitutes. His saint's day really would have fallen on a Wednesday in 1928, too.

Let's move to an even saintlier topic. It's time for tea... pots. The façade of the shop that Chrissy is so amazed by in Cock Lane is still visible today and was another of my Google Maps Street View finds. One thing I cannot say for sure is how long John James Royle's shop was occupied, but it was opened in the early twentieth century in order to showcase the English inventor's many creations.

Born in Manchester in 1850, Royle was an industrialist, who founded a foundry (ha ha) and engineering business before opening shops to sell his patented creations. These included eggbeaters, steam traps, a timed egg boiler, smokeless stoves and irons, a pendulous gas table (whatever that is), and most brilliantly a self-pouring teapot. The concept of this masterpiece was that you could put a cup underneath the spout and push down on a handle on the top for the hot tea to gush forth. I mean, forget the iPhone and the home computer! Forget televisions and aeroplanes! The self-pouring teapot was a technological game changer, and I demand that history be rewritten so that every home in Britain is provided with one. Over the last few years, I have bought two (count them, two!) teapots for my wife, both of which were useless and poured liquid everywhere. If only I'd known about Royle's invention.

And whilst we're visiting Cock Lane – which I only chose because there was a police station near it in the twenties and that decision led to all the interesting nonsense I'm spouting (pun also intended) – what about the ghost? Everything Chrissy says about the ghost of Cock Lane is true but, in order to keep the already crammed-full narrative ticking along, I had to leave out some of the details. It really was a media sensation when it occurred in 1762, but it was even more scandalous than Chrissy knew. One of the reasons that the press went crazy for the story was that, on possessing a little girl, the spirit claimed she had been murdered by her husband. The girl's father charged people to commune with the spirit and lots of well-thought-of people believed him and took up his cause. The problem with this was that the man they were accusing of murder was still alive and took them to court.

The case split the country and was seen as a dividing line between belief and scepticism, superstition and reason. Seances were conducted, massive crowds gathered outside the house and the Duke of York and Horace Walpole came to see the possession for themselves. Of course, it was all a scam, and the little girl was hiding a wooden device under her dress, which she banged once for yes and twice for no. When separated from her scheming family, the falsehood was revealed. Five people were put on trial (thankfully not including the girl) and found guilty of conspiracy against the dead woman's husband. The little girl's father was put in the stocks as part of his punishment, but as Chrissy reveals, the people of London felt sorry for him and took up a collection. The story is mentioned in three Dickens novels and one of the witnesses at the trial was a maid called Esther "Carrots" Carlisle. Good stuff!

About ten years ago, I read a Bill Bryson book all about 1927 and had planned to include any number of fascinating elements from the history mentioned there. The year is almost up (for Chrissy and his grandfather) and though I completely ignored Charles Lindbergh's accomplishments, the one thing I found time to mention was the case of Ruth Snyder. Snyder convinced her husband to take out a life insurance policy that, somewhat hilariously, paid out in the case of violent death. She tried and failed to kill him seven times, but the eighth worked a charm.

She and her accomplice attempted to make the scene look like a robbery gone wrong, but the police saw through the scheme. What's most interesting about the case is the way that the press and public became obsessed with it. It was blown out of all proportion and the trial and rumours surrounding the crime dominated the news for months. The plotters, who were also lovers, turned against one another and both were put to death, and a journalist sneaked a camera into the chamber attached to his leg in order to capture a photograph of the black widow getting her final sentence. The Gutteridge case, which also gets a mention in this book, was a similar focus of attention for newspapers across the Atlantic in Britain. A policeman was violently murdered and though the killers were soon caught, it does seem as though the police fabricated additional evidence to ensure they got their comeuppance. Grim!

And after all that murder, I feel I should cleanse your palette with something more appetising. The Shooter's Sandwich originated in

Edwardian Britain and was recently (undemocratically) chosen by The Guardian newspaper as the greatest sandwich in the world, which led to lots of food bloggers trying to recreate it. It was invented to give hunters a substantial lunch to take with them, hence the massive proportions of bread, steak, mushrooms and onions. The sandwich is pressed under heavy weights overnight to make the juices of the meat soak into the bread. It does sound tasty, but I don't think I could eat a whole one!

And now all that remains is for the fat lady to sing and then I can take a break. Considering that this book is set in Theatreland, it's surprising that I only included a paltry two songs this time around. The first, you will probably know as I certainly did. My mother was singing it one day when I was home in London, and so I checked how old it was, made sure it was in the public domain, and gave it to Chrissy to belt out. 'The Honeysuckle and the Bee' is from 1901 and, beside the fact it was written by Albert H. Fitz and William H. Penn, I found out very little else about it.

A newer, and so more traceable song is 'Somebody Stole my Gal' from 1918. The best version, of course, is by The Muppets. They recorded the song twice on the original TV show, once with the Prairie Dog Glee Club – before they stole everything in the rehearsal room – and then again by the brilliantly named Lubbock Lou and His Jughuggers. What's odd about the song is that, going right back to the twenties, I can find no version of it that sings anything but the chorus, though there are definitely verses that go with it. It was written by Leo Wood and has become something of a jazz standard, with the 1924 Ted Weems version selling a million copies. However, the reason I chose it was simply because the Savoy Hotel's house band, the Savoy Orpheans, used it in their repertoire.

That's it. No more. Just under five thousand words is a ridiculous length for one of these things, and I beg your forgiveness. In my defence, however, I didn't go into fly fishing, the factories that lined the South Bank of the Thames that would have ruined the view from the Savoy until the 1950s, the traditional childhood game of conkers, the story of the Macaroni Pastor and I even resisted banging on about music halls as I'd been planning to. I'll see you all next time. Thanks for reading.

ACKNOWLEDGEMENTS

I really am thankful for being able to find the people who know the right stuff at the right time with these books. A massive thank you has to go to Susan Scott, the archivist at the Savoy Hotel, who met me there in the summer. She provided some fascinating information, photos from the time and even read and gave me feedback on my very silly book. The always kind and charming George Blagden helped me out with advice on the reality of working on a play, and I can't wait to see him in the Bing Crosby role in "White Christmas" in the theatre this December. I expect your dressing room to be massive, George, and decorated exactly to your tastes – playing the hit(s?) of Bill Nighy from November to January.

Thank you, too, to my crack team of experts – the Hoggs, the Martins, (**fiction**), Paul Bickley (**policing**), Karen Baugh Menuhin (**marketing**) and Mar Pérez (**forensic pathology**) for knowing lots of stuff when I don't. And to my fellow writers who are always there for me, especially Catherine, Suzanne and Lucy.

Thank you, many times over, to all the readers in my ARC team who have combed the book for errors. I wouldn't be able to produce this series so quickly or successfully without you...

Rebecca Brooks, Ferne Miller, Melinda Kimlinger, Emma James, Mindy Denkin, Namoi Lamont, Katharine Reibig, Linsey Neale, Karen Davis, Terri Roller, Margaret Liddle, Esther Lamin, Lori Willis, Anja Peerdeman, Marion Davis, Sarah Turner, Sandra Hoff, Karen M, Mary Nickell, Vanessa Rivington, Helena George, Anne Kavcic, Nancy Roberts, Pat Hathaway, Peggy Craddock, Cathleen Brickhouse, Susan Reddington, Sonya Elizabeth Richards, John Presler, Mary Harmon, Beth Weldon, Karen Quinn, Karen Alexander, Mindy Wygonik, Jacquie Erwin, Janet Rutherford, Anny Pritchard, M.P. Smith, Molly Bailey, Nancy Vieth, Ila Patlogan, Lisa Bjornstad, Randy Hartselle, Misty Walker, Carol Vani, June Techtow and Keryn De Maria.

READ MORE LORD EDGINGTON MYSTERIES TODAY.

- **Murder at the Spring Ball**
- **Death From High Places** (free e-novella available exclusively at benedictbrown.net. Paperback and audiobook are available at Amazon)
- **A Body at a Boarding School**
- **Death on a Summer's Day**
- **The Mystery of Mistletoe Hall**
- **The Tangled Treasure Trail**
- **The Curious Case of the Templeton-Swifts**
- **The Crimes of Clearwell Castle**
- **A Novel Way to Kill** (Free e-book only available at www.benedictbrown.net/twisty)
- **The Snows of Weston Moor**
- **What the Vicar Saw**
- **Blood on the Banister**
- **A Killer in the Wings**
- **The Christmas Bell Mystery** (November 2023)

Check out the complete Lord Edgington Collection at Amazon

The first seven Lord Edgington audiobooks, narrated by the actor George Blagden, are available now on all major audiobook platforms. There will be more coming very soon.

THE "BLOOD ON THE BANISTERS" COCKTAIL

The Savoy Hotel is inseverably linked to cocktails, and there are a few good reasons why. The first is that the hotel was instrumental in popularising cocktail culture in the UK through its "American Bar", the name of which was given to bars that sold cocktails in the late nineteenth century. The Savoy also published its own recipe book in 1930 with 750 cocktails in it which were supposedly compiled by then bartender Harry Craddock. And a major reason for the fame of that book is the inclusion of several cocktails that are believed to have been created in that hallowed bar.

In the very first Lord Edgington, I spoke about the former head bartender Ada Coleman, who first concocted the Hanky Panky. For his part, Craddock is particularly associated with the wonderfully titled Corpse Reviver #2 and the White Lady. **The White Lady** already existed in various forms a decade before the book was published, and though who exactly has the right to claim the title as the cocktail's creator is not clear, it seems quite likely that Craddock created what would go on to be the definitive recipe. He took out crème de menthe and brandy that previous recipes had called for, restored the gin and then added a bit more for good measure, which leaves us with these proportions…

> ¼ **lemon juice**
> ¼ **triple sec** (e.g. Cointreau)
> ½ **gin.**

The Savoy Cocktail Book just gives the instructions to "Shake well and strain into cocktail glass" but most recipes serve the drink in a coupe glass. In the thirties, bartenders started adding egg white and sugar syrup for those who found it too sour. The much-debated history is fascinating, and I really recommend the article about it on diffordsguide. com where two other potential originators' names are also thrown into the ring.

You can get our offical cocktail expert François Monti's brilliant book "101 Cocktails to Try Before you Die" at Amazon.

WORDS AND REFERENCES YOU MIGHT NOT KNOW

Down your alley – seems to have been more common in the twenties than *up your alley*.

Speed merchant – someone who drives fast.

Rozzers – slang for police officers from the late 19th century.

The greatest city in the world – I accept that this is a hard claim to prove. I must say that I love Paris and New York, but for the pure city experience – in 1927, at least – I doubt many places would have compared to London.

Folded up – we would know say that a business or enterprise *folds*, but that doesn't seem to have been in use at the time.

Histrion – a mildly insulting word for an actor.

Feeder – the actor who facilitates a joke. The term straight man wasn't used until the fifties.

Uxoricide – the murder of one's wife.

Green Street – it leads off Leicester Square in London and I'm glad that I didn't rely on the modern map I was looking at, as this road is now called Irving Street after Henry Irving, but that change didn't occur until 1939. On that street, you can visit a statue of the famous actor, and the Irving society continue to lay a wreath there in February each year to commemorate his birth.

Criss-cross – a misunderstanding.

Puppyishly – I thought I'd invented this word, but no! It exists.

BBC – the British Broadcasting Corporation was only known by that name from New Year's Day 1927, before which it was the British Broadcasting Company, a private organisation which had already found a big audience over the previous four years, due in no small part to the coverage it gave to the general strike of 1926.

Two-facedness – another self-explanatory word which I was very happy to find in the dictionary.

Downfaced – sad… boo hoo.

Tootsicums / stampers – toes / feet.

Scrolled – not to be found in the dictionary (even the OED) it's presumably a Cornish word that means *grilled over the fire on an iron plate*.

Give someone a bye – this comes from cricket. A bye is an extra run (i.e. a point) given to the batting team when the ball passes the batter untouched. It has come to mean *give someone a free pass*.

Protean – from the myth of Proteus, it means shifting and unpredictable.

Short shrift – shrift was the space of time allowed for a criminal to confess before execution. And to give short shrift means to deal with something quickly, not giving it much importance.

Pettish – petulant / peevish

Jackdaw / twitterer – chatterboxes!

Cotton boll – the soft round capsule which holds the seeds on a cotton or flax plant.

Flusterment – a tizzy.

Blisters – swine, bounders, annoying people.

Blue funk – a low mood.

Novemberish – feeling grumpy.

Ill-to-do – the opposite of well-to-do.

Timmynoggies – gadgets / thingummies.

Gaud – gaudiness.

Open-faced – honest seeming.

Dramaturgist – a playwright.

Rookeries – slums.

Confuddled – befuddled and confused.

Criminous – guilty or accused of a crime.

THE IZZY PALMER MYSTERIES

If you're looking for a modern murder mystery series with just as many off-the-wall characters, try **"The Izzy Palmer Mysteries"** for your next whodunit fix.

Check out the complete Izzy Palmer Collection in ebook, paperback and Kindle Unlimited at Amazon.

ABOUT ME

Writing has always been my passion. It was my favourite half-an-hour a week at primary school, and I started on my first, truly abysmal book as a teenager. So it wasn't a difficult decision to study literature at university which led to a master's in Creative Writing.

I'm a Welsh-Irish-Englishman originally from **South London** but now living with my French/Spanish wife and presumably quite confused infant daughter in **Burgos**, a beautiful mediaeval city in the north of Spain. I write overlooking the Castilian countryside, trying not to be distracted by the vultures, hawks and red kites that fly past my window each day.

When Covid-19 hit in 2020, the language school where I worked as an English teacher closed down and I became a full-time writer. I have two murder mystery series. There are already six books written in **"The Izzy Palmer Mysteries"** which is a more modern, zany take on the genre. I will continue to alternate releases between Izzy and Lord Edgington. I hope to release at least ten books in each series.

I previously spent years focussing on kids' books and wrote everything from fairy tales to environmental dystopian fantasies, right through to issue-based teen fiction. My book **"The Princess and The Peach"** was long-listed for the Chicken House prize in The Times and an American producer even talked about adapting it into a film. I'll be slowly publishing those books whenever we find the time.

"A Killer in the Wings" is the eleventh novel in the "Lord Edgington Investigates…" series. The next book will be out in November 2023 and there's a novella available free if you sign up to my **readers' club**. Should you wish to tell me what you think about Chrissy and his grandfather, my writing or the world at large, I'd love to hear from you, so feel free to get in touch via...

www.benedictbrown.net

CHARACTER LIST

Theatrical Types

Sections in brackets represent the characters whom the actors portray in the play.

Peter Canning – He may or may not die on the first page of the book – he does! A kind-hearted and professional actor.
(*Edward Buxton in his twenties* – only appears in the opening scene. Thinking about it now, he would probably have played the hotel manager or something like that later in the play.)

Harriet Taft – The actress who plays two women in the play who are swiftly murdered. We don't learn much else about her other than that she smokes like a chimney and couldn't be the killer.
(*Carolina Buxton / Emilia Buxton* – the two wives of Edward Buxton who are murdered.)

Gabriel Nelson – a beloved and hugely successful actor in his fifties who moved from comedy to serious roles and is considered one of the greats. He stars as the main detective in the play.
(*Inspector Rupert L'Estrange* – the rather arrogant, preening detective from Marius's books.)

Lillian Bradshaw – Nelson's career-long enemy. A capable but secretive actress who is admired by her peers.
(*Marjorie Whitstable* – an actress who is having an affair with Edward Buxton in the main part of the play.)

Oliver Hartley – Nelson's former comedy partner and life-long friend.
(*Edward Buxton in his fifties* in the main part of the play. He is an actor like many of his friends.)

Tallulah Alanson – a promising actress aged twenty-five.
(*Miriam Buxton* – Edward and Carolina Buxton's daughter – girlfriend to the much older Clive McCormack)

Brian Grimage – roguish fellow who became an actor to impress women and failed.
(**Clive McCormack,** another actor and old friend of Edward Buxton. He is also Miriam's boyfriend.)

Dancing Denny – cheeky cockney stagehand aged fifteen.
(In the play he initially appears as a dancer between acts, but then he takes on Marmaduke's role as a waiter and newspaper boy.)

Marius Quin – Author and the writer of the play "A Killer in the Wings" that is being put on in Daly's Theatre throughout the book.
(He has no part in the play!)

Marmaduke Adelaide – last seen in The Mystery of Mistletoe Hall and two other Edgington novels. He was Chrissy's bully at school before they became friends. He is outspoken but with a good heart and is chasing his dream of becoming an actor.
(In the play, he initially plays a waiter and a newspaper boy, but gets a promotion to play the younger version of Edward Buxton.)

Colin West – the director of the play who quits after a series of accidents and the death of Peter Canning.

Old Friends

Lord Edgington – former police superintendent, master detective, Marquess of Edgington, lord of his family seat of Cranley Hall in Surrey and a snappy dresser of some renown.

Christopher Prentiss – his grandson and the opposite of his grandfather in a number of ways, but an increasingly competent sleuth in his own right.

Chief Inspector Darrington – former colleague of Lord Edgington at Scotland Yard.

Detective Inspector Lovebrook – a cheery officer who appeared in the previous book, "Blood on the Banisters". He is also the main police officer in the Marius Quin Mystery series.

Todd – originally the Cranley Hall chauffeur, he now does a bit of everything for Lord Edgington.

Cook/Henrietta – the Cranley Hall cook.

Halfpenny – the head footman of Cranley Hall.

Made in United States
Troutdale, OR
11/14/2023

14590845R00181